"Have you forgotten who I am?"

"Not for a second," Cord said, remembering everything, his eyes caressing Raine. "You're the woman I kissed until you melted and ran over me like liquid fire. So much heat—and all of it locked away. Who are you waiting for, Raine? A well-mannered lapdog who always shows up for his meals on time?"

"Yes," Raine hissed, furious. "That's just what I'm waiting for!"

"You're lying," Cord said, his voice calm, relentless. "You're surrounded by men like that. You have been all your life—but not one of them has touched the fire inside you." Assurance rang in his voice. He was not guessing. He knew.

Dear Reader,

I'd like to start this letter by thanking all of you who have written to me regarding our Silhouette Classics. Almost all of you have been pleased to find your old favorites back in print again, and most of you have also included suggestions for books and authors you'd like to see in the future. Though we can't make all of you happy, we are trying to see that all the authors you like—even if not all the specific titles—are represented.

In keeping with that policy, an author who is a consistent bestseller every time she comes out with a new book is now making her first appearance in Silhouette Classics. *Never Give Your Heart* was the first Silhouette Special Edition written by Tracy Sinclair, but it wasn't her first book by any means. She started off in the Silhouette Romance line, where she won readers' hearts before moving on to do longer books. We think you'll enjoy this look back at her "Special" beginnings.

Next up is *Summer Games*, by Elizabeth Lowell. Though written to coincide with the 1984 Summer Olympics, this book is just as timely—and romantic— now as the day it was first published. For a look behind the scenes at the world's most prestigious athletic competition, as well as spine-tingling suspense and a compelling romance presented with the special Elizabeth Lowell touch, you won't want to let your summer pass without *Summer Games*.

Next month, look for Barbara Faith and Mary Lynn Baxter, and in future months expect to see Sondra Stanford, Joan Hohl, Kathleen Eagle and more as the best of the past keeps coming your way—only from Silhouette Classics.

Leslie J. Wainger
Senior Editor

Elizabeth Lowell

Summer Games

Silhouette Classics

Published by Silhouette Books New York

America's Publisher of Contemporary Romance

SILHOUETTE BOOKS
300 East 42nd St., New York, N.Y. 10017

Silhouette Classics edition published July 1988

Silhouette Intimate Moments edition published July 1984

ISBN 0-373-04617-0

Copyright © 1984 by Ann Maxwell

America's Publisher of Contemporary Romance

Printed in the U.S.A.

Books by Elizabeth Lowell

Silhouette Desire

Summer Thunder #77
The Fire of Spring #265
Too Hot to Handle #319
Love Song for a Raven #355
Fever #415

Silhouette Intimate Moments

The Danvers Touch #18
Lover in the Rough #34
Summer Games #57
Forget Me Not #72
A Woman Without Lies #81
Traveling Man #97
Valley of the Sun #109
Sequel #128
Fires of Eden #141
Sweet Wind, Wild Wind #178

ELIZABETH LOWELL

is a pseudonym for Ann Maxwell, who also writes with her husband under the name A. E. Maxwell. Her novels range from science fiction to historical fiction, and from romance to the sometimes gritty reality of modern suspense. All her novels share a common theme—the power and beauty of love.

for
Karen Solem

who has supported my writing in
two very different fields

appreciation

Chapter 1

RANCHO SANTA FE'S TAWNY HILLS ROLLED GENTLY UP
from the clean sand beaches of the Pacific Ocean three miles
away. Many hills wore crowns of expensive houses, their
windows and walls of glass molten gold in the late-
afternoon light. A cool salt smell from the sea mingled with
the scent of wild grass cured by a hot southern California
sun. A largely dry riverbed twisted sinuously among hills
and ravines, eucalyptus trees and granite outcroppings.
Patches of the Fairbanks Ranch Country Club's emerald
golf course remained along the river, making a startling
contrast with the sere hillsides. Man-made obstacles of
wood and rock and water crisscrossed the riverbed and
climbed the hills.

It was the obstacles, rather than the quiet beauty of the
land, that held Raine Chandler-Smith's attention. Yesterday
she had marched among the uniformed ranks of athletes

who had traveled thousands of miles to compete in the Summer Olympics. Yesterday she had been one among thousands surrounded by rippling flags and vivid, multicolored ceremonies. Yesterday she had been enthralled, humbled, and excited to be a part of a tradition that was as old as Western civilization.

But today Raine was alone, measuring obstacles that had been created for the sole purpose of testing the skill, endurance and trust that existed between her and her horse. The three-day event was to riders what the pentathlon was to traditional athletes—the ultimate test.

Unconsciously, Raine breathed in deeply, savoring the strange scents. The combination of odors was haunting, older than civilization or man, as old as hills and sea and sunlight. Raised in Virginia and Europe, Raine found the dryness of a California summer both alien and fascinating. She stretched and shifted the weight of her rucksack, making the water bottle inside gurgle companionably. As she moved, her camera and binoculars knocked lightly against each other below her breasts. She took another step, winced, and decided that it was time to take the pebble out of her hiking shoe.

With the supple ease that characterized all of her motions, Raine balanced on one foot while she probed for the pebble that had been poking into her arch. Despite her innate coordination, Raine didn't think of herself as graceful. At eleven, she had been five feet, seven and three-quarters inches of angular girl who despaired of ever being as at ease on the ground as she was on a horse's back. At twenty-five, Raine was lithe and gently curved, with a woman's smooth strength and the poise of a rider who regularly entered and won world-class competitions. Yet she still thought of herself as a little awkward and relentlessly average in looks. Medium brown hair, medium brown eyes and medium brown figure was the way she summed up herself when she thought about it.

Raine rarely thought about herself anymore. She had spent nearly all of her life trying to be as beautiful and as accomplished as her much older siblings. But how could a gawky brown hen compete with the two tawny swans who were her sisters, one of whom was the compleat senator's wife and the other a very successful Broadway actress? Her two older brothers were also successful, one a diplomat and the other a surgeon.

Raine had discovered horses when she was only five. It had been an elegant solution to the problem of what to do with Baby Lorraine, or Raine, as she had insisted on being called as soon as she had realized that her name was "secondhand." Horses had given Raine a way to be first. There had always been a rapport between her and the animals that were her life's work and love. When she was riding she forgot to feel awkward and inadequate. She merged herself with the rhythms of her horse and the demands of the jumps. There was a fantastic exhilaration to flying over fences and obstacles on the back of her blood-bay stallion. Only then was she wholly free, wholly alive, wholly herself.

"But if you don't get to work instead of daydreaming," Raine muttered as she retied her shoe, "you'll end up flat on your back in the dirt instead of flying. The cross-country part of the endurance event looks rougher than anything you've taken on yet."

Raine picked up the binoculars and focused on the dry riverbed twisting along the base of the hill. After a few moments she pulled a pad out of her rucksack, sketched in the line of river and hills, and scuffed at the ground beneath her feet. She bent and yanked at the grass until it pulled free. The ground was rough, tending toward tight clods of clay and small stones. Absently, she sifted out some of the pebbles and kept them in her left hand.

"Dry but not really hard going," she said to herself, making notes along the margin of the sketch. "Thank God it's not supposed to rain here during the event. This stuff looks like it would be slippery."

Raine replaced the small sketch pad and stood on the crest of the hill, thinking about the Olympic Games to come, wondering how the hills would look wearing clusters of people as well as houses. Absently, she juggled the pebbles she had kept in her hand. From time to time she threw away a small stone, until finally all the pebbles were gone. Then she brushed off her fingers, grabbed the camera, adjusted the very long telephoto lens and took a series of overlapping photos. Once developed, the slides would make a panorama of the part of the Fairbanks Ranch Country Club that had been torn up and given over to the Summer Games.

"Good, but not good enough," she said, frowning. "Wish I could walk the actual cross-country course."

But she couldn't. All of the endurance-event competitors would walk the course for the first time, together, the day before the event. Ten days from today . . . culmination of a lifetime of work.

Until the day before the endurance event, Raine would have to be satisfied with reconnoitering along the outskirts, extrapolating course conditions as best she could at a distance. She had never ridden over such a dry land in her life; it worried her that she wouldn't have the same instinctive understanding of the terrain that she had on the East Coast or in Britain or France.

Raine's lips curved in an ironic smile. In a way, it was fitting that the most important contest of her life should find her on the outside looking in. She'd spent a lot of time like that, watching the world at a distance. Most of the time she preferred it that way. Sometimes, though, when she heard lovers laugh softly, touch each other as though they were more precious than gold, a man bending down to his woman, smiling . . .

Abruptly, Raine picked up the binoculars again. She scanned the land below, hardly seeing the rich honey sheen of sunlight on grass or the blue-black dance of shadows beneath the wind. She concentrated on a grove of eucalyptus, noting that the smooth-trunked trees were rather like horses, huge yet graceful, powerful yet elegant. She wondered if the drifts of dried leaves and peeling bark she saw at the base of the trees would be slippery or if the ground itself would be damp. She couldn't tell from where she was and she couldn't get closer without crossing the Olympic boundary markers.

With a sigh, Raine turned her attention away from the dense shadows and the gray-green leaves shimmering in the late-afternoon light. She didn't notice the man who watched her from the depths of the eucalyptus grove, concealed by shadows and by the absolute stillness of his body as he waited for her attention to pass over the grove, over him.

Even when she turned and disappeared over the crest of the hill, Cord Elliot didn't move. He crouched in the fragrant shadows and waited for a long six count. When no one reappeared at the crest of the hill, he stood up in a single powerful movement, still concealed by trees, listening with the concentration of a man whose life depended on the acuteness of his senses. After a moment he flowed out of the grove, moving as discreetly as a shadow.

Cord's sand-colored bush jacket and jeans blended with the tawny grass as he went up the slope, choosing a narrow crease in the hillside that would bring him out just behind the place where the woman he had been watching had

stood. Using every bit of natural cover, Cord climbed
swiftly until he was just below the crest of the hill. Then he
dropped flat and eased up to the top, making sure that his
head never rose higher than ripe grass swaying in the wind,
for his black hair would be conspicuous against the golden
hillside.

His ice-blue glance raked the downhill side, searching for
the woman who was entirely too curious about the site of
the Olympic endurance event. A quick glance revealed no
one moving over the land.

*All right, honey. Where did that nice smooth walk take
you? Over by those boulders? No, not enough time. The
next grove. Yeah. Why are you kneeling there? Holes.
You're digging holes, for Chrissake. Why? What choice
piece of hell are you planting there? And why there? Why
not on the course, where the horses will come thundering
by, exhausted and yet still game, running their guts out
because they were born to it and because their riders are
there with them, as tired and tough as the horses. Is that
what you're after? Do you ache to kill something that's
stronger and ·better than you'll ever be? Or will you be
happy just turning the spectators into a hell's kitchen of
dead and dying?*

Motionless, Cord lay just below the crest of the hill,
watching. He was too far away to see precisely what the
woman was doing. Military binoculars dug into his chest,
but he ignored them. The angle of the sun was just right for
flashing off the binocular lenses, giving away his location.
For now he would wait. As soon as the woman turned
away, though, he would come down off that hill. Then he
would ask some questions.

And she would answer every one of them.

Pale blue eyes watched as Raine stood. She let the last
fragrant eucalyptus leaves crumble between her fingers and

drift away in the fitful wind. She brushed off her khaki slacks and faded chambray blouse. The pungence of eucalyptus still clung to her like an invisible shadow, mingling with the summer scent of grass and heat.

"Well," she said quietly to herself as she looked around at the dusty earth, "at least it won't get muddy under the trees no matter how many horses churn through." With new respect and appreciation, she stared up into the towering crown of a nearby eucalyptus. "It's a long time between drinks for you, isn't it? You could give lessons to a camel. Makes me thirsty just thinking about it." Without looking away from the tree, Raine reached into her rucksack for her water bottle.

In the next instant she was hit from behind. Dazed, totally unprepared, she let her riding reflexes take over. She tried to fall loosely, rolling with the impact rather than fighting it. Even so, her breath was knocked out. By the time she could breathe again she was flat on her face in the leaves and dust, pinned to the ground by a heavy weight. Her binoculars, camera and rucksack had been stripped away. She tried to get up, only to be brought down again ruthlessly.

"Don't move." The man's voice was cold, flat.

Instinctively, Raine obeyed.

Then she felt hands moving over her body with a familiarity that no man had dared for years. Even as she stiffened, she realized that for all its intimacy, the man's touch was oddly impersonal. The world spun crazily as he flipped her over and laid her flat again. She felt the muscular weight of his leg pinning her legs to the ground, the iron power of his forearm against her throat. So long as she was utterly still she could breathe. If she tried to move she would choke.

Raine lay on her back and fought not to panic as she

stared up into the unyielding planes of the man's face. She
felt his hand move over her shoulders, under her arms, over
her breasts, her stomach, between her thighs. She made an
involuntary sound, fear and anger and protest combined
into one inchoate syllable. A winter-blue glance raked over
her face as the man's hand continued down her body to her
right ankle, removed her shoe, then repeated the process on
her left leg. He tossed the shoes beyond her reach. They
landed on top of the rucksack, binoculars and camera,
which he had also thrown aside.

"Name."

It took Raine a moment to connect the man's curt
command with the information he wanted from her. "R-
Raine."

"Last name."

"S-Smith," Raine said, swallowing, trying to ease the
dryness of her mouth.

"What are you doing here."

Raine closed her eyes and fought to control the chemical
storm in her blood. She was used to dealing with adrenaline; the first thing competitors learned was how to control
the body's response to stress. The second thing competitors
learned was how to think under pressure. She began
thinking very quickly, and decided that if the man were
going to hurt her, he would be doing so, not asking her
questions. As soon as that thought occurred, fury replaced
fear. Her eyes opened clear and very hard.

"Who the hell are you?" demanded Raine.

The man's forearm moved slightly, cutting off her air.
The pressure was lifted almost immediately. Pale eyes
watched her to see if she had taken the hint. She had. The
next time she spoke, it was to answer his question.

"I'm looking at the country," said Raine.

"Why."

No inflection, just the same flat demand that had characterized his every word.

"I'm an Olympic rider."

Something flickered in the man's eyes. "Prove it," he said, his voice still flat. Yet even as he spoke, his body changed subtly, becoming somehow less . . . predatory.

"I left Dev at Santa Anita," Raine said curtly, her voice thinned by anger and the aftermath of fear.

"Dev?" he asked, inflection and curiosity enlivening his voice.

"Devlin's Waterloo. My horse."

"Describe it."

"Seventeen and a half hands high, stallion, blood-bay with no white, three-quarters thoroughbred and the rest either Irish or—"

"Good enough, Raine *Smith*," murmured the man, with an odd emphasis on her last name. His body changed as he looked down at her, becoming less hard and more forgiving, less impersonal and more male. He moved his arm, releasing her neck from restraint. He didn't remove the weight of his leg across hers, however. Nor did his wariness vanish. It was as much a part of him as the darkness at the center of his ice-blue eyes. "As for who the hell I am," he smiled slightly, "you can call me Cord Elliot."

Raine stared, fascinated by the countless icy glints of blue in Cord's eyes. She was held by the unexpected beauty of his eyes as surely as she was pinned by his weight. Suddenly she was aware of Cord as a man, all of him stretched along her, his body hard and warm, quick and dangerous, his hair as thick and black as her stallion's mane.

"Olympic rider, mmm?" continued Cord, looking at the lithe body lying so quietly half beneath his. "That explains why you fell all relaxed and controlled, yet you didn't know how to counter the simplest unarmed combat tricks. You're a product of very civilized training, not Cuban or Lebanese commando camps.''

''Commando camps?'' said Raine on an ascending note, wondering if she was in the hands of a madman after all.

''Don't sound so shocked,'' said Cord dryly. ''They exist.''

''What are you talking about?''

''Terrorism,'' answered Cord almost absently, his attention caught by the soft swell of Raine's breasts as she breathed in sharply, and by the warmth of her legs pinned beneath his thigh.

''Terrorism! Of all the absurd—! Do I look like a terrorist?'' she demanded angrily.

''No fangs, huh?'' suggested Cord with grim humor. ''Honey, the last terrorist I had my hands on was dressed in a yellow silk ball gown and stank of hate and cordite.'' He saw Raine's confusion and added helpfully, ''Cordite is gunpowder.''

''She?'' asked Raine, her voice rising again. ''The terrorist was a *woman?*''

''Men don't have a corner on violence.''

''But—''

Cord continued talking as though Raine hadn't interrupted. His glance moved over her more intimately than his hands had when he had frisked her for weapons. ''You don't smell like a terrorist.'' He bent his head closer to her neck and inhaled slowly. ''You smell of sunlight and dried grass and the shadows beneath eucalyptus trees.''

Raine saw the tiny, sensual flare of Cord's nostrils as he breathed in her scent. She found herself holding her breath like an amateur rider approaching a big fence. When she spoke, her voice was almost husky. She felt suddenly defenseless, angry, and utterly disturbed. She challenged Cord almost recklessly, willing to risk his anger in order to escape the sensuality of his appraisal.

"Even if some terrorists are women," she snapped, "what harm could I be doing out here alone?"

"Setting bombs."

"That's ridiculous," scoffed Raine.

"What were you scattering around?" asked Cord almost absently, as though he didn't care what the answer was. But his eyes were very clear, very intent.

Raine blinked, sensing the intensity beneath Cord's casual pose. "I—little stones. I was throwing little stones. It's a habit. I go for walks and pick up small stones and toss them as I think." Then, hotly, "Besides, I don't have room in my rucksack for bombs."

"No? Det cord and explosive caps don't take up much space. Neither does plastique or phosphorus, for that matter. You could even fit in a stick or five of good old-fashioned dynamite. All the things that go boom in the night." Cord's voice shifted, clipped and hard. "Why were you digging?"

"To see what the going is like," she said, then expanded her explanation when Cord's only response was a silence that had the effect of making her want to explain herself. Later she would realize that such silence could be a very effective interrogation technique. Now, however, she was too off-balance to do more than respond. "I wanted to know whether the ground is hard or soft, dry or wet, how stable, what to expect on a downhill run when Dev's hooves cut deep. That sort of thing."

"You weren't going to set little explosives so that when the horses came down the hill they'd have a preview of hell?"

Shocked, Raine could only stare. ". . . No," she said, trembling, "oh no. No one would be that sick."

Cord looked at her for a long moment. When he spoke his voice was different, cynical and very tired. "If you believe that, little girl, you shouldn't be let out alone after dark. Remember the Munich Olympics? If you're too young to remember that, how about the IRA bombing the Queen's Palace Guard? Pieces of men and horses all over the place."

"Stop it . . . !" whispered Raine in a strangled voice, horrified.

"I'm trying to."

Cord gave Raine a long, searching look before he shifted his body, easing the weight of his leg over hers, but not quite freeing her. If Raine tensed for a sudden movement, he would feel it instantly.

Raine looked at Cord's tan face, sensing that she was being weighed in a way that was totally unfamiliar to her. After a few moments she saw the subtle shift of his heavy black eyebrows, the easing of the tension around his icy blue eyes, the relaxation of the hard line of his mouth. She sensed that whatever danger she might have been in from Cord was finally past. With that came the realization of just how terribly vulnerable she had been. If Cord Elliot had been another kind of man . . .

Raine began shaking, a reaction to being knocked off her feet and flattened beneath a stranger's hard body. She tried to control herself, but a small sound escaped as she shuddered again and again.

Cord felt the shudders that went through Raine and knew exactly what was happening. The shock of being overwhelmed had worn off. She knew she was safe, but now she was thinking of what had just happened. And what could have happened. He saw her thoughts in the fragile glimmer of tears magnifying the green and gold of her hazel eyes, in

the delicate curve of her trembling mouth, in the ripples of
fear moving visibly over her clear skin.

An odd feeling of shame grew in Cord, odd because he
had simply been doing his job in the safest, most efficient
manner he knew. She could have been reaching for a
weapon in her rucksack. That was why he had knocked her
down. Yet, even though his act had been justified according
to the terms of the world he lived in, Cord felt as though he
had violated Raine in a fundamental way.

Because he had. Between one instant and the next, he had
demonstrated just how frail her security and her world
really were, how vulnerable she was, how unexpected and
dangerous life could be. It was a cruelty that he regretted,
however necessary it might have been at the time. And now
she was lying very close to him, her eyes dilated and her
lips pale, her hands clenched as she fought not to show how
badly she had been shaken.

Raine bit her lip, trying not to cry aloud, ashamed of the
physical reactions to fear that she could not control. She felt
Cord move, felt his hands pulling her against his body,
hands that were gentle rather than hard, strength that
cherished rather than threatened her, long fingers stroking
her hair soothingly. His voice was deep, calming, and his
arms were a solid barrier protecting her from fear.

"It's all right," Cord murmured, smoothing Raine's hair
with his palm as he tucked her head against his chest. "I
won't hurt you. I'm sorry I frightened you. You're safe
with me, Raine, I promise you."

Raine could no more control her reaction to Cord's offer
of protection than she could control the shudders wracking
her body. Her hands came up to his chest and her fingers
clung to his shirt, seeking the resilience and strength
beneath. His words ran together into a dark velvet sound
that sank beneath her fear, reassuring her even as his

strength reassured her. He had showed her how frail her
safe world really was; the knowledge that he would also
protect her was a relief as great as her fear had been.

With a last, shuddering breath, Raine brought herself
under control. As she looked up at Cord, tears made silver
trails through the dust on her cheeks. She saw his eyes
change, dark centers expanding as he memorized her
features and the shine of tears on her smooth skin. Warm
fingers slid beneath her tangled hair as he bent and very
gently kissed the tears caught in her eyelashes.

"I'm so sorry," said Cord, his voice husky. "I wish to
hell I hadn't frightened you. Raine . . ." he whispered,
"beautiful name, beautiful eyes, beautiful . . ."

Cord's mouth brushed over hers so lightly that Raine
thought she had imagined it. But she didn't imagine the
silver glimmer of her tears on his lips, the subtle tightening
of his body against hers, and the warm flush of sensation
spreading beneath her skin.

"Are you all right now?" asked Cord, lifting his head
and measuring Raine with pale, intent eyes.

Raine nodded, afraid to trust her voice. Then, hesitantly,
she whispered, "I'm sorry."

"For what?"

"Being such a—such a child."

"We're all children when we're taken by surprise," Cord
said, smoothing tendrils of rich brown hair away from
Raine's face.

"Not you."

Curiosity expanded the blue-black center of Cord's eyes.
"How do you know?"

"No one has taken you by surprise for a long time,"
Raine said softly, positively.

"You have, just now." Cord looked at her with an

intensity that was almost tangible. "You're an unusual woman, Raine Smith. Very unusual. And beautiful."

Reflexively, Raine shook her head. Chestnut hair fell forward, tickling her full lower lip. With an impatient movement, she pushed the hair behind her ears. She didn't think of herself as attractive, so she assumed that when a man complimented her it was meaningless flattery.

Cord felt the withdrawal stiffening Raine's body and released her immediately. He knew that if he tried to hold her she would fight him. He already felt as though he'd pulled the wings off the most intriguing butterfly he'd ever seen; he didn't want to feel like a rapist in the bargain.

But as Raine sat up and reached for the rucksack, Cord's hand shot out and wrapped around her wrist. Startled, Raine turned quickly toward him. As she stared at him, she realized that he hadn't had time to search the rucksack for weapons in the time since he'd knocked her down. Motionless, she waited for him to make a move.

Cord looked into Raine's startled hazel eyes for a long moment, then slowly released her wrist.

"You still don't trust me, do you?" asked Raine, surprise and something very close to disappointment in her voice.

Cord hesitated. "I'm ninety-eight percent sure you're who and what you say you are. The other two percent," he added calmly, "could be the death of me."

Raine snatched her hand back from the rucksack. "I just wanted my comb."

"Then get it."

"No. You get it. And take your time," she added quietly. "We'll both feel safer if you're one hundred percent sure."

A long arm reached past Raine. Cord retrieved her shoes, flexing the soles as he gave them to her. He lifted the rucksack onto his lap. While Raine put on her shoes, Cord rummaged expertly through the contents of the blue rucksack. When he was finished, he turned back to her. In his right hand was her comb. In his left hand was her small sketch pad.

"May I?" he asked, indicating the sketch pad.

Raine nodded as she took the comb from Cord's hand. While he flipped through the contents of her sketch pad, she began to unsnarl her shoulder-length hair. She combed carefully, favoring her right arm, which had taken the brunt of her fall. She'd had much worse bruises, though. She ignored the modest messages of pain her upper arm sent and concentrated on taming her flyaway hair.

Raine's hair had just enough natural curl to give it thickness, body, and a mind of its own. The curl showed as an unquenchable tendency to turn up at the ends. In the slanting light, her hair showed a surprising amount of gold, giving it a sun-shot appearance that added depth and interest to the dominant chestnut color. Raine didn't notice that, however. She simply combed her hair, wincing once or twice as her arm protested, impatient with the ache in her arm and the undisciplined, slippery mass of her hair. Her temper wasn't improved when she couldn't find the clip that Cord had knocked out of her hair when he had taken her to the ground with stunning force.

Raine turned to find Cord watching her, the sketch pad forgotten in his hands. "Well?" she said, arching her left eyebrow, trying to ignore the rush of sensation beneath her skin when she realized that he had been smiling as he watched her comb her hair.

"Water bottle, pencils, rawhide thongs, sketch pad, tape recorder, film, an apple, a chocolate bar, an elastic bandage and a buckle."

"A buckle?" said Raine, startled. "Let me see."

Cord reached into the rucksack and unerringly brought out a buckle no bigger than his thumbnail.

"So that's where it went," groaned Raine. "I was polishing Dev's tack when Captain Jon called me. I didn't have time to put the buckle where it belonged and I didn't want to lose it, so I put it in a safe place . . ." Her voice trailed off.

"How long ago was that?" asked Cord, laughter stirring just beneath the surface of his deep voice.

"Five weeks," admitted Raine sheepishly. "I'm forever putting things in safe places and then forgetting where I put them. Captain Jon swears I need a keeper."

"Don't you have one?" asked Cord, his eyes intent, his voice casual.

"No. And if I did," added Raine in a crisp voice, "I'd promptly lose him, too."

"That would depend on the man," Cord pointed out smoothly, smiling. But there was no laughter in his voice, rather a mixture of emotions too complex to easily separate or name.

Raine's eyes widened fractionally as she looked at the man who was so close to her, watching her with unnerving intensity. Self-consciously, she lifted her right arm to push back the hair that kept wanting to fall across her mouth. The movement made her wince almost invisibly. Cord saw it, though; his pale eyes saw everything.

"Let me see your arm," said Cord, holding out his hand.

"It's nothing," shrugged Raine, meaning exactly what she said.

Cord waited, his hand out.

"Really," she protested, "it's probably just a friction bruise." But even as Raine spoke, she was obeying the silent command that radiated from Cord. Grumbling, she pushed the faded blue sleeve of her shirt as far above her elbow as she could. "See?"

A red welt marred Raine's fine-grained skin. The welt began a few inches above her elbow and disappeared beneath the bunched blue cloth. The sleeve had torn at the shoulder seam. It sagged downward, revealing the top of the welt. Tiny beads of blood glistened redly.

Before Raine could protest, Cord hooked a finger in the torn seam and yanked quickly. The cloth gave way as though made of smoke rather than fiber. As Cord looked at her scraped flesh, his lips flattened. Wordlessly, he pulled a clean handkerchief from his pocket, wet the white square with water from the bottle, and held the soaking cloth gently against her abraded skin.

"Hurt?" Cord asked gently, watching Raine's eyes.

Raine started to speak, swallowed, and shook her head, caught by the self-recrimination she sensed in Cord. "It's all right," she said as she tentatively touched his sleeve. The tension and hard muscle beneath the sand-colored cloth was almost shocking. "Cord? Believe me, I do much worse to myself twice a week."

"But you didn't do this to yourself," he said softly. "*I did.*"

There was nothing Raine could say to that, so she simply watched as Cord worked on her arm. The contrast between the muscular power of his shoulders and the exquisite gentleness of his fingers as he cleaned the abrasion sent unfamiliar sensations coursing through Raine. Cord looked up, saw Raine watching him, and let his fingers slide slowly from the inside of her elbow to the pulse beating beneath the soft skin of her wrist.

"Forgive me?" he murmured.

"I—of course," she said, knowing it was true but not entirely sure why.

"I don't have any antiseptic," Cord said, looking critically at the abrasion. "I suppose I could use the oldest remedy."

"What's that?" asked Raine, bemused by the man who could thoroughly frighten and then thoroughly reassure her in the space of a few minutes.

"Kiss it and make it well," said Cord, his voice as deep as the shadows pooling beneath the fragrant trees.

Raine's lips parted slightly with surprise and an invitation that she wasn't even aware of.

"But," continued Cord, his voice dark and smooth, flowing over her, sinking into her, "when I kiss you, it won't be like a parent kissing a child. It will be very healing, though. For both of us."

Raine felt her pulse accelerate beneath Cord's fingertips and knew that he felt it too. She looked away quickly, confused by her reaction to him. She was not the type to lose control of herself merely because a man touched her wrist and spoke to her. It was Cord's unexpected gentleness that unnerved her, the danger and the strength and the yearning in him, a hunger that called to depths in her that she hadn't known existed.

Cord removed the wet cloth, examined Raine's arm again and said matter-of-factly, "We'll wash it better tonight. Are you through here?"

Raine felt off-balance, caught between Cord's assumption that he would be with her tonight and his quick question. Wryly, she realized that it would be a useful technique for controlling a conversation. First you throw in an assumption that may or may not be true and then you follow it quickly with a totally unrelated question. The person answering the question is caught between protesting the assumption and fielding the question.

So rather than challenge the assumption, Raine answered the question—and then realized that in doing so, she had tacitly accepted the assumption that Cord would be with her that night. Just as she had accepted his statement that he would kiss her, and in doing so, had all but invited him to do just that.

"That was pretty slick," Raine said, feeling outmaneuvered but not particularly resentful.

"Thank you," Cord said, smiling. "You're pretty quick yourself."

Her left eyebrow lifted in silent skepticism. "Next to you, I'm distinctly slow. And I'm not through here. There's at least one more hilltop I have to cover."

"That way?" Cord asked, gesturing toward the empty hills and twisting ravine that were the site of the endurance event.

"Not quite. It's a case of look but don't touch, at least until the day before the event. So," said Raine, pointing toward a hilltop that was not inside the Olympic course markers, "I'll have to settle for that one."

"Are you planning on finishing before dark?"

"Yes."

"Pity," murmured Cord. "I'll bet this place is dynamite by moonlight."

Raine's expression changed as she remembered the brutal uses to which dynamite could be put.

"Sorry. Bad choice of words," said Cord.

As he stood, he took Raine's left hand and pulled her easily to her feet. She and Cord spotted her missing barrette at the same instant. He scooped it up before she could, caught her hair in one hand and clipped the chestnut mass in place. When he was finished, he gently stroked her gold-shot hair. She felt the warmth of his breath on her neck, and a touch that could have been his lips.

"Your hair smells like sunlight," Cord murmured. Then, as though he had said nothing at all, he asked, "Where do we go from here?"

Chapter 2

CORD HAD DONE IT AGAIN, ONLY THIS TIME THE ASSUMPtion was buried in the question. *We.* Where do *we* go from here? Talk about an open-ended, fully loaded question. . . . Raine gathered her fraying concentration and bent over to pick up her rucksack. Cord beat her to it, swinging the rucksack up easily over one shoulder. Sketch pad and pencil appeared in his hand again.

"You handle the camera," Cord suggested mildly, picking it up off the ground and flipping the strap over her neck. He replaced her binoculars, too. "I'll take care of the sketches."

"Were they that bad?" asked Raine without resentment, knowing that her sketches were ungainly and all but indecipherable to anyone but herself.

"Let's just say that you don't threaten da Vinci."

"Do you?" asked Raine.

"You can tell me tonight, when you look at my, er, sketchings after dinner."

"Mr. Elliot—" began Raine, determination plain in the lines of her face.

"Aren't you hungry after all your walking around?"

"Of course, but—" said Raine.

"Good," interrupted Cord smoothly. "You drive me to Santa Anita and I'll buy you dinner. Fair trade, don't you think?"

"But—"

"Two dinners, then," he said, smiling down at her. "You drive a hard bargain, lady. And my name is Cord, not Mr. Elliot."

Raine's teeth clicked together in frustration. She hadn't felt so overmatched since she had unwisely taken on both her older sisters at once.

"Lead me to your hilltop," said Cord. Subdued laughter made his voice even deeper than it usually was. Then the laughter slid away, leaving only hunger and intensity as he looked down at her. "If you want me to leave, I will. But I'd much rather stay. I'll be good. I promise you."

Slanting light fell across Cord's eyes, making the countless splinters of blue within the ice-pale irises glitter like crystal. Against the dark, male planes of his face, his eyes seemed impossibly vivid, fringed in lashes as dense and black as midnight. With an effort, Raine forced herself to look away from Cord. She had come out here to reconnoiter land, not a man.

As she looked at the countryside, she saw that the hills were empty, the houses few and distant. Twilight welled up out of nameless ravines, shadow pools spreading and joining, forerunner of darkness to come. Suddenly Raine was glad that Cord was there. He had inadvertently yanked her out of her warm, civilized world of equestrian competition and forced her to remember that there was another, much larger and colder world out there, a barbarian world where violence rather than safety was the rule.

"What about your work," asked Raine, "whatever it may be? Don't you have something you have to do?"

"My work is the same as yours."

"You're a rider?" she said, her voice lifting with astonishment.

"Not in the way you mean," Cord answered, the corner of his mouth turning up in a very male smile. "But we're both here for the same kind of work today—a quick reconnoiter of the cross-country course."

"If you're not a rider, what are you looking for?"

"Places to hide and seek, fields of fire and radio dead spaces, sniper angles and ambush sites."

Cord's casual acceptance of that kind of violence shocked Raine. She watched in confused silence as he took a very small walkie-talkie unit out of his hip pocket, extended the telescoping antenna and spoke quietly. She understood neither his words nor the crackling that issued from the flat black rectangle. Apparently the response was satisfactory, for Cord collapsed the antenna and replaced the unit in his pocket.

"What sort of things does a rider look for?" asked Cord, setting off toward a hill overlooking the riverbed that wound through the Olympic course.

Numbly, Raine followed. When Cord repeated the question, she took a deep breath and began to explain her world to a man whose world could hardly have been more alien to her if he had come from another planet.

"Today, I'm just trying to get a feel for the country. It's not at all like Virginia," she added dryly.

Cord's sideways glance was quick, penetrating; but all he said was, "You don't have a southern accent."

"My father is with the foreign service. I've lived in too many places to have any kind of accent at all." Exclusive boarding schools also didn't encourage accents, but there was no reason to go into that. "I'd know what to expect if twenty horses went over the Virginia hills in front of me, but a dry land is different." Raine frowned. "I'll have to tape Dev's legs more heavily than usual, I think. The going will be hard in places."

"Watch the water jumps. A lot of clay around. Slippery as hell."

Raine looked at Cord. "Are you sure you aren't a rider?"

"Not professionally, not since I was eighteen."

"You're too big to be a jockey," said Raine, assessing Cord's six-foot-plus height in a sweeping glance. "Strong shoulders and legs, steady hands and great balance. Did you hunt?"

Cord's lips curved in silent laughter. "Yes, but not the way you mean. I ate what I shot, and when I rode it was for pay as well as pleasure. Rodeo."

Intrigued, Raine waited for Cord to say more about his past. When he didn't, she asked, "Why did you give it up?"

"Vietnam," he said briefly, opening and closing the subject with a single word.

"And then?" Raine asked, unable to curb her curiosity about the man walking beside her.

"More of the same."

She waited, then persisted. "And then?"

"There wasn't any 'and then' for me," Cord said bluntly.

"You're still in the army or marines or whatever?"

Cord stopped and swung toward Raine, his eyes narrow. He looked her over from her hair to the toes of her hiking shoes. "Funny," he said sardonically, "you don't look like a cat. No furry ears or long tail or whiskers. But you're as curious as any cat I've ever known."

"And you're a man used to asking rather than answering questions," said Raine, her voice neutral.

"Curiosity, and claws, too," muttered Cord. For a long moment he looked down at Raine's oval face, at her hazel eyes with their surprising glints of gold and green, at the feminine mouth that was quick to smile but wasn't smiling now. "What do you really want to know, Raine?"

"I—" She stopped, unable to answer for the simple reason that she didn't know.

Raine had seen men who moved like Cord before. Men walking discreetly through embassy halls. Men watching the crowd while the crowd watched a statesman speak. Men whose job it was to guard diplomats and foreign dignitaries and people whose names and titles and true functions were shrouded in files only a few officials were cleared to read. Men whose very lives were state secrets. Men like her father. Men like those who guarded her father. Raine hadn't thought about such men in years, since she had stopped seeing her parents for more than a few hours at a time.

"I don't know what question I was trying to ask," said Raine finally. "It's been a long time since I've been around a man like you."

"A man like me?" Cord smiled, but there was little humor in the hard line of his mouth parting across white teeth. "Two arms, two hands, two feet, two legs, ten fingers—"

"And one gun in the small of your back," said Raine.

Cord looked surprised for an instant; then his face lost all expression. He watched her as he had when he first saw her walking the hills, winter eyes and icy speculation.

Raine tried to smile, and failed. "So I was right. You're a man like my father, and like the men who guard him."

She tried to control the absurd disappointment the discovery had brought to her. A man like her father, giving his time and energy to an uneasy combination of ambition and idealism. A man like her father, who had little time for the wife he loved, and less time for his own children.

"Your father?" asked Cord, his voice too disciplined to reveal anything, even interest.

Raine hesitated, then shrugged. She was usually careful not to mention her family connections. But there was nothing usual about the situation or the man walking beside her—or her response to the man. It would be better if Cord knew. Better to end the attraction now, retreating behind an armor of old wealth and impeccable, powerful names.

"Justin Chandler-Smith. A man who routinely thinks in terms of international politics," Raine said quietly, regretting the impulse that had brought conversation around to her family. But it was too late now. It had been too late since she had found out that Cord, too, lived a life that put work first and everything else second. "My father's recommendations make or break countries and cultures. He lives with scenarios of human viciousness, betrayal, and violence. It's a horrible way to live, always aware of the worst side of human nature, where men are evil and death serves a political purpose."

"Somebody has to live in that world," Cord said quietly, "or it would be the only world left for everyone to live in."

"Yes," Raine said distantly, "that's what my father says, too."

"You don't believe him?"

Raine shrugged. "I'm sure he's right. He always is." Then, with a harshness she couldn't conceal, "But did he have to live with it all the time? Wasn't anything else important to him? His wife? His kids? Anything at all?"

"Maybe it's because his family was so very important to him that he gave himself to protecting them," suggested Cord quietly.

"Maybe," said Raine, her voice flat. "And maybe he just likes that violent world better than the other one."

"Is that the question you wanted to ask me? If I like the world I live in?"

Raine tilted her chin almost defiantly as she met Cord's pale eyes. "Yes," she said distinctly, "I think that's the question I had in mind."

Cord hesitated, looking down at the woman who apparently so disliked being associated with her father that she refused even to use his full name. "My work is satisfying in many ways," said Cord finally. "Exciting, at times. Alarms and excursions," he continued, his voice lightly mocking, but the mockery was aimed at himself rather than her. "Saving civilization from barbarians, winning and losing and fighting again, life and death as close together as bullets in a clip."

Cord's voice faded as he remembered how it had been fifteen years ago, when he was twenty-one and everything had seemed so clear. Lately it seemed that there was more death than life, more doubt than certainty. He had lost patience with people who believed in simple slogans, easy solutions, and the inevitable victory of civilization over barbarism. He had learned in the hardest possible way that happiness was a rare gift rather than a God-given right, that men had died and continued to die so that others could live, and that sometimes in the hours before dawn it seemed that the barbarians were winning because civilization just didn't give a damn.

Cord pulled his mind away from the downward spiral of his thoughts. He knew the danger of what he was feeling. He had assessed his emotions as unflinchingly as he assessed a black street when he was outnumbered five to one. He was getting cold inside. It was called burning out. Darkness without dawn, winter without spring. Burnout. Maybe it was time to let someone else take his place in the thin bloody line standing against the barbarians. Someone who found more excitement than disillusionment in the battle, someone who didn't feel cold all the way to his soul.

Someone who hadn't frightened a woman called Raine.

"Cord?" asked Raine softly, sensing his distance from her and the winter chill beneath his calm exterior. "I'm sorry. I don't have any right to attack your work. It's not your fault my father never had enough time for his family." Her hand moved in an appealing gesture that ended with her fingertips brushing Cord's sleeve. "And I'm not naive or stupid. I know that your work is necessary. It's just that I don't like thinking about it."

Cord gently lifted Raine's hand from his sleeve. He looked at the slender fingers with their clean, carefully kept nails. He ran his thumb over the calluses on her palm, which had come from a lifetime of holding reins and lead ropes. He kissed the smooth center of her hand, a caress as natural and warm as the late-afternoon light.

"There are times I don't like thinking about my work either," said Cord quietly. "So tell me about your work, Raine Smith-only, no Chandler. How did you come to be an Olympic equestrian?"

Raine felt her throat tighten at the echoes of weariness and disappointment she heard in Cord's voice. There was a deep current in him, a need more compelling than simple sexual desire . . . although desire was there too. She couldn't help but respond to the hunger and strange gentleness of him, and to the deeply buried, nameless yearning she sensed.

When Cord laced his fingers through hers and began to lead her along the margin of riverbed and hills, Raine made no objection. Instead, she simply accepted the intimacy of his palm against hers as though they had always walked this way.

"I started riding when I was five," said Raine, not looking at Cord as they walked, for she was afraid of shattering the fragile warmth of the moment. "I was an afterthought—an accident, really. Eight years younger than my closest sibling. I resented always being smallest and last and worst at everything the family did. So I found something no one in the family did, and then I did that better than anyone in or out of the family. Horses. Mom and Dad didn't really care, beyond a certain relief. It gave me something to do besides turn things upside down at home."

Cord smiled faintly. "You mean you weren't a perfect little angel?"

"I was a perfect little witch," said Raine succinctly. "I didn't know it at the time, of course, any more than I knew why I was so determined to succeed at riding. I just went through life hell-bent on being best."

"Sounds just like your father," murmured Cord.

"Do you know him?" asked Raine, startled.

"A lot of people know Chandler-Smith," Cord said easily, neither evading nor really answering Raine's question. He turned at the top of the small rise and gestured toward the riverbed. "Not much light left for a lens as big as you're using. Better get shooting."

Raine reached for her camera, then realized that her hand

was still securely held in Cord's. She looked up—and found herself reflected in his clear, light eyes. He slid his fingers from between hers so slowly that the slightest pressure of his skin moving over hers was transformed into a lingering, sensual caress. When he was no longer touching her, she felt strangely lost, as empty as the cloudless sky.

With fingers that trembled just enough for Cord to see, Raine adjusted the focus ring on the telephoto lens. He took out the sketch pad and pencil and began reducing the surrounding terrain to dark slashes across white paper. He finished more quickly than she did, for she was having trouble holding the camera still.

Raine took a deep breath and let it out slowly. When there was no more air in her lungs, she gently triggered the shutter, hoping that she wouldn't jar the camera while it was taking the picture. Cord had been right; there was barely enough light left for any but long exposures, and she hadn't brought a tripod to steady the camera. With a sense of futility, she heard the shutter open and close too slowly. She simply couldn't hold the heavy lens absolutely still long enough to get a decent exposure.

"Use my shoulder," said Cord, kneeling easily in front of her.

Raine hesitated, then propped the long lens on Cord's shoulder. She bent over, sighted, adjusted the focus and shot. Cord didn't move.

"A little to the right," she said.

Cord shifted his body, then froze again. Raine tried to work as quickly as she could, knowing how difficult it was for Cord to remain immobile. But instead of concentrating on overlapping the shots to form a seamless panorama, she found herself staring at the sleek black line of Cord's hair against his neck. She caught a wisp of fragrance and inhaled deeply, savoring the subtle citrus scent of aftershave blend-

ed with the clean male smell of him. Tanned skin stretched
smoothly over the tendons and muscles of his neck,
motionless but for the almost hidden beat of his pulse. What
would it be like to touch that pulse as he had touched hers,
to feel it accelerate beneath her fingertip? What would it be
like to—

"Finished?" asked Cord.

Raine gathered her scattering thoughts. "One more. A
little further to the right."

Cord moved, then became motionless again. Raine took
another picture, then one more for insurance.

"Done," she said. "If you ever want to change careers,
I'll give you a high recommendation as a tripod. Where did
you learn to be so still?"

"In the jungle," said Cord simply, rising and turning
toward Raine in one fluid motion. His quickness startled
her, as did his words. He smiled crookedly when a wisp of
her hair that had been teased free by the wind floated lightly
over his lips. "I could give you a map of the endurance
event accurate to the last centimeter, margins full of notes
on crowd control and sniper scopes, trajectories and hiding
places, targets of opportunity and equations for the disper-
sion of various gases under different conditions of wind and
humidity. But you wouldn't want that, would you? Not
even if I erased all the ugly notes. You wouldn't want an
unfair advantage over the other riders."

Raine nodded, unable to speak. *Gas. Sniper. Target.* All
of her life she had seen careers like her father's, like Cord's,
solely in terms of what it had meant to her as a child—a
father who was hardly ever there when she wanted him to
be. But now she was seeing that career in other terms.
Suddenly, she had a visceral understanding of the danger
implicit in Cord's work.

Life, even Cord's immensely vital life, was vulnerable, and death was always there, waiting for the unlucky or the unwary or those who had no one to protect them. At least her father had a wife who waited for him, children, a home, a place of love and warmth to retreat to when the other world began to freeze all that was human in him. Cord had no such retreat. He had spent his life guarding a gentle world that he had never been lucky enough to live in. He could easily die without ever knowing that warm world.

Sniper. Bombs. Ambush. Death.

The realization both chilled and saddened Raine, sliding through the defenses she had been trying to build against Cord. There was something in him that she could not refuse, something that called to her in a wordless, compelling language. Was he hearing that same language, feeling the same pull? Was that why he stood as she did, silently, almost stunned, feeling as though her world had been turned upside down and shaken until she fell out?

An electronic beeper shrilled in the stillness. Without looking away from Raine, Cord moved his hand automatically to his belt. With his thumb he punched out a code that acknowledged receipt of the summons.

Raine's expression changed, showing a resentment that was quickly replaced by an appearance of indifference. Only at that instant did she realize just how much she had been looking forward to driving back to Santa Anita and having dinner with Cord Elliot. The realization made her angry. She was a fool to be interested in a man who was like her father, so involved in his work that he lived his life at the end of an electronic leash. She had left that world behind once. She would never enter it again, no matter what the lure.

"You'd better hurry," Raine said coolly, taking the

sketch pad and pencil from Cord, then putting them away in the rucksack she slid off Cord's shoulder. "The nearest phone is back at the clubhouse."

"Raine."

Cord spoke her name so softly that she almost didn't hear. Then his hands came up to her shoulders, holding her in a gentle vise.

"Come back with me," Cord said quietly, urgently, looking at Raine as though he were afraid that she would vanish the instant she was no longer reflected in his eyes. "Don't stay out here alone. The world is full of men hungry for warmth, men who would kill for a single smile from lips like yours. And some of those men would simply take what they wanted, destroying everything."

Raine looked up at Cord, sensed his male power and need, his body trained for death and his eyes hungry for life. Her resentment crumbled, shattered by the same man who had broken apart a world she hadn't questioned since she was a child. Tears gathered in her eyes, blurring Cord's outline, leaving only the crystal intensity of his gaze.

"Don't be afraid of me," Cord said sadly, stepping back, retreating, releasing her. "I'm not one of the barbarians. I won't take anything that you don't want to give."

Silently, Raine shook her head. "You've risked so much," she whispered, "you've given so much, and yet you've never known the warm world you make possible for others. You could die without knowing that world, like a sentry barred from the very fire he protects. And," she said huskily, "I could die. You made me realize that this afternoon. Life doesn't last forever. It just seems that way."

The rucksack slipped from Raine's fingers as Cord drew her close. His hands framed her face as he bent over her, moving slowly, never using his superior strength to hold her captive. If she wanted to evade him, all she had to do was step away. She did not. She tilted her face toward his, suddenly as hungry to be close to him as he was to touch her.

Cord's lips moved over the chestnut arch of her eyebrows, the smooth skin at her temples, the soft hollow beneath her cheekbone, kisses as delicate as a breath. Raine shivered and leaned closer to him, totally off-guard. She hadn't expected such gentleness, his hunger restrained until it showed only in the tension of his arms. Her fingertips traced his veins from wrist to elbow and back again in gentle, searching caresses that said more about her own hunger than she knew.

Cord's fingers tightened, drawing Raine still closer to him. He felt her breath flow warmly over his neck as his mouth traced the line of her jaw with slow, melting kisses. He knew he should stop, knew he was taking unfair advantage of her, first frightening her and then comforting her and finally making love to her, always a step ahead of her, a master of unarmed combat keeping a novice off-balance until there was nowhere to turn but into his arms.

Yes, he should stop. He would stop. But not yet. Not until he had come just a bit closer to her fire, warmed himself just a bit longer, driven out just a bit more of the chill that had crept like an enemy into his soul, ambushing him when he least expected it. He knew he had no right to hold a woman like Raine, a woman made for one man's love, not for casual liaisons with men whose lives belonged to war.

But she was so warm in his arms, and he was so cold inside.

Raine's lips opened willingly as she shared the kiss, inviting Cord more deeply into her warmth, inviting him to dream about a place by her fire. When his tongue moved over hers, she made an involuntary sound of pleasure and surprise. Her fingers slid beneath his short sleeves and over the hard muscles of his arms as though she had suddenly lost her balance and must cling to him or fall.

Her response went through Cord like a shock wave. He fought an almost overpowering surge of hunger. He wanted to take Raine down to the golden grass and make love to her until nothing else was real, no past or future, no rights or wrongs, nothing but sunset sliding into night, a man and woman alone, two lovers turning and twining and blending intimately, two flames burning as one in a world of crimson silence.

Raine sensed the hunger in Cord, heard the almost silent groan from deep in his chest as his tongue slowly caressed hers, felt his tearing reluctance to end the kiss. She clung to him without realizing it, aware only of his muscles flexed beneath her hands, the salt-sweet taste of him on her lips and tongue. She didn't want the kiss to end, to stand apart from him once more, to send him alone into the descending night.

Finally Cord forced himself to lift his mouth, knowing that if he didn't stop now he might not be able to stop at all. The hunger gripping him was new, an unknown quantity. It was not simple lust. He had learned long ago to control his own sexuality. What he felt now was as though a dam had given way deep inside him, releasing torrents of need that were as complex and unexpected as they were powerful, sweeping everything before them.

Cord closed his eyes and fought to control himself, but the afterimage of Raine's parted lips burned behind his eyelids. *Do you know what a temptation you are, Raine Chandler-Smith?* he asked silently, afraid to speak aloud and frighten her again. When he trusted himself to look at her once more, he saw himself condensed in wide hazel

eyes looking up at him. Need turned in him deeply, as hot
and bright and new as a knife just brought from the forge.

"You're coming back with me," Cord said, his voice
very certain. It wasn't a question or even an invitation, but
a simple statement of fact.

Raine knew it would be futile to object. Nor was there
any reason to. For one thing, there wasn't enough light left
for photography. For another, it would be foolish to keep
wandering alone over the unknown land with darkness
coming down. And, she admitted to herself, there was the
fact that she wasn't ready to leave Cord yet.

Cord retrieved the rucksack, laced his fingers through
Raine's and began walking back toward the country club.
Lights from distant houses glowed in the rose sunset,
making the sky overhead a deep, radiant blue by compari-
son. Raine walked silently, matching her strides to Cord's
longer ones even as he slowed to accommodate her. They
exchanged a look of almost startled recognition, smiled,
and continued walking, their strides evenly matched.

When they reached the clubhouse, there was a helicopter
sitting in the parking lot. The chopper was small, sleek, and
lacked either military or civil markings. Raine had seen her
father climb into similar vehicles and disappear for weeks at
a time with neither word nor warning. Her fingers tightened
in the instant before she controlled herself and released
Cord's hand.

Cord felt both the tension and the sudden release, and
knew that Raine had guessed the helicopter was for him.
She was Chandler-Smith's daughter. She knew all about
uncertainty and unexpected good-byes. Knew it and hated
it, her resentment plain in first the tightness and then the
retreat of her fingers. Other women had found Cord's job
romantic, the secrets of his work tantalizing, the danger
implicit in the gun he wore almost erotic. But not Raine.

She knew Cord's work for what it was, a deadly enemy of intimacy.

Silently, deeply, Cord cursed the life he led, running up against its demands like a mustang coming up against a fence for the first time in its wild life. With a hoarse sound Cord pulled Raine into his arms, holding her tightly, ignoring the clash of binoculars and camera, feeling only the resistance of her closed lips.

Raine clenched herself against Cord for a long moment, but found it impossible to deny him. When her mouth softened she heard her name spoken once, relief and hunger and apology; and then he kissed her until she forgot everything but the taste and feel of him. Passion and restraint, strength and yearning, danger and safety, gentleness and ruthlessness, everything that he was and could be were poured into a single kiss. He had breached her safe, predictable world, shattering her defenses and demanding a place next to the civilized, womanly fire that he had guarded for so many years without ever knowing its warmth.

When Cord finally loosened his arms and stepped back, Raine could hardly stand. She closed her eyes but still saw him, his thick black hair and blazing ice-blue eyes, the lines of his face harsh with need and his mouth shockingly sensual as he looked down at her, wanting her.

"Tomorrow night," he said. "Seven o'clock. Dinner."

"No," she said, shaking her head, her eyes still closed. "You don't know where you'll be tomorrow night."

"I'll be wherever you are. Seven o'clock. *Look at me, Raine.*"

Raine opened her eyes and shook her head helplessly. "Seven o'clock," she said, but her tone said only that she didn't believe Cord would be there.

Before Cord could speak, the helicopter ripped to life, its rotor spinning until the body of the craft trembled like a beast crouched at the point of springing on its prey. Cord handed Raine the rucksack, then turned and walked quickly away, his black hair rippling in the backwash of the great blades slicing through the twilight.

Raine stood, eyes narrowed against tears and the harsh wind spinning off the black rotor. She braced herself as the chopper leaped into the air, churning the twilight into a chaos of flashing light. Hands clenched at her sides, she closed her eyes as Cord's helicopter became smaller and darker, fading into night, leaving only an afterimage of a blinking red light on her retina and a fading echo in her ears.

When Raine opened her eyes again, she was alone.

Chapter 3

RAINE STOOD NEXT TO DEV IN THE STALL. SHE WAS dwarfed by the stallion's height and muscle. She brushed his bright mahogany-red coat with long, sweeping strokes. Dev didn't need the grooming any more than he had needed the extra time she had spent talking soothingly to him. The horse was neither unkept nor restless. At the moment, though, Raine felt she was both.

Patience was not Raine's strongest point. She knew it, and allowed for it. Or tried to. The weeks before any three-day event were difficult enough. The weeks before the Olympic three-day event were impossible. The syndrome that Raine labeled "competition madness" set in. There was little more to be done in terms of training either horses or riders. The horses were all but bursting with vitality. Other than an hour a day of undemanding riding and a few hours spent grooming and walking, the horses didn't require anything. Hard work or long hours in the ring were counterproductive, making the horses stale rather than eager for the coming test.

The same went for the riders. They, too, were in the peak of physical condition, figuratively champing at the bit for the competition to begin and the suspense to end. Because they were athletes, the riders knew better than to deaden the cutting edges of stress with alcohol or drugs. Nor could they work themselves into a blessed state of numbness, for that would sour them as surely as it would sour their horses.

Many riders—and other athletes—relieved the stresses of competition madness with an affair. It was a common and covertly accepted practice, a pragmatic and delightful means of killing time without jeopardizing competitive fitness. More than one man had explained this very logically to Raine. Just as logically, she had explained that she preferred long walks and unnecessary groomings of Devlin's Waterloo to empty bedroom games.

Only once had Raine given in to competition madness. She had been in Europe, competing for the first time with world-class equestrians. She had been out of her depth in more ways than one. As a result, a French rider had seduced her almost effortlessly on her twenty-first birthday. She had mistaken his Gallic appreciation of women in general for a particular appreciation of Raine Smith. He had been disconcerted to discover that she was a virgin, and worse, a Chandler-Smith. He had been kind, though, telling her beautiful lies for several weeks as he eased himself out of her life, taking with him her innocence.

Since then, Raine had been very careful to date no one who was associated with her work. Which meant, in effect, no one at all. She enjoyed the men she was constantly with, joking and trading equestrian advice, planning surprise birthday parties and being a babysitter-of-last-resort for the married riders. Humorous, unflappable, generous, a hell of

a rider, younger-sister-in-residence, mind like a whip . . .
and untouchable. All of those words had been used to
describe her. All were correct, so far as they went.

But none of those words described the emotions beneath
her surface, the loneliness and yearning that Raine was so
careful to conceal. Until yesterday, when a stranger had
knocked her flat and then gently held her, looked at her as
though he saw through the facade to the womanly warmth
beneath, and then kissed her and bathed both of them in fire.

With a whispered curse, Raine threw Dev's brush into
the tack box hanging on the wide stall door. She had
thought a lot about what had happened yesterday; the
darkness beneath her eyes was proof of that. The only
rational explanation she had was that what had happened
out in that lonely twilight had been the inevitable product of
her precompetition nerves and Cord's high-stress work. She
had been literally knocked off-balance, all her normal
certainties shattered. He had been on a hair-trigger adrenaline ride, not knowing if she was a terrorist carrying death
in a rucksack.

Given those facts, and the subsequent shattering of
normal social reserve, was it so surprising that Cord had
kissed her and she had responded? They were simply
human, a man and a woman with more adrenaline than
common sense coursing through them. Nothing mysterious
or even unexpected, once she thought about it logically. It
couldn't have been any more than nerves. It certainly
couldn't have been a silent recognition of the other half of
herself, a filling of inner hollows that had waited empty and
unknown for a lifetime, a joining more complex and . . .
dangerous? . . . than she could accept.

Nerves, nothing more. Competition madness.

Period.

"Raine?"

Startled, Raine spun around. "Oh. Hi, Captain Jon. I didn't hear you come up."

The captain leaned on the stall door but didn't offer to come in. He had a very healthy respect for the stallion's heels. "Phone call for you."

Automatically, Raine glanced at the watch on her wrist. Five-thirty. A little late for any of her family to be calling her—or a little early, depending on whether it was her brother in Japan or her mother in Berlin. Perhaps it was her sister, calling before the latest round of political fund-raisers. Or, even more likely, it was one of the increasing number of reporters who had discovered that Raine Smith, Olympic equestrian, was also Lorraine Todhunter Chandler-Smith, daughter of old wealth and older power.

Captain Jon stepped away from the stall door as Raine patted Dev's rump and walked out of the stall into the broad aisle that went between rows of stalls. Hot-blooded horses stood quietly, watching everything that happened with liquid brown eyes, coats gleaming with health. As the two people walked down the aisle, horses poked their heads over stall doors. Some of the horses whickered softly as they scented Raine, asking for a word or a touch. Raine responded almost absently, stroking velvet noses with her fingertips as she walked toward the phone at the end of the aisle.

"I called your name three times," Captain Jon said. "Maybe I should get you a beeper."

Raine scowled and muttered a word that wasn't normally part of her vocabulary.

Captain Jon's white eyebrows lifted. "I didn't think it was that bad an idea."

"I don't like electronic leashes," she said succinctly.

"No kidding," he said in a too-innocent tone. The American slang sounded odd coming from the Eton-educated Swiss aristocrat.

Raine gave Captain Jon a narrow glance, then relented with a smile. "Sorry. Comes of being raised with the damn things. Birthdays, Christmas, Thanksgiving, the Pan-American Games—it didn't matter. Somewhere in the world, hell is always breaking loose. Beep-beep and good-bye."

Captain Jon didn't argue. He knew better than anyone that Raine still resented the fact that her father had managed to attend only three of the dozens of competitions Raine had been in over the years.

"Worry about your own piece of the world," advised the captain, rubbing his hand through his thinning gray hair. "Leave the rest of it to the pros."

Men like Cord, thought Raine, but she said nothing.

"Speaking of the rest of the world," said Captain Jon, "there's been an update in the security regs. Riders going to look over the country around Rancho Santa Fe have to use the buddy system." He looked at Raine covertly, surprised by the sudden tension he saw in her expression. "It's not an unreasonable request," he added. "Ever since Munich, Olympic athletes have been a target. I've seen the country around the endurance course. There's damn-all out there but hills, obstacles, and what's left of the original golf course."

"I know. I was there yesterday."

"Alone?"

"Most of the time." Raine picked up the phone near the end of the aisle before the captain could ask any other questions. "Hello," she said crisply.

"Seven o'clock," said a deep voice.

Raine didn't know that she went pale as she heard the

voice of the man that she had already relegated to the pigeonhole marked "Competition Madness." She hadn't really expected to hear from Cord again. She certainly hadn't expected her heart to lurch and then race while adrenaline poured into her blood as though she had just taken a hard fall. Hearing Cord's voice had brought yesterday back all too vividly, first the fear and then the safety.

And then the fire.

In the background Raine heard other voices coming through the phone, oddly pitched voices riding broken waves of sound punctuated by bursts of static.

"I know you're there," said Cord, his voice both gritty and intimate. "I can hear you breathing. I just wish I were close enough to feel your breath too, and see the pulse beating in your soft throat."

Raine could tell by Cord's voice that he had guessed— no, *known*—that she would be in full retreat from yesterday and him. He had stopped that retreat effectively, reminding her of the very things that both frightened and fascinated her. He was as much in charge as he had been when he had surprised her in the hills. And she was as much off-balance.

"Don't you ever play fair?" she asked finally, keeping all but the least quiver of emotion out of her voice.

"I'm a hunter, Raine. I don't play at all."

"Well, I'm no dumb bunny, Cord Elliot," she said coolly.

"I know. In fact, I feel rather like Actaeon must have felt when he hunted Diana beneath her own moon. Not a sport for the fainthearted." Cord's laugh was rough yet soft, a purr from an animal that was definitely not a domestic cat. "Seven o'clock, Raine. Wear whatever you like. Or, like Diana, wear nothing at all."

Cord hung up before Raine could say anything. It was just as well, she admitted ruefully to herself; she couldn't think of anything to say.

"Everything okay?" asked Captain Jon, looking closely at Raine's face, first pale and now flushed.

"Sure," said Raine distractedly, replacing the phone. "The person I was talking to is just rather, er, disconcerting."

"Anyone I know?"

"Doubt it," said Raine, frowning and fingering the plastic-coated badge that was clipped to her collar. The badge identified her as an Olympic competitor with access to all equestrian areas. "I just met the man yesterday."

"Oh?"

Raine looked down at her hands and arms, dusty from hours of cleaning Dev's stall and brushing his healthy red hide. Wear anything she liked, hmmm? Well, Mr. In-Charge Elliot, be prepared to have *your* wind knocked out for a change. But first, a bath.

"I won't be in the mess hall tonight," she said.

Captain Jon shrugged. His athletes were older than most Olympic competitors. He didn't cluck over his riders, unless they had it coming. Then he could mother-hen with a vengeance. Besides, Raine had never given him a bit of trouble, not even when she had fallen for that smooth-talking Frenchman. Although he had dumped her just before a big meet, she had kept her concentration, proving that she was a world-class competitor. It was her performance that day that had convinced Captain Jon that Raine was Olympic material.

"Found a man, eh?" he asked, smiling widely.

"Right," she said, knowing if she denied it, Captain Jon would find out anyway and decide that Cord was more important to her than he was. "He knocked me right off my feet."

"Isn't that 'swept you right off your feet'?"

"Not this one. Knocked me right out of my shoes."

The captain chuckled, assuming it was a joke. "Don't worry about curfew. You can use the break."

Raine hurried through the huge grounds of Santa Anita park toward the employee parking lot where she kept her car. There weren't too many people around—a few reporters and horse pundits, a score of groupies, competitors walking and riding and schooling their horses. Even though some of the equestrian events were already taking place, there were still men hammering and building with a frenzy that came from working toward deadlines that should have been met weeks ago.

The racing season had ended only in June, however, not leaving much time for the conversion of a flat racing track into a show-jumping ring, dressage ring, practice rings, exercise areas, massive new bleachers on all sides, and the multitude of quarters required for both men and animals. As Santa Anita was removed from other Olympic venues, or competition areas, and there were few other female equestrian competitors, Raine had quarters by herself in a nearby motel.

The motel was more accustomed to high rollers than high jumpers, and was decorated accordingly with an abundance of gilt and mirrors. Not quite whore's Christmas decor, but close enough to make Raine smile every time she thought of it. The motel was handy to Santa Anita, however. The water was unfailingly hot, the sheets were changed every day and the towels twice daily. That was all she asked of any lodging, and more than she usually got.

As she opened the motel door, the cool, neutral smell

peculiar to rented rooms and air conditioning washed over
her. At least it wasn't like stepping into a refrigerator. After
the first two days, Raine had convinced the maid that a
temperature in the upper seventies was much preferable to
one in the sixties.

Raine swept into the bathroom, peeling off grubby
clothes as she went. The water in the black-tiled shower
came out in a thick, hard, pulsating spray that rapidly
reduced her to jelly. With a groan of sheer pleasure, she let
hot water knead tight muscles that were the only exterior
sign of Olympic pressures. The days and hours and minutes
before the beginning of the three-day event unrolled before
her like eternity.

With the skill of long practice, Raine turned her thoughts
away from the competition to come. There was nothing she
could do about moving time faster except to distract herself.
And, she decided with a thin smile, Cord qualified as one
hell of a distraction. She wasn't in the running for an affair,
but dinner and the chance to flap the unflappable Mr.
Elliot . . . that was entirely different.

Humming quietly, Raine dried her hair and set it in big
hot rollers. She rubbed a perfumed cream over her body,
put on makeup with a sparing, skilled hand, and wandered
over to the closet wearing little more than fragrance and an
anticipatory smile. She bypassed the tailored formality of
her dressage clothes—silk hat and starched linen shirt,
black coat with tails, clean riding pants with a razor
crease—and went directly to the five evening outfits that
were a necessary part of world-class riding equipment. The
Olympic Equestrian Team was supported by donations. The
wealthiest donors often threw stylish parties that riders
were urgently "requested" to attend. Raine, raised in an
atmosphere of political reality, knew better than to balk at

such "requests," and had acquired a wardrobe suitable for such affairs.

She ignored the floor-length, gold-shot bronze dress of Indian silk, and the crimson *soie* pants and filmy top from Italy. Her fingers hovered over a black, ankle-length sheath that was slit to mid-thigh in the front. Then she remembered Cord's long-legged stride. Even with the slit, the black dress would be like wearing hobbles. She settled on a rustling mass of jade-green watercolor silk. The top of the dress overlapped without fastening, making a deep V to her waist. Although the silk rarely revealed more than a hint of curving breasts, the artfully draped folds seemed always on the verge of coming undone. A pleated belt of the same material finished the knee-length dress.

Still humming, Raine pulled on some very sheer, very French pantyhose. The deep neckline made a bra impossible. It didn't matter. She wasn't built to overflow any bounds of propriety. She stepped into the dress, closed the invisible side zipper, and arranged the neckline so that it concealed far more than it revealed. The deep, shimmering green of the dress made her skin look like porcelain lit from within by flame. A long, handmade gold chain followed the neckline of the dress, weaving light into glimmers of gold that were picked up and repeated by her hazel eyes. Emeralds glowed among the gold links and winked in each earlobe, echoing the green flecks in her eyes.

She fastened on a pair of very high, almost nonexistent evening sandals made of wisps of butter-soft gold leather. Pulling out rollers with both hands, she went back into the bathroom to comb her hair. Even disciplined by hot rollers, her hair was as stubborn as any horse she had ever tried to school. She combed out the crackling, silky mass until it was a wild cloud around her shoulders. Then she gathered the slippery chestnut hair in her hands and built a smooth, sophisticated coil on top of her head. Finally she pulled free a few curling tendrils, letting them fall softly around her temples and ears and the nape of her neck. A few more tendrils escaped on their own, providing an arresting contrast to the sleek discipline of the chestnut coils.

Raine looked at the result in the mirror and nodded to herself. "You'll never stop traffic, but you don't look like you just crawled out of a haystack, either."

She turned away, not seeing what others would see: elegance and poise. Gold-shot hair, and eyes alive with intelligence and humor; the tantalizing curve of neck and shoulders; the feminine swell of breasts beneath silk that teased even as it concealed. She was not beautiful in the usual sense of the word, but she was a woman to tempt any man who had the eyes to see her and the confidence to pursue what he saw.

Raine straightened up the room with the ingrained neatness of someone accustomed to living out of suitcases. When she was finished, she looked critically at her fingernails. Short, buffed rather than polished, they looked almost childlike next to the elegance of her dress. She shrugged and put the matter out of her mind. Long, brightly painted nails were a nuisance around the stable.

Raine looked at the incredibly thin gold watch that had been her father's gift to her after he had been forced to leave the Pan-American Games before he could see her event. Seven o'clock.

There was a brisk knock on the door that fairly shouted of Cord Elliot's male confidence. Raine almost smiled, knowing that she didn't need to call out and ask who was there. She went to the door, took off the chain and opened the door without checking to see who was on the other side.

"Are you always so trusting?" asked Cord disapprovingly.

Raine started to answer but found herself staring instead. Where was the rough stranger who had ruthlessly knocked her down and searched her yesterday, in a few moments shattering her secure world? Cord was dressed impeccably in navy blazer and silk tie, white silk shirt and fine charcoal wool pants. The elegant clothes served only to enhance his male grace and strength, quietly proving that clothes were only as good as the man who wore them. With a sinking feeling, Raine realized that he'd done it again, knocked her off-balance, left her floundering and at a loss while he remained in complete control.

Cord looked down into the quiet face of the woman who had troubled his thoughts since the instant he had decided that she wasn't a terrorist bent on death. The ripped blue blouse and faded riding pants were gone, as was the dust-and-tear-streaked face. She stood before him proudly, her wealth and position and poise pulled around her like medieval armor. Princess-at-work. Touch-not.

He had expected the social armor. In fact, he had dressed for it. He was an old hand at getting past barriers, at camouflage and passing unseen in every kind of crowd. He had lived with savages and prime ministers, could converse with barbarians and Ph.D.'s. So he smiled down at Raine as his senses quickened with her scent, the chestnut coils and teasing tendrils of her hair, the subdued glint of emerald against the sensuous lobes of her ears, the sheen of smooth silk against smoother skin, feet arched as delicately as a dancer's.

Not a princess. A queen. Centuries of wealth and power condensed into a deceptively slender form. Cord wondered whether Raine had dressed specifically to intimidate him, then decided that her clothes were a reflexive defense against the rest of the world. Like a fawn freezing at the first hint of a wolf, Raine was letting her exterior conceal the heat and life inside. He smiled at the thought, a slow smile that did nothing to conceal the male intensity of his appraisal.

She smiled at him in return, a tentative curve of lips, wistful and aloof and so beautiful to him that he couldn't restrain a sudden, silent intake of breath. He held out his hand. Automatically, she took it. When his lips found again the warm center of her palm, her fingers curled slightly in sensual response.

"My compliments to your fairy godmother," Cord murmured, looking at Raine with eyes that were hooded, their dark centers wide.

"Cinderella was a scullery maid, not a stable hand," said Raine lightly, dismissing the compliment as she had dismissed so many before, not believing in her own attractiveness.

Yet Cord's response to Raine's changed appearance affected her the same way his lips against her palm did: frissons of warmth racing through her. She had anticipated the same combination of surprise and retreat from Cord that she had seen in other men when she had dressed with the wealth and elegance that were her heritage. Those men had been disconcerted, almost uneasy. They had been expecting a socially gauche rider and had been presented with a woman who had graduated from Europe's finest finishing schools and social circuits. It wasn't a life she had particularly enjoyed, but it had had its uses, especially as a deterrent.

Until now. Cord had been attracted rather than repelled. And she was again off-center, again feeling as though she had to cling to him for balance.

"Ready?" he asked.

Raine scooped her purse off the table. Cord put his hand behind her elbow, guiding her out of the room. He shut the door, checked that it was locked, and ushered Raine toward a black Pantera crouched like a big cat in the parking lot. He handed Raine into the low-slung sports car, fastened her seatbelt, closed her door firmly and got in the driver's side. She watched covertly as he folded himself into the low seat with the easy coordination that marked all of his movements.

"Anything you can't eat?" asked Cord as he brought the car to life.

"Curry," she said, sighing. "Unfortunately, I love the taste."

Cord gave Raine a sympathetic look before he eased the Pantera out into traffic. "How about Asian food?"

"Love it. Chinese, Japanese, Korean—"

"Vietnamese?"

"Never tried it," she admitted.

"If you don't like the appetizers, I'll take you somewhere else," he promised.

Raine relaxed into the leather seat as the car accelerated with an eagerness that reminded her of Dev. The engine's sound rose an octave, sending discreet messages of raw power into the passenger compartment. Raine watched approvingly as Cord controlled the car with small, certain movements of his hands, an economy of motion that spoke of skill and confidence.

"You must have been a good rider," she said as Cord downshifted coming into a curve.

Cord gave her a sideways look before returning his attention to the heavy traffic. "Why do you say that?"

"Your hands. Quick. Sure. Calm. Sensitive." As Raine spoke, she remembered the feeling of his hands framing her

face and was glad that the light in the car was too dim to
reveal the pulse beating more rapidly in her throat.

"Legacy of a misspent youth," said Cord wryly. "Family tradition. My great-grandfather and grandfather were
mustañeros—wild-horse hunters. They would follow the
mustangs on foot, keeping them always on the move, never
letting them eat more than a few bites of food or drink more
than a few cups of water. They'd literally walk those
mustangs into the ground."

At Raine's startled sound, Cord looked sideways.

"It's true," he assured her. "The horses would move in
a broad circle, keeping to the water holes and grazing lands
they knew. Two men could work a herd, leapfrogging each
other as they cut across the country from water hole to water
hole, arriving ahead of the horses and then stampeding
them off to the next water hole. After a while the horses got
so hungry and thirsty and sore footed that you could walk
right up and put a rope on them. They would follow you
anywhere for a hatful of water."

Raine turned slightly in the seat, caught by the shadow
quality of Cord's voice, darkness and textures of emotion
transformed into a very masculine, soothing timbre. It was
the kind of voice that she could listen to endlessly, like
music.

Cord kept talking, unaware of Raine's intent eyes. It had
been a long time since he had thought about the people and
places and scents of his childhood.

"Dad went on the last of the hunts when he was only
nine. The good horses were gone by then. Nothing left but
slab-sided scrub beasts as mean as the rock desert men had
crowded them into." Cord shook his head, remembering
the old photos, faded and curling, across his father's
bedroom wall, pictures of mustangs and *mustañeros* long
since dead. "Granddad and Dad took to breaking the rough

string, other men's horses that were either too green or too mean to be ridden. Granddad was a regular shaman. Had a voice that would mesmerize the meanest stud.''

Raine smiled to herself, thinking that Cord had definitely inherited his grandfather's gift. Listening to Cord's voice was like being wrapped in velvet.

''I learned to ride on horses that no one but my dad would touch. I learned to move confidently, cleanly, and never to turn my back. I also learned that even the most savage horse can be gentled, given time, patience, and,'' grinning, ''enough apples.''

Cord fell silent, suddenly remembering the tickling feel of an apple being lipped off his palm by a horse that had finally learned to trust.

''Dev could have used a man like you,'' said Raine quietly.

''Was your horse a hard case?'' asked Cord.

''Yes, but he had reason. The first time I saw him, I was sixteen, walking a one-day-event course with my father. We saw Dev go down, throwing his rider. By the time we got there, Dev was still down, his front legs tangled in the bars of a fixed jump. His rider was standing next to him, cursing and kicking and whipping Dev as hard as he could. Dev's eyes were rolling white and wild, and bloody foam was dripping from his body. Any other horse would have panicked and broken both legs trying to fight free, but not Dev.''

Cord gave Raine a quick glance, saw her eyes narrow as she stared through the windshield; but it was the past she was seeing, a past that still had the power to make rage slide hotly in her veins.

''What did you do?'' asked Cord when Raine said nothing more.

''I grabbed that cruel, brainless bastard and shoved him

into my father's arms," Raine said. "Then I stood and talked to Dev until his eyes stopped rolling. When he finally let me touch him without flinching and baring his teeth, I went to work easing his legs free of the bars."

"That took a lot of nerve," said Cord quietly, picturing a younger, smaller Raine working in dangerously close quarters with a stallion that was half out of its mind with pain and fear.

"There was no other way to get the job done," she said matter-of-factly. "When I coaxed Dev to his feet, he was bloody and scraped and lathered all over, trembling in every limb. Yet he stood and watched me with his ears up, his eyes calm, the picture of well-mannered attention. I stood there holding the reins and I knew I couldn't give a horse like that back to a sadist."

Cord waited, glancing sideways, trying to equate the elegant woman in the seat next to him with the brutal episode out of her past. If he saw only the silk dress and emerald earrings, her words sounded preposterous. If he remembered the woman who had fought not to panic when she was helpless beneath a stranger's intrusive hands, then her words made sense. An elegant, vulnerable woman, yes; but also a woman who didn't flinch from doing what had to be done.

"I asked that obscene idiot what he thought the horse was worth," continued Raine, unaware of Cord's intense appraisal. "He said, 'A bullet. He's too old to geld and too mean to ride.'" She hesitated, remembering what had happened next. It was one of the few times in her life when her father had been there when it counted. "So my father pulled his gun, shucked out a bullet, and flipped it to the man."

"That's one for our side, Blue," said Cord beneath his breath.

Raine turned with a swiftness that showed she had heard. "That's my father's nickname. You know him, don't you?" she asked, accusation in her voice.

"A lot of men know him. I doubt that he knows Cord Elliot, though," Cord added with a crooked half smile, as though enjoying a joke that he wasn't ready to share yet.

Raine hesitated, then accepted what Cord had said. It was true. A lot of men who were strangers to Justin Chandler-Smith knew his nickname. Her father had worked in many embassies overseas, as well as in the State Department in the U.S. His titles had varied with the assignment: undersecretary; assistant to the secretary; or the oldest joke of all, chief assistant to the assistant chief. All the titles were meaningless. In the covert world her father inhabited, men without leverage held resounding titles. Men with true power moved discreetly, gray eminences in the marble corridors of power. It was a system used by all world powers, though few carried it as far as the Russians, who routinely gave their highest KGB men the cover job of chauffeur in Russian foreign embassies.

"Did you have any trouble with Dev?" asked Cord, turning into a small parking lot and changing the subject in the same neat maneuver.

"I had to retrain him entirely. I turned him out to pasture for three months before I even tried to put a bridle on him. It took more than a year to bring him up to the most basic level of schooled responses. It was worth it, though. Dev was born for eventing. He has more sheer guts than any horse I've ever ridden. Brawn and brains, too," she added wryly. "He's saved my fanny more than once on a downhill jump. His only drawback is that he won't tolerate strange men handling him. As for riding him—every man who has tried has ended up on the floor."

"And you?" asked Cord as a parking attendant trotted over, eager to get his hands on the Pantera.

"Dev hasn't dumped me intentionally," said Raine. "I've hit the floor more than once out of my own stupidity, though."

"Somehow," said Cord, "I can't picture you being stupid." He turned sideways and ran his fingertip from the softness of Raine's earlobe to the pulse accelerating in her throat. "Taken by surprise, yes. Next to treachery, surprise is the best way to take a highly fortified position."

Raine stared, off-balance again, wondering if Cord would ever stop surprising her.

Chapter 4

AS RAINE SHOULD HAVE EXPECTED, THE RESTAURANT Cord chose was a surprise. She had assumed an Oriental restaurant would have the usual mock-Asian decor—red tassels and wall hangings from Taiwan. But the Year of the Rainbow was decorated with continental restraint and richness. Heavy linen and crystal, bone china and silver napkin holders. It took Raine a moment to realize why the place settings looked bare; there was no flatware on the table.

The menu was also a surprise. It was printed in ideographs with French translations. At least, Raine assumed the French was a translation; she couldn't read ideographs. The only price appeared at the very bottom of the menu. The figure assured her that the food was either marvelous or served on platinum plates. Perhaps both.

She couldn't help wondering how Cord managed to

afford elegant clothes, transportation and restaurants. What she had heard of his background didn't suggest inherited wealth. And while people who worked for the government at the highest levels were paid well, they weren't paid that well. Many diplomats were forced to supplement their salaries with personal wealth just to be able to entertain on the scale their jobs required. The United States might be one of the richest countries on earth, but its diplomatic budgets were decidedly thin.

Raine looked up and saw Cord watching her openly, his ice-blue eyes vivid in the candlelight, his thick black hair gleaming with life. He was very close, having chosen to sit at a right angle to her rather than across the table from her.

"If you like haute cuisine after the French manner," he said, "order from the right side of the menu. If you're feeling adventurous—or would trust me to order for you—go to the left side. And don't worry about the lack of silverware. They'll bring you the proper tools to eat whatever you choose."

Cord watched as Raine read the French side of the menu with a speed that suggested utter familiarity with the language and cuisine. He smiled quietly to himself and waited, watching candlelight shimmer and slide over the chestnut coils of her hair with each small movement of her head. A wisp of her hair floated forward, tickling the corner of Raine's mouth. Cord tucked the silky tendril back in place. As he removed his hand, he let his fingertip trace the rim of her ear. She gave him a startled look, then an almost shy smile that made him wish they were alone in a fortress, the doors locked and bolted against the world outside.

"I'm feeling adventurous," Raine said, turning to the left side of the menu.

"Not trusting?" Cord asked with a wounded expression and a wicked light in his eyes.

"Adventurous," she said firmly, refusing him the satisfaction of being trusted.

"There's a lot to be said for adventure," Cord pointed out with a smile.

"Then let's just say I'm hungry enough to eat anything."

Amusement danced in Cord's eyes, but he was wise enough to say nothing at all. Gently, he pulled the menu out of Raine's grasp and set it on top of his own menu, which he hadn't bothered to open.

The waiter materialized. Cord spoke in a sliding, singsong language. After a discreetly startled reappraisal of his client, the waiter began scribbling ideographs on his pad. When Cord was finished, the waiter made a few recommendations. Cord took one and discarded the others. The wine steward came over. They conferred over the list in two languages, neither of which was English.

Raine smiled with a mixture of amusement and appreciation. Cord reminded her of her father, a man at home in several tongues and utterly fluent in the oldest language known to man—power. When Cord looked up, Raine saluted him silently. He gathered her hand into his, watching her expression as he spoke.

"No inherited wealth, just the best education Uncle Sam and experience could provide," said Cord. He smiled slightly and added, "The steward was polite enough not to wince at my French accent."

"Inherited wealth only means money, not the brains to use it. And there's nothing wrong with your accent," she said, defending Cord instantly.

"Tell that to a Parisian."

"You can't tell *anything* to a Parisian," retorted Raine.

Cord's dark pupils dilated. "The queen is very kind to her soldier," he said softly.

He lifted Raine's hand to his lips, savored the sweet-

smelling skin for an instant with the hidden tip of his tongue
before he lowered her hand again. The caress was so casual,
yet at the same time so intimate, that Raine could barely
control the shiver that went through her.

"I'm not a queen," she whispered through suddenly dry
lips, "and you're hardly a common soldier."

Cord simply looked at Raine, making no effort to conceal
the hunger in his eyes, a hunger reflected in the slow
movement of his thumb over her fingertips. When the wine
arrived, he went through the ritual of tasting it almost
indifferently, not even releasing her hand. Yet Raine knew
that if the wine had been inferior, he would have noticed
and sent it back instantly. Cord Elliot was not a man to
accept second best in anything.

The wine was both delicious and unfamiliar, a Fumé
Blanc that exactly complemented the exotic meal. There
was shrimp paste broiled on narrow strips of sugarcane,
tiny crepe-like wrappers containing a mint leaf and crisp
julienne of marinated vegetables, miniature meatballs sim-
mered in a piquant sauce, shrimp that tasted like rainbows
and melted in her mouth. There were other dishes too,
temperatures hot and cold and tepid, tastes sweet and
vinegar and salt, flavors and textures and colors combined
in endless array, a feast for the eyes as well as the palate.

The meal came with silver chopsticks and a lemon-
scented fingerbowl. Raine watched Cord, ate the appropri-
ate foods with her fingers, and used the fingerbowl as she
would after any meal. The chopsticks, however, baffled
her. The cuisines she was familiar with would have used a
tool shaped like a chopstick to skewer and broil chunks of
meat, not to eat anything as tiny and elusive as rice.

"Like this," said Cord, taking Raine's hand and posi-
tioning the chopsticks correctly. "Keep the chopsticks
almost parallel to the plate, instead of vertical as you would

a fork. Now, hold the bottom one steady and move the top one. Or vice versa. I'm not a purist. Whatever works.''

Raine became more adept as the meal progressed, but still lost about one out of three tidbits. Cord used the chopsticks with a dexterity that fascinated her. She found herself divided between admiration and exasperation as she watched him eat. When yet another succulent shrimp escaped her, exasperation won out. Deftly, Cord picked up the shrimp in his chopsticks and held it near her lips. Automatically she opened her mouth and took the morsel.

Cord looked hungrily at the white gleam of Raine's teeth, the pink tip of her tongue, the sensual fullness of her lips as they closed for an instant around his chopsticks. The memory of a twilight hill and the taste of her on his tongue went through Cord and settled deep inside, the sweet heaviness and aching of male hunger. Resolutely, he looked away from her mouth; tonight he wanted to prove to her that he was a gentleman as well as a man trained in violence. He wanted to seduce her in more than a merely physical way. He wanted her to trust him. Everything about Raine told him that Justin Chandler-Smith's youngest daughter was neither worldly nor wild when it came to men.

She was wise, though. With a feeling close to anger, Cord wondered who had been the one to teach her to distrust a man's admiration and touch.

By the time the dinner was over, Raine was thinking of ways to discreetly loosen her silk belt. For the last ten minutes she had been telling herself that she would take just one more bite of crisp vegetable or one more rainbow bite of shrimp. But each bite had demanded another from a complementary dish, foods and flavors blended with such sophistication that the palate always wanted just one more taste. Finally she groaned and put her chopsticks on their ivory rest.

"No more," she said firmly. "Take it away, please. Save me from myself."

Cord smiled, pleased that Raine had enjoyed the unusual meal. A woman could say polite words and push food around a plate, but only someone who truly enjoyed the flavors would have eaten with Raine's enthusiasm. "Are you sure? I can feed you if you're just tired of using chopsticks."

Absently, Raine flexed her right hand where muscles she had never used protested the unaccustomed strain of holding chopsticks. "You could feed me," she agreed with a crooked smile, "but could you digest it for me?"

Laughing, Cord shook his head. The waiter reappeared and cleared the table with discretion and speed.

"Dessert?" asked Cord, taking Raine's hand again.

"Impossible."

"Coffee? Liqueur?"

"Would you believe a walk to the car?" said Raine. "If I don't get out of here, I'm going to pop."

Cord spoke to the waiter. The man returned with two pieces of hand-dipped chocolate candy wrapped in gold foil. He also had a Styrofoam cup of coffee laced with Armagnac. The plastic lid and cup were startling against the heavy silver tray.

As Cord escorted Raine out of the restaurant, he saw the laughter just beneath her serene exterior. He tucked her in the car, slid in the driver's side and said, "What's the punch line?"

Raine tried and failed to smother her amusement as the parking attendant handed Cord the coffee and candy. "Styrofoam and sterling," she said, laughing aloud.

"The waiter tried to talk me into taking one of their china cups," said Cord dryly, "but I held out for the real thing."

Raine balanced the coffee in one hand and the chocolates

in the other as Cord drove the Pantera through darkened streets and onto the freeway. She fed Cord his candy, ate her own, and carefully pried off the plastic lid on the cup. The marvelous aromas of Colombian coffee and French Armagnac expanded to fill the interior off the car.

"Go ahead," said Cord without looking over at Raine, knowing that the coffee had tempted her. "I got it for both of us."

Cautiously, Raine sipped at the hot, heady liquid.

Cord's hand went to the tape deck. There was a soft click; then the haunting strains of Debussy moved over both people like a caress. After an initial instant of surprise at Cord's taste in music, Raine sighed and gave herself over to the lyric beauty of the sounds. When Cord lifted the coffee cup out of her hand, the sliding warmth of his fingertips over her skin became another kind of music.

The opposite lanes of the freeway slid by in a silver-white dazzle, a river of light sixty feet wide and hundreds of miles long. Directly ahead, the river was a shimmering ruby flow where random amber lights winked as invisible cars changed lanes. When the music finally faded into silence, Raine was all but mesmerized by the beauty of the night and the quiet male presence at her side. She watched the world slide by, saying nothing until they were off the freeway and parked in a lot high on a hill overlooking Los Angeles.

"Where are we?" asked Raine lazily, stealing the cup away from Cord and taking the last sip from its fragrant depths.

"Griffith Observatory," said Cord as he shut off the engine. "You see," he murmured, taking the empty cup from Raine's fingers and putting it on the floor, "if I could, I'd give you the moon and the stars in hopes that you would forgive me for frightening you yesterday. But I can't," he said, unlocking their seatbelts and lifting her across his lap

with a fluid motion. "So I'll give you the next best thing. A
guided tour of the universe."

As Cord's mouth brushed over Raine's lips, her cheeks,
her eyelashes, his fingers smoothed the sensitive nape of her
neck. When his lips returned to hers, the tip of his tongue
moved tantalizingly over the curves of her mouth. Unconsciously, her lips parted, wanting more of his sensual touch.
With melting gentleness, his teeth closed over her lower lip
and his tongue caressed the soft, captive flesh.

Raine felt herself losing her balance again . . . but she
didn't care. She was surrounded by a warm velvet world,
nowhere to fall but Cord's arms and he was holding her as
though she were made of moonlight and dreams. With a
shiver of pleasure, she relaxed against him, her hands
sliding over the soft wool of his coat, instinctively drawn to
the silk beneath. Her fingers moved up his shirt, enjoying
the muscular resilience of him.

Cord's arms tightened around Raine as he felt the restless
seeking of her hands rubbing over his chest, heard her tiny
sigh as her fingers tangled in the hair at the nape of his neck.
With a final caress, he released her lip, taking instead her
mouth, searching her darkness and warmth as though she
were wholly undiscovered territory. Not one hidden surface, not one warm texture escaped his slow, intimate
exploration. He captured her tongue with his own and drank
deeply of her sweetness, his hunger growing in heat and
heaviness until a slight shift of her hips against his thighs
made him groan deep in his chest.

Reluctantly Cord separated his mouth from Raine's,
feeling as though he were tearing off his own skin. He saw
her dilated eyes, her flushed cheeks, her quick, shallow
breaths and knew that she was as aroused as he was. Gently
he pressed her head against his chest, held her close,
rocking her very slowly. The depth of his hunger for her

surprised him, as did the depth of her response. Her subtle
shifts and hesitations had told him that she was a sensual
rather than an experienced woman. Yet she had opened to
him like an undefended valley, inviting and warm for the
soldier coming down from the frigid heights of a mountain
pass.

Raine slid her arms around Cord, enjoying the solid feel
of his flesh. He radiated a strength and vitality that
reminded her of Dev. She had never felt quite so safe as she
did right then, and so cherished. All the relentless pressures
weighing her down had evaporated in Cord's presence.

"You were right," she said softly. "Kissing you is a
healing thing."

She felt Cord's breath stop, then resume. Slowly, his
hand stroked the length of her dress from shoulder to waist
to knee. Silk whispered seductively, asking to be stroked
again. His finger tilted up her chin. Gentle kisses touched
every contour of her face, lingered over the softness of her
lips.

"You're very beautiful," he whispered.

When Raine opened her mouth to protest, Cord's tongue
slid between her teeth, silencing her with a sweetness that
made her shiver. It was a long time before he lifted his head
and looked down at her with eyes more silver than blue,
their centers dark with passion.

"If I don't put you back on the other side of the car," he
said regretfully, "we'll miss that guided tour of the universe."

Raine's breath caught at the hunger that burned in Cord's
eyes, and at the exquisite gentleness of his hands moving
over her skin. "I thought this was the tour," she said,
unable to conceal the catch in her voice or the quiver of her
response to his long caress.

Cord watched Raine's eyes as though he could see the

truth reflected in their hazel depths. "Is this a new world for you?"

"Yes," she said simply.

"It's new for me, too," he said, and bent down to kiss her with a gentleness that made her want to melt and flow over him.

Headlights flashed through the windshield when another car pulled into the parking lot. Laughter and conversation drifted through the Pantera's open window as people walked toward the observatory's entrance. Resolutely, Cord eased Raine back into her seat. Without a word, he got out and walked around to her side of the car.

Raine watched Cord's lithe stride, the male grace of his body, and felt unfamiliar sensations race over nerve endings she hadn't known she had. When he reached in to help her out of the car, the simple touch of his hand on hers made muscles tighten deep within her body. She stared up at him with an almost dazed look. Being seduced by the charming French rider hadn't been nearly as exciting as simply being kissed by Cord Elliot. The realization dismayed her, making her distrust her own responses. Yet when Cord smiled and took her hand, she couldn't bring herself to withdraw.

Slowly, they walked toward the domed planetarium, barely noticing the glittering, jeweled carpet of Los Angeles spread from horizon to horizon at their feet. The interior of the building was cool, the ceiling shaped like a hemisphere, the seats oddly slanted so that people looked up rather than forward. Silently, hand in hand, Raine and Cord sat and waited in darkness for the universe to condense across the arched ceiling.

Stars materialized, countless silver shimmers scattered across the featureless black ceiling-sky. The stars moved in graceful swirls, fading down the sides of artificial night until a single spiral galaxy filled the viewing area in stately disarray. A polished voice began to speak, pointing out the relationship of the planet Earth to the languidly turning galaxy known as the Milky Way. The tiny sparkle of Earth's sun along one arm of the galaxy increased and the rest of the galaxy expanded until stars blurred and ran in silver streamers down the ceiling to vanish in the black walls. The Solar System grew until individual planets could be seen gliding at the end of invisible leashes around the burning center of the Sun.

The balanced dance of force and counterforce, attraction and retreat was as seductive as Debussy or the haunting fragrance of Armagnac and coffee. Each planet was featured separately: the ochres and tawny browns of Mercury; the fierce heat beneath Venus's brilliant, seething cloud cover; the fragile silver and blue beauty of Earth; Mars's empty, red-brown surface; the great red Eye of Jupiter, set immovably in fluid, multicolored bands of cloud; and Saturn's incredible rings, curves of silence and beauty turning endlessly around their own frozen center.

Raine watched without moving, enthralled by a perspective that was as new to her as the alien landscapes condensing and vanishing in silent counterpoint to the narrator's serene voice. Some of the views were composite photographs taken by space-faring machines. Other views were drawn by artists with rigorous scientific backgrounds. The combination of the factual and the fantastic was as shocking in its own way as being knocked off her feet by Cord.

The Solar System was huge and mysterious, the universe unimaginably vast, the possibilities literally infinite. For all its variety of people and geography, within the perspective of the larger universe, Earth was only a wisp of a dream circling an unknown star; and human life was simply a dream within that dream.

Slowly, light seeped into the auditorium. Raine blinked, still lost within the vastness and beauty of what she had seen. The sense of infinity suspended within eternity was oddly comforting to her. Life was both fragile and tenacious, brief and able to embrace eternity. She sighed with a pleasure that was unlike anything she had felt before. The new sense of being rooted in a vastly larger reality was like being taken out of a cage and set free to soar on endless currents of possibility. She hadn't known that the cage was there until the door was opened. Now she would never go back.

"That was wonderful," said Raine slowly, turning toward Cord. "How did you know that I needed that? I didn't even know it myself."

Cord's fingers tightened over hers. "I knew I needed it. I thought you might. It's easy to get so tangled in one small reality that you can't see forest, trees, or the hand in front of your face. Concentration is fine. Usually it's the only way to get a job done. But sometimes too much concentration ties you in tiny little knots."

"Competition madness," said Raine. "Nothing else seems real but the contest ahead. The world shrinks and shrinks and *shrinks* until it's all you can do to take a deep breath. You have to find something to distract yourself or you suffocate."

Cord stood and pulled Raine to her feet. "That's the way it is in my job," he said, putting his hand on the small of her back as they walked out of the planetarium into the warm darkness. "I guess you could call it a kind of competition madness."

Raine looked sideways and saw the thin gleam of Cord's teeth. His smile was more grim than amused. She knew without asking that the stakes Cord played for were lives rather than medals or ribbons. She wanted to ask what, precisely, Cord's job was, but a lifetime of ingrained reticence about classified work made the question stick in her throat.

"Can you walk in those sexy little sandals?" asked Cord.

Raine looked down at the three tiny straps and outrageously high heel on her right foot. "Depends on what you mean by walk," she admitted. "Anything less civilized than a sidewalk might be a problem."

"If it gets too bad, I'll carry you."

Cord guided Raine onto a paved pathway that wound along the edge of the hills. A fitful wind sent shivers of sound through the silence, distant voices and nearby trees whispering among themselves. After a few moments the path led to a secluded loop overlooking the valley below. Southern pines grew along the viewpoint, their black trunks and airy branches making lacy patterns against the random illumination of city below and stars above. Each city light was vivid, distinct, an echo of the vastly larger stars flung in diamond brightness across the sky.

Everything seemed magnified: the soft scrape of leather soles on pavement, the rub of needles against branches, the fluid ripple of sprinklers on another hill, the whisper of silk caressing Raine's legs. The air smelled of resin and summer flowers and freshly watered grass. The city lights below were stitched together with the ruby and silver threads of countless freeways. Warm air flowed over Raine's skin, tugged gently at her hair. Cord's fingers moved caressingly over hers, sending streamers of invisible warmth through her.

Raine drew a deep breath, letting herself expand into the limitless night. She felt as though she were in a new world, each sense intensely alive, everything around her brighter, better, more vivid and complete. She raised Cord's hand to her mouth and brushed her lips over his skin. The gesture was so natural that she didn't realize what she was doing until she had done it. Cord's thumb moved slowly over her fingertips, telling her how much he had enjoyed the spontaneous touch of her lips.

"Now I know how Dev feels after I wash and groom and polish him and then ride him dancing into a ring," Raine said dreamily. "Everything is ahead, anything is possible."

Cord's thumb traced Raine's cheekbone and the hollow beneath before settling on the corner of her mouth. When he tilted her face, her lips parted naturally and her arms moved to circle his waist. He took her hands, kissed each palm, and placed her arms around his neck, not wanting her to feel the gun nestled in the small of his back. At the beginning of the evening she had been afraid of him at some level. He knew that without any doubt, for sensing fear was his business. He guessed that her fear had as much to do with her past as with his job, but he didn't want to remind her of either just now, because for the moment fear had been forgotten.

When Raine's fingers rubbed over Cord's neck and into his hair, he arched against her touch like a great black-haired cat. Her fingers clenched almost painfully in the rough silk of his hair as his response swept through her, taking her breath with its power. Her nails raked not quite gently over his skin in silent demand that he lower his head and kiss her.

Cord laughed and caught Raine's lower lip between his teeth. His hard tongue teased her while he slowly devoured her lip. Raine made a small sound of pleasure and desire. Strong hands moved from her face to her shoulders and then down her spine to her hips, molding her to the hungry length of his body. When he felt her shudder of response, he groaned softly and cupped the resilient warmth of her hips in his hands. She made a startled sound and tried to move back, only to find herself held by the teeth gently gripping her lower lip.

The instant that Raine discovered she was imprisoned in a sensual vise, Cord released her. Off-balance, she clung to the hard support of his upper arms, staring into his ice-blue eyes. Only they weren't icy now but smoldering with passion, a silver blue hot enough to burn. He bent his head and licked her lips with tiny, catlike strokes, a primitive caress that made liquid fire run and gather inside her. Helplessly, she said his name, a name he stole from her tongue as he claimed the warm territory of her mouth for his own.

The kiss deepened as each of them sought to become part of the other. Cord's hands kneaded down her spine to her hips, touching each feminine curve, holding her against the growing heat and heaviness of his own desire. His fingers shaped the deep cleft of her buttocks, then slid lower, seeking the smooth curve of her inner thighs. This time she did not withdraw at the intimacy. Her arms tightened around his neck as she arched against him, wanting only to be closer and then closer still.

Cord's hands moved back up to Raine's shoulders and then down her arms to her waist, savoring the feminine curves of her body. Fingers spread wide, he traced the line of her ribs beneath the thin silk. His thumbs brushed over her nipples, then moved on before she could do more than gasp at the fire leaping inside her. He murmured against her lips, words without meaning except as another kind of caress, the dark velvet of his voice both soothing and inciting her.

His teeth closed delicately over her ear. He traced its shape with the hardened tip of his tongue, then thrust into her with slow strokes that made her cling to him. His fingers

eased beneath the chestnut coils of her hair, holding her
immobile as his tongue reclaimed her mouth. His other
hand smoothed her throat, savoring the race of her pulse.
Then his caress moved with slow inevitability down the
deep neckline of her dress, sliding beneath silk until her
breast nestled in his hand.

Raine knew that she should protest, but the only sound
that came out of her throat was a tiny moan of pleasure as
Cord's thumb circled her nipple. Taut, aching with a hunger
and need that she had never known before, Raine gave
herself over to the endless sensuality of Cord's touch. She
felt an instant of coolness as he brushed aside the fold of
silk covering her, then a searing pleasure when he bent and
took her into the heat of his mouth. Teeth and tongue moved
over her gently, then suckled her with a fierce tenderness
that made her cry out, defenseless against the fire he could
call from her depths. Eyes closed, trembling, she clung to
him for balance.

Raine was too inexperienced to understand what it did to
Cord when her hips moved against him with instinctive
invitation. He knew, though. Knew that he was at flash
point with a woman he had no right even to touch. He had
no right to seduce her into giving him a place at the center
of her fire. She was the queen and he was the soldier
destined to guard the castle rather than warm himself at the
fire.

That was what Cord's common sense said, but it was a
small voice crying in a wilderness of passion and hunger
and something more, emotions more gentle and complex
and vastly more consuming than lust. He wanted to protect and ravish Raine at the same time, to keep her from
harm and burn her to her core the way he was being burned,
to die and be reborn in her arms and she in his.

Yet he had no right. It was not her wealth or her family that defeated him. It was her vulnerability. As a child she had been a casualty in the undeclared war that was her father's life. It would be no different with Cord. He would wound Raine again, and himself, tearing himself apart between two irreconcilable needs, career and love locked in an endlessly destructive downward spiral until love was dead and duty was ashes. He had seen it happen to too many of his friends, their wives burned out, haunted, cynical. He could not do that to Raine, who trusted him more than she knew—Raine, who had become too precious to risk breaking.

It took all of Cord's considerable discipline to gently disengage himself from Raine's warmth. He held her against his chest as he had in the car, rocking slowly, soothing both of them in the only way he would permit himself to do. When he would have ended even that undemanding embrace, Raine made a sound of protest and moved closer.

"It's late," said Cord, even though his arms tightened around her. He closed his eyes, savoring the warmth and fragrance of Raine as she stirred, her palms moving slowly over the silk of his shirt. "You have a curfew."

"Captain Jon told me not to worry. He thinks I work too hard anyway."

"Do you?"

Raine's shoulders lifted beneath Cord's hands in a shrug. "I love my work. But . . ."

"But?" he asked. His fingers kneaded lightly, smoothing away the tension he felt returning to her neck and back.

"But right now," Raine said, turning her face up to Cord, "I don't want to go back to that world. Not yet. I've never felt quite like this."

Cord looked down into Raine's wide hazel eyes. "How do you feel?" he said, knowing he shouldn't ask but unable to stop.

"New. No past but tonight. No future further away than the next instant when you'll touch me. . . ."

Raine's honesty was more devastating and more intimate than an experienced lover's knowing caress. She was an invitation Cord couldn't refuse and couldn't accept and couldn't ignore.

"Raine," whispered Cord, his voice thick with restraint and need, "you don't know what you're doing."

"Does it matter?" she asked, sliding her hands up to his face, then pulling his head down to her lips. "You know enough for both of us."

"That's the problem," he said roughly.

Cord saw the instant of realization hit Raine, the embarrassment staining her cheeks. The body that had been pliant in his arms twisted and was free with a speed that reminded Cord that Raine was a highly trained athlete.

"I'm sorry," she said in a strained voice. "That was incredibly stupid of me."

And it had been. Just because Cord Elliot was the first man in her life that had made her ache with hunger, that didn't automatically mean he felt the same way. She had turned down enough men. It was only logical that one would turn her down eventually. A man as experienced as Cord would want an equally experienced lover.

"Raine—"

"You're right, of course," she said, cutting across whatever sophisticated, kind, *experienced* explanation Cord was going to offer. She didn't want to hear it. She'd heard all that mattered. "I do have a curfew. Thanks for the guided tour. I'll take a cab back to Santa Anita."

Raine turned and began walking blindly along the path, knowing only that she had to get away. She no longer saw the scintillant display of city lights or the shadow dance of black trees and warm wind. She saw nothing but her own humiliation. Not that Cord had intended to humiliate her. He had been a gentleman until she had refused to take a hint. Even then, he had been no harsher than he had to be to get her attention.

High heels wobbled warningly beneath Raine's feet as she increased her pace. The sandals weren't made for speed or distance, and she desperately wanted both right now. She could hear Cord coming closer, closing the space between them with long, determined strides.

"I'll take you home," he said quietly.

The hell you will, thought Raine. She tore off her shoes with two quick motions and began to run down the path, confident that she would quickly outpace Cord. Part of her Olympic training involved running distances up to five kilometers. She had never particularly cared for the required exercise, although she had appreciated the results.

Tonight, though, she welcomed the physical release that running provided, the freedom of racing through darkness away from the man who didn't want her. Her coiled hair, already loosened by Cord's probing fingers, came wholly undone. She shook her head, sending hairpins flying and hair streaming back over her shoulders. Jade-green silk flowed in a dark caress up her thighs as her stride became even longer, legs flashing in the occasional patches of illumination along the path.

Anger and humiliation were transformed into adrenaline coursing through Raine, feeding her desire to run. Part of her realized that she was heading away from the planetarium, into the black recesses of the huge park. But she didn't care. She ran lightly, soundlessly, a green flame racing among the shadows and pools of light along the path, wildfire running free in the night.

Something hard clamped onto Raine's arm, spinning her around until she crashed into a hard wall of flesh. In the instant that Raine realized she was caught, Cord surrounded her. One of his hands tangled irrevocably in her hair, chaining her. His arms closed around her, crushing any thought of rebellion. He invaded her mouth, forcing her to accept the intimacy of his tongue thrusting into her softness as he held her immobile, consolidating his victory.

The transition between freedom and capture was so swift, so overwhelming, that for a time Raine couldn't have fought even if Cord had permitted her to. When she finally tried, Cord countered her untrained struggles with an ease that would have frightened her if she hadn't sensed that it was hunger rather than a desire to punish her that was driving Cord. Whatever she had thought back on the overlook, Cord wanted her now with an honesty that was more shattering than any words, any touch could have been.

Raine's body changed beneath Cord's hands, softening and flowing over his male surfaces, surrendering what he had already taken; and in doing so, making a mockery of terms such as victory or defeat, flight or capture, invasion or surrender. She felt the shudder of desire go through him, felt as much as heard the groan that began deep in his chest, felt and was inflamed by the sinuous movement of his hips as he lifted her and then let her slide down the hard length of his body, showing her exactly how much he desired her.

"I thought you didn't want me," Raine whispered when Cord finally freed her mouth.

Cord laughed once, harshly. "Kiss me," he said urgently, his eyes looking hungrily at Raine's mouth even as he lowered his head again. "I want to feel your tongue moving over mine."

"Cord—"

"*Kiss me.*"

Raine opened her lips, inviting the sweetness and heat of Cord's mouth even as she sought his tongue. She kissed him as he had kissed her, hunger and honesty and passion shivering through her with each stroke of flesh sliding moistly over flesh. Her hands moved beneath his jacket, seeking the hard, coiling male strength of him. Her fingers searched beneath his tie, slid boldly into the opening between buttons on his shirt. Even as her fingers found his skin, his hands cupped her breasts beneath the folds of green silk.

She couldn't help the broken sound that escaped her when his fingers teased her nipples until they were hard peaks begging to be kissed. His teeth raked down her neck, neither too light nor too cruel. He had just enough restraint not to leave loving marks on her, staking out her unblemished flesh as his own. But he wanted to. He wanted to discover and claim every bit of her softness and feminine hunger, to feed and then possess the heat that was inside her, to spend the night listening to the soft cries pouring out of her as she burned in her own fire.

With hungry hands, Cord kneaded Raine's hips, enjoying the tantalizing flex and play of muscle as she moved against him. He felt her hands slide around his body beneath his jacket, seeking to bring him even closer to her. Her head tilted back as he lifted her hips into the heavy ache of his desire. He felt the sweet tension and shivering in her as she responded. Her nails raked down his spine—and found the gun nestled in the small of his back.

There was an instant of stillness followed by a withdrawal that couldn't have been more complete if Raine had turned and run away again.

"I wouldn't have expected Blue's daughter to be afraid of a holstered gun," Cord said in a husky voice, "but if it bothers you that much, I'll take it off."

"It's not that," said Raine, feeling numb and foolish and totally off-balance. But she would not reach for Cord this time. She would find her balance on her own, because she remembered now. "I'd forgotten what you were."

"What I am," said Cord bluntly, "is a man."

"Yes," Raine said, her voice distant and sad at the same time. Her hand slid beneath Cord's jacket once again, only this time she continued below his waist until she felt the hard rectangle of the electronic pager nestled securely in its case below his belt. "You're a man who has clothes specially tailored to conceal the bulge of beeper and gun. Or is that your spare ammunition clip?"

"No," Cord said, his voice even. "The clip is on my right side."

Raine didn't bother to verify it. She felt cold. Unconsciously, she rubbed her hands over her arms, trying to warm herself. Cord swore softly, viciously, a residue of hunger and a frustration that went much deeper than desire. He should have known better than to get involved with a woman like Raine. She was wealthy, successful, gently raised—and burned beyond recovery on the subject of certain types of work. His type of work.

"I'm more than a gun and a beeper," said Cord, his voice savage.

"Are you? My father isn't."

"Crap!" snarled Cord. "Your mother sure as hell doesn't think so."

"I'm not my mother. I want more from a man than money and position."

"Blue loves your mother very much."

"Perhaps," said Raine politely.

"You don't think so?" challenged Cord.

"Depends on what you call love," Raine retorted. "Being left without warning again and again, never being able to count on the man who 'loves' you for something so simple as a shoulder to sleep on, never knowing if he's coming back—"

"He always has. Other men might screw around," Cord said bluntly, "but Blue never did."

Raine's laugh wasn't pleasant. "Not surprising. Only a wife would put up with a man wearing a beeper. A mistress would tell him to go to hell."

"Or a daughter?" suggested Cord sardonically.

"Wife, mistress or daughter," Raine snapped, "the beeper means the same thing: second place in a two-entry race. I had all I could take of that as a child. The kind of work my father does is important, addictive, and carnivorous. But then, I'm not telling you anything you don't know, am I?"

"No," Cord said, his mouth as grim as his voice. "I knew how you felt the instant my beeper went off yesterday. That's what I meant tonight when I said that you didn't know what you were doing. I knew you didn't want me, even though you thought you did."

"I wanted you," Raine whispered, shivering, torn between her hunger and the cold of childhood memories.

"Not enough to see past the gun and beeper. Not even for one goddamned night. I suppose I should be grateful. Neither one of us is the one-night-stand type. Sure as hell you would have hated me in the morning." Cord bent and picked up the purse and sandals Raine had dropped when he caught her. "Put your shoes on."

Raine tried to, but couldn't because her fingers were

shaking. With an impatient sound, Cord reclaimed the sandals and fastened them on her. In silence, they walked back to the car. The silence remained until Cord pulled up and parked several doors down from Raine's motel room.

"Give me your key."

Raine stared at Cord.

"Don't worry, Baby Raine. I'm not planning to spend the night between your white sheets."

"I don't like that name," she said tightly.

"I know." Cord's smile was barely more than a knife-edge of teeth. He opened Raine's purse and took out the room key before she could object. "Stay here."

Cord walked to the door, tested gently to see that it was still locked, then lifted the key with his right hand. As he did, he caught movement out of the corner of his eye. He spun around, his left hand pulling out his gun in the instant before he recognized Raine. She retreated two steps and then caught herself angrily. Even though Cord didn't look very civilized at the moment, she knew he wouldn't hurt her.

"I told you to stay in the car," he said curtly.

"Why should I?"

"Because there might be a bomb behind this door, just waiting for the key to be turned."

Raine's hand came up to her mouth in an involuntary gesture of shock. "But then you—you'd be the one to—"

"That's my job," Cord said. "Go back to the car."

"But—"

"Relax. I'm more worried about someone waiting in the room than a bomb."

Raine spun and walked back to the car without another word. Cord opened the motel room, went inside, and listened for a minute, holding his breath. Nothing moved, nothing breathed. He flipped on the light, searched the places big enough to hide a man, and found exactly what the odds said he should: nothing. He went back out to the car, then walked Raine to her door.

"You live in a beautiful castle, with a fire burning in every hearth," said Cord, standing very close to Raine, watching her with eyes that were as clear and empty as ice. "I wish to hell there were a place by all that fire for me." He gave Raine a fierce, yearning kiss before he turned and went to his car, leaving her standing with his taste on her lips and her nails digging into her own palms.

He didn't look back.

Chapter 5

RAINE LEANED AGAINST THE STALL, HER ELBOWS ON THE bottom half of the Dutch door, her back to the dusty yard that separated rows of stables. The yard was wetted down twice daily, but the southern California heat evaporated water almost as quickly as it came out of the sprinklers. Although it was very early in the day, a dry wind already stirred among the fragile leaves of pepper trees, making lacy shadows shiver and run over the ground. The breeze lifted Raine's hair, blowing it over her face.

Ears pricked, Dev snorted and investigated the flying strands of Raine's hair with quivering nostrils. Raine watched Dev breathe deeply and snort repeatedly as he drank her scent. She wondered if it was only the wind that was making Dev nervous today. Since the moment he had caught her scent, he had been walking on eggs.

"What is it, boy?" she asked softly, holding out her hand.

Dev sniffed her hand, then her arm, then her neck with consuming interest.

"Hey," said Raine, backing away from the horse's intense inspection, "I know I didn't shower this morning, but I smell a lot worse after a workout and you've never objected."

Dev snorted a long comment, then resumed snuffling over every inch of Raine, reserving his most particular interest for her hair, face, neck and hands. The last time Dev had showed such a persistent interest in her, she had been wearing a new cologne. But whatever artificial scent she had on was left over from last night, and it was the same cologne she had worn for years. Nothing had changed—except that last night she had let a man's hands and mouth move over her as though he owned her.

A flush of color spread beneath Raine's skin as she realized what had happened. Dev was fascinated by her scent because it *was* different. Traces of Cord Elliot lingered on her skin, in her hair, behind her ears, in the hollow of her throat, between her fingers where she had rubbed them through Cord's hair. Invisible traces to her, but not to the stallion's acute senses.

Cord's male scent was all over her, blended with her own.

Raine gritted her teeth and waited for Dev to accustom himself to the new scent. The horse's unerring accuracy in finding each place that Cord had touched her proved unnerving when it wasn't embarrassing. She only tolerated the thorough inspection because it was easier than going back to the motel and taking a shower.

After a final, long snort, Dev turned away and lipped indifferently at the straw on the stall floor.

"Finished?" asked Raine sarcastically. "You're sure, now? I'd hate to have you mistake me for someone else."

Except for a flick of a black-tipped ear, Dev ignored her. Raine turned to the wheelbarrow she had brought up to the stall and pried off a few thick flakes of baled hay. The hay had been shipped all the way from Virginia so that Dev wouldn't have his digestive system upset by new food. Later in the morning he would get a special round of corn and oats and vitamins. For now, though, Dev would get the bulky food. Raine tucked the hay under one arm and went into the stall, closing the lower half of the door behind her. She slapped Dev's gleaming mahogany haunch.

"Move over, or no breakfast."

The stallion shifted aside good-naturedly. Raine dumped the hay in the manger and let Dev's strong teeth tear apart the inches-thick slabs of hay. While he ate, she raked out his stall. There was no lack of stable help to muck out Dev's quarters, including girls who would have little to fear from Dev's heels. Even so, Raine preferred to care for the horse herself. Watching how Dev ate, how he moved, even how he breathed, all added up to her own version of a daily checkup of the stallion's health. If anything was wrong with Dev, no matter how subtle, Raine would notice.

She cleaned Dev's hooves, working quietly, each hoof braced between her bent legs. If the stallion hadn't been cooperative, the job would have been impossible. As it was, all Raine had to do was touch a fetlock and that hoof was presented politely for her inspection. When each hoof was clean and she had satisfied herself that each shoe was on securely, she brought in fresh straw for the stall. She made several trips, scattering straw lavishly. Naturally, by the time she came back with a last armful, Dev had produced more manure for her to take care of.

"Never fails," Raine muttered, grabbing the rake and taking care of the problem. "Feed one end and the other goes to work."

Dev ignored her. Raine reached into the box that held Dev's personal grooming tools. She went to work on him with a soft oval brush, bringing the already gleaming hide up to a high red gloss. From the yard came the sound of voices, too distant for Raine to make out individual words. The subtle shifts of tone, however, told her that Captain Jon was one of the people talking. With half attention, she listened to his voice come closer.

"None of the animals I've pointed out would give your men any problem," said Captain Jon in his clear tenor. "This next one, however, is different. Devlin's Waterloo should never be handled by anyone but his owner, Miss Smith. In a pinch, the stallion will tolerate being handled by me, but I'm bloody careful about making sudden moves. Not that the horse is vicious, mind you. He was abused by a man and has never forgotten it."

There was silence broken by the subtle whisper of a soft brush over Dev's softer hide. Finished with breakfast, Dev stood three-legged, his head hanging, his eyes closed, the picture of serenity. He groaned his pleasure as Raine's careful grooming scratched all the places he couldn't scratch himself.

"Are you telling me *that* is the terror of stable twelve?" asked a deep, amused voice from behind the stall door.

Raine managed not to drop the brush when she recognized Cord's voice. She finished a long stroke down Dev's haunch. The stallion turned, head up, ears pricked forward. She saw the flare of his nostrils when he scented Cord Elliot. As though comparing scents, Dev nosed Raine, then turned around and began a thorough smelling of Cord.

Cord stood without moving, watching Dev's black muzzle while it traveled lightly from his fingertips to his ears.

"Hello, Devlin's Waterloo," said Cord calmly, unafraid

of the huge stallion's attention. "Are you trying to tell me I should have taken a shower this morning?"

Raine flushed and looked away. She fervently hoped that she would be the only one to figure out why Dev was so interested in Cord's scent—and so unafraid of a man who was a stranger.

"Bloody fascinating," muttered Captain Jon, watching Dev's ears, the early-warning system of any horse's temper. The stallion's ears were up, interested but not nervous. "Dev isn't afraid of you. And," finished Captain Jon, giving Cord an appraising look, "you aren't afraid of him."

"I was raised around horses," said Cord easily. Very slowly, he lifted his hand, watching the stallion's ears.

Dev snorted, then sniffed Cord's fingers with renewed interest.

"I'd scratch your ears for you," murmured Cord, "but I don't think you're ready for that, are you?"

Dev whuffled a soft answer, blowing warm air over Cord's neck.

"You're a beauty," continued Cord, his voice velvet and deep, as mesmerizing as a moonlit river flowing through darkness. "You're big as a mountain, but so well made that you seem more like fifteen than seventeen hands. Healthy, too. Look at those muscles slide when you move . . . graceful as a woman and strong as a god. My great-granddaddy would have killed to get his hands on a stud like you. Red hide and black socks, mane and tail like slices of midnight. The devil's own colors. But you aren't a devil, are you? You're an angel dressed to go sightseeing in hell."

Dev stood and listened, bewitched by a shaman's voice, forgetting even to sniff the oddly familiar scent of the man who stood so quietly before him.

"Raine," said Cord, not shifting the tone of his voice at all, "come over and stand in front of me."

SUMMER GAMES   95

It took Raine a moment to realize that the velvet words were directed at her. She moved slowly, pulled by an invisible leash. Cord neither looked away from Dev nor moved as Raine came and stood in front of the stall door. Cord's voice never ceased, words and nonsense words intermixed into a soothing river lapping at consciousness, draining tension into boneless contentment.

"Turn around and face Dev," said Cord.

Again, it took Raine a moment to respond.

"Don't be startled," murmured Cord. "I'm going to put my arm next to yours." Cord followed his words with action, slowly bringing his arm forward until it lay along Raine's. His voice continued all the time, sound flowing soothingly. "Slowly raise your hand and pet Dev."

Raine obeyed, almost as mesmerized as her horse by the spoken music of Cord's voice. As she moved, so did Cord, their arms lifting as one. Dev didn't flinch when her hand, with Cord's covering it, scratched the sensitive area behind the stallion's ears. Cord continued speaking, a murmurous, mesmerizing flow of sound, nonsense interspersed with meaning.

"Slowly ease your hand down to your side," said Cord.

Raine's hand retreated to her side, moving with a dreamlike slowness. Dev didn't seem to notice the instant that her hand was gone and he was standing as placid as a cow while a strange man scratched itchy places with unerring skill.

"Move away from me slowly," murmured Cord, "along the stall door. Very, very slowly. That's it. Good."

Raine moved, fascinated by what was happening.

It took a few moments for Dev to realize that his mistress was gone and in her place was a man who was neither wholly familiar nor wholly strange. By the time Dev was aware of what had happened, it was too late for panic or anger. The contact was established. Dev's ears wavered, then settled at a relaxed half-mast position. The stallion sighed and nudged Cord's skilled hand, accepting it.

Cord continued talking for a moment, praising Dev lavishly, using his voice and touch to reward the stallion's acceptance. When Cord removed his hand and stopped talking, Dev looked vaguely surprised. He snorted once, resoundingly, gave Cord a bemused look, and turned his attention back to Raine.

"Bloody incredible," said Captain Jon, looking from Dev to Cord. "I don't care what your job is, Elliot. If you aren't training horses, you're wasting yourself."

"I had an edge," said Cord, smiling slightly, looking at Raine.

Raine knew then that Cord understood exactly why Dev had been so interested in Cord's scent; Cord had smelled of Raine, just as she had smelled of him.

"An edge!" snorted Captain Jon. "You had the whole bloody campaign in the palm of your hand and you knew it. That's a rare gift, man. Use it." Then, as an afterthought, "If the rest of your men are a tenth the horseman you are, they can be underfoot all you like. I'll withdraw my complaints immediately."

"Your men?" said Raine, looking at Cord. She realized that he was dressed in blue jeans, work shirt and a denim jacket, nothing to distinguish him except the aura of power that he wore as naturally as he wore the casual clothes.

"Sorry," said Captain Jon. "I haven't introduced you. Miss Raine Smith, Mr. Cord Elliot. Mr. Elliot is with Olympic security."

Cord held out his hand. Years of ingrained politeness made Raine take it.

"Hello, Raine," said Cord, his voice suddenly velvet and dark again.

"Don't use that shaman's voice on me," she said coolly, but she couldn't help the warmth that raced through her when his hand closed over hers. "I'm not as good-natured as my horse."

"I know," Cord said, his voice suddenly flat, uninflected. He turned back to Captain Jon, who was looking both puzzled and more than a little curious at the undercurrents flowing between the two. "I met Raine a few days ago, but we've never been properly introduced," said Cord. "In fact, Raine is the reason I amended the security regulations to include taking a friend along for any inspections of the endurance course."

"Then you're the chap who swept her off her feet," said Captain Jon with a sideways look at Raine.

"Is that what she said?" asked Cord, his voice bland, the center of his eyes very black against the pale blue irises.

"Not quite," Raine retorted. *"Knocked* me off my feet was how I put it. More accurate, don't you think?"

Cord smiled crookedly. "You think I'm more truth than poetry, is that it?"

Raine started to agree, then remembered the feeling of being held by Cord, changing as he touched her, a new world opening before her. And then the cold steel gun, the old world coming up to claim her.

"That's the way life is," Raine said, her voice sad. "More truth than poetry." She looked away to speak to Captain Jon, only to realize that he had withdrawn unobtrusively.

"Your picture is misleading," said Cord.

"What?" she said, off-balance again, turning toward him.

"Your picture," said Cord, touching the laminated ID badge clipped to Raine's collar. "Is that the best the photographer could do?"

Raine shrugged. The picture had been taken just after she had arrived in California. She had been jet-lagged and exhausted, having spent the previous forty-eight hours without sleep, her head in a basin as the last word in Asian flu bugs ravaged her system until she devoutly wished to die. Her normally clear skin had looked thick and sallow, her eyes had been ringed by darkness, and her hair had hung like wet string around her face. When the photographer had said "Smile!" her lips had thinned into a pale, humorless line.

"I'd been sick," she said succinctly.

"I believe it." Cord shook his head. "I might not have jumped you if your file picture had looked more like the real you. But then, it probably wouldn't have mattered. Photographs are tricky. You can get badly burned depending on them. When you started reaching into that rucksack, you left me no choice but to take you down."

Raine started to disagree hotly; and then she remembered last night, when Cord had taken the key out of her purse and opened the door to her room. To a man who spent his life knowing that every key could trigger a bomb, the idea that she might have a weapon in her rucksack would be inevitable, not incredible. Her glance went to Cord's badge. It had his name and the word "Security," followed by a code number that assured access to every nook and cranny of any Olympic site.

Beneath the laminated plastic, the face in Cord's picture was hard and unyielding, older than he looked now. The flash had highlighted the narrow sprinkling of gray that would one day become a solid forelock of silver, pure and vivid against the black thickness of his hair. In the picture, Cord's eyes were as hard and transparent as glacier ice, almost no blue showing, and the line of his jaw was grim.

He looked like what he was, a man accustomed to secrets, a man who wore a gun and knew how to use it.

"Your picture looks more like you than you do," said Raine slowly.

Cord's expression changed subtly, like a mask slipping into place. He looked more like his picture now. Cold. "I was angry when that picture was taken. I had just been pulled off a matter that I'd been working on for a long time."

"And assigned to Olympic security?" guessed Raine.

Cord hesitated. The pause was familiar to Raine; it was her father's response when she asked questions and she didn't have the security clearance to hear the answers. But, unlike Justin Chandler-Smith, Cord answered.

"Yes."

"Will you go back to the, er, 'matter' when the Summer Games are over?" persisted Raine, though she knew she shouldn't be asking questions. Nor should she be holding her breath to hear his answer.

Again the hesitation. Again the surprising honesty of Cord's answer. "I don't know. The matter may be concluded by then. If it isn't, I'll see it through to conclusion." Cord added softly, unexpectedly, "I owe them that much, Raine."

The blend of harshness and yearning in Cord's voice made emotions twist through Raine, anger and sympathy and a yearning that was too much like Cord's. "You don't owe me any explanations or answers," she said tightly. "I know how the game is played."

"Do you?" he asked, watching her with an intensity that made his eyes narrow.

"I grew up with it, Cord. Have you forgotten who I am?"

"Not for a second," he said, his voice caressing Raine as he looked at her lips with eyes that remembered everything. "You're the woman I kissed until you melted and ran over me like liquid fire. So much heat—and all of it locked away from men like me. Who are you waiting for, Raine *Chandler*-Smith? A well-mannered lapdog who always shows up for his meals on time?"

"Yes," Raine hissed, suddenly furious. "That's just what I'm waiting for!"

"You're lying," said Cord, his voice calm, relentless. "You're surrounded by men like that. You have been all your life—but not one of them has touched the fire inside you."

"How do you know?" she challenged. "I might have had a string of lovers as long as Dev's tail."

"You might have, but you haven't." Assurance rang in Cord's voice. He was not guessing. He knew.

"You've read my file," she said coldly, outraged at the invasion of her private life.

"No. I read *you*. And everything I see tells me I'm right. If you liked lapdogs, you'd be riding a lapdog. You'd be cool and regal on top of an impeccably mannered dressage horse. If you liked lapdogs, you sure as hell wouldn't be riding a blood-bay stud as big and mean as a falling mountain."

"Dev isn't mean," said Raine quickly. "Not with me, anyway."

"No, not with you," said Cord, his voice changing again, smoky velvet. "You can reach inside the hardest creature and hold its heart beating in your hand."

Raine felt herself falling again, off-balance, as unprepared as Dev for Cord's ability to slide through defenses that had routed all comers for as long as she could remember.

"That isn't right," she whispered, thinking aloud.

"No, it isn't. But it's just what you do, Raine."

Raine simply shook her head, unable to speak or even to believe what Cord was saying.

Dev nudged Raine vigorously, all but knocking her off her feet. Automatically she reached for the stallion's halter rope, hanging high on the wall beside her. She clipped the rope onto Dev's halter.

"It's time for Dev's walk," Raine said in a strained voice.

Cord looked at the loose halter. It would offer almost no restraint if the stallion decided to bolt. "That's it? Just a regular halter?"

Raine looked at the halter, sighed, and went to the tack box. She returned with a different halter. It was almost a hackamore—a bridle without a bit. So long as Dev behaved, the special halter would remain loose around his muzzle. If he acted up, a pull on the lead rope would cause a strap across Dev's nose to tighten, cutting off the flow of air through the stallion's nostrils. It was as effective as a steel bit in terms of control, but gave the horse greater freedom to eat and drink in the stall.

"Good enough?" she asked coolly.

Cord nodded. "Leave it on him all the time. That's a request, but I can make it official."

"Dev is a gentleman."

"With you, yes. With the rest of the world, he's hell on four hooves."

"Not with you," Raine retorted almost resentfully as she led Dev out into the yard.

Cord bent close as Raine walked by. "That's because I smelled like you," he said, his voice deep. "I noticed it this morning, like the scent of spring on the wind. But it isn't spring, is it? It's winter all year round with you."

"That isn't fair," she whispered, but he heard.

"Not much is, or hadn't you noticed? Open your eyes, Baby Raine. There's a world out there you haven't seen."

"I've seen it," Raine said, her voice as harsh as his. Her eyes were defiant. Splinters of dark green flashed as she turned her head to face Cord. "It didn't impress me as a good place to live in. A fine place for dying, though. Or hadn't *you* noticed?"

"Is that what you're afraid of—dying?"

Raine tilted her head to one side as she considered the question. "No," she said finally, "I'm afraid of being like my mother, waiting for the man she loves to be assassinated. Waiting alone, because he's too busy saving the world to live with her. That's what I'm afraid of, Mr. Cord Elliot—loving the wrong man."

"So you haven't loved any man."

"My choice."

"A lonely choice. More lonely than your mother's. She's at least waiting for someone."

"A choice that was forced on her. Dad was just a lawyer when she married him."

Cord moved close in a single, gliding stride. "When you find the tame *gentle*man of your dreams, Baby Raine, what will you do when he takes one look at you and runs like hell?"

"What do you mean?" whispered Raine, wanting to look away from Cord but not able to. The intensity in him was like a net suddenly thrown over her, holding her immobile.

"Look at yourself. Rich. Graceful. Pedigreed back to the Dark Ages. Smart and strong and elegant, a rapier turned on a master smith's forge. A *gentle*man could probably get past all that, but what about the rest? What about the wildness burning inside you? The risk-taking part of you that saw seventeen hands of savage horse and said, 'This is mine.' There's part of you that loves danger. Like your father. Like me.''

"That's not true," Raine said, her voice raw.

"Like hell it isn't." Cord's laugh was harsh and humorless. His voice was a knife cutting away her certainties, her world, leaving her no place to hide. "You complain that my job or your father's is risky. What the hell do you call taking Dev over blind downhill jumps when he's so tired you can hear the breath groaning through him? Whatever you call it, your little dream *gentle*man will turn pale and go looking for a nice, safe, timid dream *gentle*woman to marry."

Raine's nails dug into the lead rope she was holding. She shook her head unconsciously, denying the truth in Cord's words. "I'll find what I want," she said, her voice husky and certain. "When I do, I won't need adrenaline and risks to fill my life."

Cord's voice changed, velvet again as he bent over her, so close that he could sense the warmth of her. "What do you want?"

"A man who loves me enough to live with me," said Raine simply, her eyes brilliant with unshed tears, tears that would never be shed because she had learned that tears didn't make any difference in the world her father lived in.

Cord closed his eyes, hearing the hurt and hunger beneath her words. "Raine," he said softly, "you wouldn't recognize your man if he stood in front of you. You're afraid of loving."

"And you're an expert on love?" she said, her voice hard and dry.

"No," he said softly, "I'm an expert on dying. On not loving. On being lonely. On looking at castles from the outside. On finding a woman worth having and then watching her bar the gate against me because I'm just a soldier, not a king."

Raine shook her head slowly, defenseless against the emotions flowing beneath Cord's words, a hunger like her own. "That's not why." She looked at Cord, so close to her, quiet and yet dangerous, hungry and yet aloof, as powerful and yet as vulnerable as Dev had been the day she had found him down and tangled helplessly in his own strength. "No," Raine whispered, her voice strained. She stepped away from Cord until she came up against the stallion's massive body. "I can't live the way my mother has. It would destroy me."

Cord stood without moving as Raine spun and walked quickly away, leading the huge blood-bay stud as casually as though he were a pony. The cold that Cord had sensed inside himself congealed into ice. He had looked over a lot of castle walls, shrugged and gone on, caring only for the next mountain range, the next skirmish beyond the valley, the next battle in a war older than he was.

But somewhere between all those valleys, the mountains and battles had become higher and colder, chilling him so subtly, so deeply that he hadn't even noticed until a woman had given him a few moments next to her fire. She had showed him the possibilities of life and warmed him all the way to his soul. Then she had talked of courtiers and kings and turned away from him, locking him outside the castle again, away from the fire . . . mountains all around, their icy reaches waiting as they had always waited for men like him.

Cord didn't want the mountains anymore. He had heard all the variations of their siren call, height and distance, victory and exhilaration, loss and despair. He had taken mountain ranges and passes one by one, held or lost them until the battle moved on to a different range. Then he had walked down through green valleys on the way to the next mountain, the next pass, the next battle. For there were always more mountains and passes singing to him, rank upon rank of heights, eternity stretching before him, a battle without end.

There were times when he couldn't remember what it felt like not to climb, not to be cold, not to fight. Behind him was a lifetime of skirmishes, of men who fought and men who died, memories and years sliding away into ice. He felt the years congealing inside, freezing him. Some day he would no longer know the difference between valley and pass, warmth and ice. Or he wouldn't care. He had seen men like that. Cinder cases. Burned out.

He had always sworn that it would never happen to him. He had never believed that it would. Like other men, he had assumed he would die before he burned out.

Like other men, he had been wrong.

The beeper at Cord's belt pulsed rhythmically. He heard it at a distance. Automatically, he punched out the answering code, years of reflexes taking over. He turned and walked quickly toward the huge motorhome that was parked just inside the stable fence. He didn't see the containers of flowers lining the paths between stables and yards. He didn't see the golden cataracts of sunlight pouring around him or feel the breeze or hear the vibrant murmur of bees settling delicately between fragrant petals. He saw nothing but mountains, felt nothing but ice.

The motorhome was the color of dust. It was connected to Santa Anita's power supply by several wires, only one of which carried electricity. The others were secure phone lines unobtrusively mingled with the more ordinary lines. Except for an unusual number of antennae, there was nothing noteworthy about the motorhome's presence. Many people associated with the Olympics found it easier to bring their quarters with them than to commute through the tangled traffic patterns of the Los Angeles Basin.

There was a man in a lawn chair out in front of the dusty
motorhome, a man who apparently had nothing better to do
than sit and dream in the sun. For all his outward relaxation,
however, the man's dark glance was shrewd and alert.

"Morning, Mr. Elliot," said the man, his soft southern
drawl as misleading as his lazy sprawl.

"Morning, Thorne. Any visitors?"

"No suh. Not even any rubberneckers."

"Good."

Cord unlocked the combination key-and-pressure lock on
the motorhome's side door and went inside. An air-
conditioner hummed discreetly. Inside, the decor was a
tawny mixture of gold and buff and chestnut with refreshing
jade-green highlights. A couch that made into a queen-size
bed went along the wall opposite the door, facing a game
table large enough to seat four. Television, stereo, a few
books and maps, nothing at all unusual to a casual glance. It
would take a very perceptive or suspicious person to notice
that the walls were too thick and the storage compartments
and cupboards were constructed to discourage casual access.

The interior door to the back of the motorhome was open.
On either side of the narrow hallway were a bathroom, a
kitchen, and a bedroom. The last third of the motorhome
could only be entered through another interior door. This
door also had an unusual lock. Cord was the only one on the
West Coast who knew the combination. He unlocked the
door, opened it and relocked it behind him.

The room was surprisingly large. One wall of furnishings
was utterly commonplace: a bed, bedside table, and lamp.
The other walls looked more like the cockpit of an airplane
or a modern recording studio than the master bedroom suite
of a luxury motorhome. Electronic equipment was built into
every available workspace. A separate air-conditioner

worked efficiently, keeping the room at an optimum temperature for the most sensitive of the equipment.

A computer terminal waited in the corner, screen blank. Cord pulled a swivel chair away from the radio and sat down in front of the computer. He unlocked the keyboard with a special key, entered a code number, and waited.

BLUE MOON CONTACT BLUE HERRING flashed on the screen.

Cord punched in the acknowledgment, swiveled to a radio telephone that had already been fitted with a scrambler, punched out another series of code numbers, hung up, and waited. After a few minutes, the phone rang.

Cord picked up the receiver. "How's the fishing?" he asked.

"They're rising, buddy." The voice floated up out of the speaker on a soft wave of static that lapped at the silence of the room.

Cord smiled grimly at the excitement he sensed beneath the radio-flattened voice of "Blue Herring." Al was a man who still looked forward to the next range of mountains, the next freezing pass, the next battle. "That so? What kind of fish do you have out there today?"

"Barracuda."

Cord's breath came in silently. "You're sure?"

"Sixty percent. Department of Fish and Game confirmed sighting on basis of file photo taken at extreme range. I know how you feel about photos, buddy, but I thought I'd pass on the nibble."

"Where did he surface," said Cord curtly, his face hard, his voice uninflected.

"LAX. Last night."

Cord thought quickly. The assassin known only as Barracuda had been spotted at Los Angeles International Airport by Immigration officials. Or, to be precise, a man

who resembled the only known photograph of Barracuda
had been spotted. If the match was correct, it would be a
coup. Cord was one of the few people who had seen
Barracuda close up and had gotten away to tell about it. As
far as Cord was concerned, Barracuda's file photo was next
to useless. It was a profile shot that didn't show the
assassin's most outstanding feature—a narrowness between
the eyes that had moved Cord to dub him Barracuda.

"Who ID'd him?" asked Cord.

"Good old Eagle Eye."

Cord traced the line of his chin with one knuckle as he
assimilated the information and extrapolated possibilities.
His eyes were narrow, intent, focused on a different world.
If Mitchell had been the one to ID Barracuda, Cord couldn't
afford to ignore it. Mitchell had an uncanny knack for
fitting grainy black-and-white still photos over moving,
three-dimensional faces. That was why Mitchell had been
assigned to Customs and Immigration in LAX for the
duration of the Olympics, when foreign nationals of all
kinds would pour into LA.

"Probable target," demanded Cord.

Al's laugh was as thin as a knife. *"You, if he sees you."*

"Of course," said Cord impatiently. Barracuda had
wanted to kill him for a long time. An assassin's success
depended on anonymity as much as skill or nerve. "Does
he know I'm here, though?"

There was a soft, static-filled pause. *"Doubtful. The boys
upstairs figure that Old Blue is the target. Backup target is
Baby Blue."*

This time Cord's breath came in with an audible sound.
Baby Blue was the code name for Raine Chandler-Smith.
Cord swore beneath his breath. It was well known how
proud Blue was of his youngest daughter—at least, everyone but the daughter in question seemed to know. Blue had

promised he'd see his daughter ride in the endurance event if it was the last thing he did.

And it well could be. Anything that made Blue's actions predictable to an assassin was dangerous. A father's desire to see his daughter perform in the Olympics was as predictable as sunrise. That was why Cord had been yanked out of his normal position as an anti-terrorist operative with the Defense Intelligence Agency and assigned as liaison to Olympic security. Blue's boss had wanted the best available protection for Chandler-Smith, and as secretary of defense, was in a position to demand it.

"You're sure about the primary and secondary target," said Cord in a clipped voice.

"There's no substitute for good bait when you're going fishing. We've got a nice, juicy night crawler on the hook."

"So the worm finally turned," Cord muttered, wondering which member of Barracuda's terrorist group had gotten scared and run for cover in the enemy's arms.

"Believe it, buddy. He's wriggling and oozing all over the place. Ugly little bastard, but he's no dummy. Blue's going to have someone's butt when he finds out that Baby Blue is on the menu."

"Blue will have to wait in line," said Cord, his voice utterly colorless as he thought of the softness and grace and surprising fire that was Raine. He had spent his life protecting people he didn't know. He knew Raine. He couldn't have her, shouldn't even want her . . . but he could see that she survived to look for her safe and gentle dream. "Tell Blue there's only one way Barracuda will get to Baby. Through me."

"But Blue doesn't know anyone called Cord Elliot," said Al innocently.

"Neither do you," retorted Cord. "Just pass the message."

"It's on its way." Then, quietly, *"Still play chess, buddy?"*

"As often as you do, *compadre.*"

Soft laughter faded into static, then silence.

Cord replaced the receiver and sat looking into space for a long time. When he focused again on the room, he was surprised to find a worn gold coin in his hand. He had taken the coin out of his pocket without fully realizing it, and had sat rubbing the smooth gold between his fingers like a talisman while he thought about assassins and Raine, the high price of life and the terrible cost of death, castle and fire, mountain and ice.

"So it's that bad, is it?" murmured Cord, turning the lucky piece between his fingers until a woman's face looked at him through slanting eyes. "Are you listening, Lady Luck, Lady Death? Or am I the one who should be listening to you?"

The woman said nothing, merely watched him from a background of ideographs. Behind her was an alien city where roofs turned up to the sky in silent supplication to unknown gods. Different culture, different reality, same world. Part of the gigantic interlocking puzzle of languages and cultures, people and desires that was life, his own life. A mélange of experience and memories and dreams . . . the smell of piñon and campfires, the eight-limbed elegance of a dancing god, flooded rice paddies the color of tears, muffled gunfire, a woman's sidelong glance through a shadowed window, the terrible green silence of a jungle when guerrillas were on the prowl.

And a gold piece bequeathed to Cord by a man he had carried on his back out of the jungle. But not in time. Green silence and death.

Cord looked at the alien coin and wondered who would be next to die.

Chapter 6

RAINE TESTED DEV'S CINCH, CHECKED HER WATCH, AND led Dev to the mounting block. The U.S. team's turn in the practice jumping ring would begin in half an hour. As time in the various rings was carefully divided among the countries, she didn't want to waste a minute by being late. She would have Dev warmed up and ready for jumping at the stroke of nine.

As Raine settled into the smooth English saddle, she couldn't help taking a quick, almost furtive look around the yard. Cord was there, leaning against one of the green stable walls, watching everyone who came and went among the tree-shaded rows of stalls. He had been nearby every time Raine moved from stall to practice ring. She even thought he had followed her to her motel room, but couldn't be sure. The car that had followed her definitely hadn't been Cord's black Pantera, yet something about the driver had been familiar; he'd had a smooth, almost catlike way of turning his head to check traffic that had reminded her of Cord.

Cord's omnipresence at Santa Anita was unnerving to Raine. It didn't matter whether she was alone or with another member of the team, receiving instructions from Captain Jon or leading Dev lazily through the linked yards; Cord was always there, watching.

At first Raine had thought that Cord's interest was purely personal, that he was pursuing her despite her stated intention of avoiding him. She had ridden over to confront him, intending to tell him to leave her alone. But she had taken one look at Cord and the words had stayed in her throat. He had glanced at her with pale, impersonal eyes, wished her a polite good morning and resumed watching the yard. His eyes missed nothing, not even the least shift of wind-ruffled pepper trees.

Raine was left staring at Cord's profile, feeling young and very foolish, hot and cold at once. The instant she had come close to him she had remembered what he seemed to have forgotten—the night he gave her a guided tour of the universe. She had seen the teasing flash of teeth and tongue when Cord spoke his brief, casual greeting. As she watched him from the safe height of Dev's back, the clean, male curve of Cord's lips had brought back memories of being kissed until there was nothing in her universe but him. For an instant she had felt again the sensual vise of his teeth holding her lower lip.

She had sat motionless on Dev's back, stunned by vivid memories of being held and caressed by the man who was so close to her now, ignoring her. When Cord had shifted position to give himself a better view of the yard, the play of muscles beneath his faded work shirt made Raine want to bend down and bury her fingers in his thick black hair, to touch him again, to run her hands over his hard body until she was so close to him that she could feel him groan with desire.

Raine had been appalled by her own thoughts, and the sudden heat and weakness coursing through her. In that instant she had discovered why people gave in to competition madness. Anything would be better than the twisting ache inside her when she looked at Cord.

And then he had turned to her, had seen the hunger in her wide, haunted eyes and soft mouth.

"I'm still wearing a gun."

Cord's words had been like a whip scoring across Raine's unguarded emotions. She had wheeled Dev and ridden off with a speed that had sent dirt spattering over Cord's feet.

The memory of that moment hadn't left Raine in the days that followed. Nor had the memory of Cord's sensuality, and her own. Even worse, she couldn't ignore the terrible feeling that she had stumbled over the other half of herself . . . and then had thrown it away, not knowing how much she needed what she had never had before.

She had been careful not to confront Cord again.

"Competition madness," Raine whispered to herself, wanting to believe that was the only source of her ache and unease.

She wanted to look over her shoulder now, to see if Cord was watching her. She was sure he was; she sensed his attention as surely as she sensed the heat rising out of the stable yard. Yet she knew that no matter how suddenly she turned, she wouldn't catch Cord looking. Even so, she couldn't shake the uncanny feeling of always being in the center of his view, a permanent reflection in his ice-blue eyes.

"It's just competition madness, you little fool," she said to herself.

Dev's left ear flicked back, then forward.

"Competition madness," said Raine firmly.

She repeated the two words all the way to the jump ring, her own private litany designed to exorcise from her thoughts the man who wore a gun and spoke with a shaman's voice. As she rode, bees in the potted flowers along the paths and fences hummed in counterpoint to her whispered words. Dev's ears flicked occasionally as he registered the erratic flight of insects or a shift in the tone of his rider's voice.

Raine took off her hard hat, wiped her forehead, and replaced the riding helmet. Today her hair was tightly held beneath the hat, no more than a few wisps curling down to tickle her hot cheeks. It was barely 8:30 A.M. and almost eighty degrees. The rising heat of the day was reflected back on Santa Anita by acres of blacktop parking lots and the massive rise of the San Gabriel Mountains just beyond the track. Despite constant attention from water trucks, the grounds were dry. Dust hung in the air, bright gold in the morning sun.

Raine held Dev's reins loosely, letting the horse pick his own pace. He shambled along with deceptive sloth, as calm as a rental nag, flicking his ears at the background noises of voices calling and horses whinnying across the parallel stable yards. Men came and went, hauling in feed and hauling out yesterday's straw. Laughter and jokes and stablegirls giggling around the tack house hid the tension beneath—competition madness.

Dev ignored the sounds. He had been at Santa Anita long enough for the background noises to become familiar. He was accustomed to the place now; the heat barely even raised a sheen of sweat beneath his gleaming leather tack. Raine noted the stallion's calm acceptance of his surroundings and smiled with satisfaction. It had been worth coming out to California early in order to ensure that Dev was accustomed to Santa Anita before the Summer Games began. Some of the other horses she saw being led around were still snorting and shying at shadows, uneasy in the midst of unfamiliar scents and sounds.

As she approached the practice rings, Raine collected Dev beneath her, tightening her contact with him until he was up on the bit and looking around alertly. Though he had never showed any inclination to fight, Devlin's Waterloo was nonetheless a stallion. When he was close to the other horses, Raine was never careless.

"First one, as usual," said Captain Jon, walking slowly toward the stallion.

Dev's ears came fully forward. He watched Captain Jon with dark, somewhat wary eyes.

"Never let up, do you, old boy?" murmured the captain. His hand came up slowly, firmly, and gripped Dev's reins just below the bit.

Dev snorted, then stood quietly.

"Nothing fancy today," said Captain Jon, looking up at Raine. "Give him fifteen minutes of light dressage. Concentrate on the counter-canter for the last five. If he's not behaving, keep after it. I'll start Mason in the ring and put you second if Dev isn't working well."

Raine nodded. Dev didn't like the counter-canter, but it was a necessary tool for dressage, endurance and show jumping.

"I'm not setting up anything higher than a meter in the ring," continued the captain. "Watch the triple combination, though. I've placed it so that you have a full stride, a half stride, then four and a half strides."

Raine sighed. Diabolical, as usual. A jump approach that was four and a half strides was just long enough to allow you to lose control of the horse, particularly if you were on an animal that liked rushing fences. Dev usually didn't. Usually. Today it might be different. She was on edge. He was humming with health; beneath his shambling act there was a great, powerful stallion eager to fly over hills and rivers and downhill jumps. In six days he would get to do just that. Until then, though, she would have to stay deep in the saddle and firm on the reins or he would be scattering bars from show jumps like jackstraws in the wind.

Raine rode Dev into a practice ring. Other horses worked around the ring, polishing whatever skills they needed to. Some practiced the absolutely immobile standing required by dressage. Others practiced changing leads at all paces. Still others moved in the elegant diagonals of dressage. Raine moved into place, keeping to the outer circumference of the ring. She rode without a whip, for Dev would not tolerate one. Any displeasure she felt with his performance would be expressed with her heels and voice.

Raine worked quietly, talking to Dev through lips that didn't move, using a voice that went no further than the horse's sensitive ears. The stallion worked willingly—too willingly. The least shift of her weight was greeted with an eager bunching of muscles that fairly screamed Dev's desire for a little violent exercise. Dev had been thoroughly trained for devouring rough country and obstacles and distances. He loved it with a fervor that had made him a great event horse. It also made him temperamentally unsuited for the mincing niceties of dressage.

"Listen to me, you great red ox," muttered Raine through clenched teeth as Dev tugged hard on the bit and danced sideways. "You'll get all the run you want in a few days. Until then, *settle down.*"

Gradually, Raine's unbending demand for a restrained walk, trot, extended trot, and all the rest of the controlled dressage movements were accepted by Dev. He balked at the counter-canter, then gave in. At least the pace was more to his liking, though still far too slow.

Raine caught a movement out of the corner of her eye and knew without turning that it was Cord Elliot. He was leaning against the ring fence at a point where Dev would pass close by. Dev's head came up and he danced in place, sensing the sudden change in his rider. Raine brought the stallion back under full control with pressure from her hands and legs.

"There's a call for you, Raine," said Cord, his deep voice carrying easily above the muffled hoofbeats of horses working in the ring.

"Later."

"It's your father."

Dev went sideways in a single, catlike leap that spoke volumes about his previous restraint. Raine swore silently and fought a brief, sharp skirmish over control of the bit.

"He's full of vinegar," observed Cord, half smiling, admiration clear in his eyes as he watched the blood-bay stallion's dance. "Aren't much for dressage, are you?" Cord added, his voice velvet and soothing. "I don't blame you, boy. Don't blame you one bit. Dressage is for people who like fences and rules."

Raine collected Dev firmly. He resisted, dancing in place, wanting to get closer to the fascinating voice.

"Bet you're one hell of a ride," murmured Cord in his shaman's voice. "Go the distance without whimpering, take a mouthful of water and turn around and do it all again. Will your mistress ever let you sire blood-bay colts, or is she going to keep you on a tight rein all your life?"

As Dev minced toward the source of the voice, his ears pricked forward until they almost touched. Raine held the horse firmly between her hands and knees, guiding him toward the exit. Cord walked along the other side of the

fence, talking the whole time. When Dev was out of the
ring, Cord grasped the reins just below the bit. Dev stood
motionless, his velvet nostrils flaring as he drank Cord's
scent and watched him with liquid brown eyes.

"Ask for operator eleven," murmured Cord. "I'll take
care of Dev for you."

Raine hesitated, then slid off the huge horse and landed
lightly on the ground beside Cord. "If you've bitten off
more horse than you can chew," she said irritably, "you
have only yourself to blame."

Cord ignored her. He led Dev away, talking quietly the
whole time. Raine watched Dev's behavior in disbelief,
then sprinted for the nearest phone, wondering what had
gone wrong with her family. She couldn't remember the last
time her father had called her. She didn't even know where
in the world he was. By the time operator eleven connected
Raine with her father, she had imagined every possible
calamity that could have happened to her family.

"Daddy?" said Raine urgently as soon as she heard his
voice, thinned by distance and static but still unmistakably
Justin Chandler-Smith. "What's wrong?"

"Nothing. I just wanted to be the one to tell you that I'll
be with your mother for the Olympics."

"You will?" asked Raine doubtfully, years of hope and
disappointment mingling in her voice. "You'll try to be
here?"

"I *will* be there, Baby Raine."

Raine laughed and shook her head. "I'm not a baby
anymore, Dad."

"You never were," he said ruefully. "Not really. Comes
of being the fifth child, I suppose. You were going to be as
old as your brothers and sisters or know the reason why."

"Speaking of siblings, are you sure everything is all
right?"

"Positive. All six of us will be there."

"Impossible," said Raine dryly. "The six of you haven't been in the same place at once since William was old enough to drive."

"The six of us never had a seventh competing in the Olympics. I'm not going to miss this one, Raine. I mean it."

Raine swallowed in spite of a throat that suddenly wanted to close. Before now, her father always had hedged his promises with the phrase "if I can."

"You don't have to," she said quietly. "If not this time, there's always another."

"Not for you, baby. I've got a cast-iron hunch that you're about through with wanderlust and adrenaline. If I don't see you ride this time, I doubt there will be another chance."

Raine's hand tightened on the phone. Her father's calm words swept through her, leaving certainty in their wake. He was right. She was tired of living on the road, tired of the relentless rounds of training and competition and pressure, the excitement that was a little bit less each time, diminishing so slowly that its loss could only be measured over the years. She still looked forward to the Olympics, still wanted very badly to compete and win. But she knew now that it would be the last time she hungered for world-class competition.

"How did you know?" she whispered. "I just found out myself."

"You're a lot like me. But you're smarter. A whole lot smarter. It took me a long time to figure out what I was missing. Well, I'm not going to miss it anymore. Look for me, Baby Raine. I love you."

Raine was too surprised to answer. By the time she whispered, "I love you, too," her father had already hung up. She replaced the receiver and stood staring across the yard, seeing nothing at all.

"Bad news?" asked Cord.

Raine blinked and turned slowly toward Cord. She focused on his eyes, almost transparent, with splinters of vivid blue radiating out from the dark centers. They were the most unusual eyes she had ever seen.

"Raine?" asked Cord, his voice gentle. "Is everything all right?"

"Daddy says he's coming to the games," said Raine, her voice clear and almost childlike. "Always before he said he would *try*. This time he promised. He's never promised before."

Cord's mouth flattened into a grim line. "Don't tell anyone else. If anyone asks you if Blue is coming, lie. And then tell me who was asking questions about your father."

The change in Cord's voice from gentle to harsh was like a slap. Raine flinched and stepped back, off-balance again. "Why?"

"Why?" repeated Cord in disbelief. Then his voice went as cold as the ice color of his eyes. "Grow up, Baby Raine. There are people in this world who would kill your father if they could find him. But they can't. That's the reason his schedule is always unpredictable. It's called survival. If you were an assassin and you knew your target had a daughter competing in the Summer Games, what would you do?"

Raine closed her eyes. "No," she whispered, shaking her head, not wanting to believe.

"Yes," retorted Cord. "Why the hell do you suppose Blue has missed so many of your competitions? Why the hell do you suppose he never came to his children's graduations? Why the hell do you think he's missed every Broadway opening night your sister ever had? Why the hell—"

"I didn't know," Raine said, her voice tight as she cut across Cord's relentless words.

"You didn't want to know," he said flatly.

"Daddy never told me," said Raine, her hands clenched.

"He didn't want you to know. If he knew I was telling you now, he'd have my butt for batting practice."

"Then why are you telling me?"

"Maybe I don't believe a father should have to be a moving target just to convince his daughter that he loves her."

"I never asked for that," said Raine, her voice shaking. "I just wanted to feel like part of the family instead of a fifth wheel. I wanted to feel like I belonged! Is that so much to ask?"

The anger went out of Cord as he saw the trembling of Raine's pale lips, the tears that she refused to shed, the corded lines of her throat as she fought to control her voice. He wanted to gather her into his arms, to stroke and soothe her until her eyes were no longer haunted and her face no longer pale.

"No," said Cord wearily, "it's not so much to ask. Just everything. Just the whole world in your palm, spinning like a bright blue ball. Some of us aren't meant to belong, Raine. Some of us have to turn the world upside down and shake the hell out of it until we make our own place in it." Cord watched her with eyes that were suddenly intent. "And that's just what I'm going to do," he said thoughtfully, his voice calm and very sure. "Shake that beautiful world until there's a place in it for me."

But not yet. He had to wait until a certain "matter" was wrapped up. Then he would be free. Until then . . .

Cord handed over Dev's reins and turned to go.

"Cord," Raine said urgently, putting her hand on his arm.

She didn't see the sudden tension in his expression, or the hungry way he watched the fingers resting on his arm. He looked at her hazel eyes, more brown than green now, almost as beautiful as the tempting curves of her mouth.

"What?" asked Cord, keeping his voice neutral with an effort.

"What if I called Dad and asked him not to come?"

Cord hesitated, wanting to take Raine's hand, to run his thumb over her fingertips and touch the center of her palm with his tongue. "If it would make you feel better, go ahead. It won't change anything, though. Sometime in the last few months I think he discovered that he'd missed getting to know quite a woman. The fact that she's his daughter just makes it worse. He's coming, Raine. Hell or high water, he's coming."

Raine remembered her father's words, the absolute certainty in his voice, and knew that Cord was right. Justin Chandler-Smith was coming to see his daughter ride. Raine's fingers closed with surprising strength over Cord's wrist. "I don't want to make it easier for someone to kill him!" she said, her voice breaking. "Cord, *please*, what can I do to make him believe that?"

"He already knows. Why do you think he's worked so hard to protect you from knowing that he's a target? Only Lorraine knows how dangerous his work is, and even she doesn't know precisely what his work involves. Not because he doesn't trust her, but because it's another way of protecting her. What she doesn't know, no one can force her to talk about."

Raine became very pale beneath her tan. The thought of her mother as a target had never occurred to her. "What can I do to protect him?" asked Raine.

Cord would have smiled, but the intensity of Raine's

emotion made that impossible. "There are a lot of very well trained, very competent people protecting your father."

"Are you one of them?" Raine asked slowly, looking at Cord with hazel eyes that were very dark, shadowed by emotion.

"I have a nice spot all picked out for Blue on the endurance course," said Cord, neither admitting nor denying Raine's conclusion. "Great view of the action, and only exposed on one side. I'll be watching it with him."

"Is that what you were doing when you jumped me, looking for a safe place for Dad?"

This time, Cord smiled very slightly. "Still angry about that, aren't you."

A strange look crossed Raine's face as she considered that incident from another point of view entirely. As she thought, she absently waved away a bee that had mistaken her bright riding helmet for an oversized flower. "No," she said, lowering her hand as the bee buzzed away, "not anymore. You didn't really have much choice, if you're supposed to be protecting my father. You had no way of knowing who I was."

A shout from the direction of the practice area distracted Raine. Cord followed the direction of her glance and saw Captain Jon walking toward them.

"Your turn in the ring," said Cord. He laced his fingers together to make a flesh-and-bone stirrup. "Ready?"

Automatically, Raine accepted the aid in remounting Dev. She was up on the tall stallion's back before she had a chance to feel more than an instant of Cord's smooth strength as he boosted her into place.

"Take care of her, boy," Cord murmured in a voice that went no further than Dev's black-tipped ears, "or I'll have your red hide for a wall hanging."

Raine settled firmly into the saddle, collected Dev, and

moved toward the practice area at a smart trot. She wished she could collect her mind as easily. She felt as though someone had taken her nice, carefully mapped-out world, turned it upside down and shaken it until she was forced to look at old realities from entirely new perspectives. Her picture of her father had shifted subtly, irrevocably. Nothing had changed, not really . . . and everything had. She couldn't remake the past, but she could look at its pieces arranged in a new way, a different pattern, different truths.

Her father did love her. She had always known that, but she hadn't always admitted it. It was easier to be angry at him than to try to understand the choices he had made. Yet, even that understanding wasn't enough. She couldn't accept a life lived as her father had. Not for herself. Not for the children she someday hoped to have.

Loving a man like Cord would destroy her.

Yet she wanted Cord as she had never wanted any man. Each time she saw him, talked to him, touched him, it became harder to pull away, to bar the castle gates and bank the fires inside while he was outside, wanting her.

"—listening?" snapped Captain Jon.

Raine collected herself and searched her subconscious for the words she must have heard while she was thinking about Cord instead of Captain Jon's instructions. "I take the triple jump once clockwise, once counterclockwise," she said, repeating the captain's instructions. "Then I go through again, changing leads twice, getting Dev to take the jumps unexpectedly, on the wrong lead."

"Good. He's got to know that when you say jump, he bloody well jumps whether or not he's on the right lead. Now, on the second round, that last jump is set at a right angle into the ring fence. Watch that Dev doesn't run out along the unfenced side just because he's on the wrong lead."

Dev went through the first series of jumps like a perfect gentleman. As he slowly cantered around to approach from the opposite side, a group of equestrians walked by just outside the ring. The riders talked among themselves as they watched the muscular stallion's progress over the low, tricky jumps.

Then one of the horses screamed, twisted sideways and bolted straight into one of the American riders waiting for a turn in the ring. The American horse went down; its rider slammed into the fence with a sickening crack. The horse that had bolted burst through the fence and hurtled into Dev.

Between one instant and the next, Raine found herself fighting to stay in the saddle. The world slowed, then stopped, allowing her to see everything with terrible clarity: the American rider down and tangled in the fence, his horse scrambling up, favoring its foreleg; a strange horse coming through the fence, shattering it, the rider barely hanging on, scrambling desperately to control his berserk mount; the horse slamming blindly into Dev, the world jerked from beneath her, horses and men frozen in place.

And then it all speeded up horribly as she was hurtled beneath the plunging horse, dusty ground rushing to meet her, no time to duck, no time to roll out of the way of the flying hooves, no time even to throw up her hands to protect her head.

Raine hit the ground and lay without moving.

Cord was running, had been running since he first saw a horse plunge blindly through the fence toward Raine. He put his hands on the top rail and vaulted the ring fence without breaking stride. He saw Dev stagger, then turn savagely on the horse that had slammed into him and was threatening to trample Raine. With a stallion's chilling scream, Dev attacked. His teeth bit cruelly into the other horse's flank. The horse squealed frantically and leaped beyond reach, finally unseating its rider. Dev turned as the man pulled himself to his feet and staggered in Raine's direction.

Dev reared and screamed again, ears flattened to his skull, bared teeth gleaming, eyes rolling white. His neck moved with a deadly, sinuous motion as he threatened the rider who was too dazed to realize what was happening. Cord hit the rider with a flying tackle that carried them away from the motionless Raine and out of Dev's immediate reach.

"Get the hell out of here," snarled Cord, all but throwing the man over the ring fence.

Cord turned and faced the raging blood-bay stallion alone. Cord wanted to run over and throw himself down by Raine, to turn the world right side out again. But if he moved quickly, Dev would attack. He was standing over his mistress like a huge guard dog, responding to her unnatural stillness with a stallion's protective instinct. It took only one look to tell Cord that Dev would kill any man who approached. Only Raine could handle Dev now; and Raine was unconscious.

"Easy," murmured Cord, his shaman's voice like a caress over the quivering stallion. "Easy, boy. I'm not going to hurt your mistress. Remember me? I'm the one who smells like Raine," said Cord, extending his right forearm, the arm that Raine had held only moments before, when Cord had believed that there was time to wait before he took down Raine's castle gate and began to live with warmth instead of ice. But now there was no more time, only Raine lying in the dust.

"Easy, Dev. Easy." Cord's voice poured over the horse like a warm river, ceaseless, soothing, bewitching with hints of moonlight sliding among deep currents. "Put those ears up, boy. Smell me . . . remember me. I won't hurt you or Raine. That's it," said Cord quietly, praising each subtle shift in the stallion's attention, each minute quiver of the horse's ears. "Smell me, boy. I smell like her. . . ."

Behind him, Cord heard the shouts and startled cries die away as everyone's attention was riveted on the ring and the fallen rider, the soft-talking man and the stallion quivering on the break-point of rage and fear, instincts violently battling with a shaman's voice for control of Dev's power-ful body. Voices called out, offering advice and warnings. With each new male voice, Dev shuddered as though a whip had fallen on his sweat-blackened hide. Cord wanted to shout at the men to shut up, but if he raised his voice, Dev would explode.

Suddenly, clearly, Captain Jon's calm tones cut across the rumble of male advice. "I will personally horsewhip the next man who speaks. If any man can get close to that stallion now, it's the man in the ring."

"But—" began one rider.

"Belt up."

Though Captain Jon didn't raise his voice, there was an immediate and total silence. Cord's mesmerizing words continued without pause. After a few minutes, Dev's ears shifted nervously as he stretched his head down to Raine. Velvet nostrils expanded and quivered as the horse's muzzle moved over his rider's motionless body. Raine's stillness was puzzling, unnerving.

"Let me look at her," said Cord, gliding closer with almost invisible movements of his feet, words and nonsense in a continuous river of sound that gently washed away Dev's uncertainty and fear.

Ears not quite flattened, Dev stretched his powerful neck toward Cord. Black nostrils expanded, quivered, scenting again the mixture of Cord and Raine on the man's sleeve. With a long breath that was almost a groan, Dev's ears came up. He nosed Cord, then Raine. Cord praised the stallion even as his strong fingers closed around the reins. Dev shuddered, but made no move to evade Cord's control.

Despite the urgency screaming inside him, Cord was careful to move slowly as he knelt next to Raine. She was face down, arms flung out as though to deflect a blow. Delicately, his fingertips found the soft skin of her neck. He held his breath and sought for the least sign of her life. He let his breath out, slowing his own heartbeats so that he could feel hers no matter how faintly or far apart they came.

Cord felt the even beat of Raine's life flowing just beneath his fingertips. He closed his eyes as relief swept through him with stunning force.

"Alive," said Cord, pitching his voice to carry. His voice was still soothing, though, for Dev was still half-wild.

"Do you want me to take Dev?" asked Captain Jon.

Skin rippled nervously along the stallion's sweaty body when the captain spoke.

"Not yet," said Cord. "I'll—"

Raine groaned and tried to get up, fighting for the breath that had been knocked out of her.

"Lie still," said Cord quietly, enforcing his words with a hand on her shoulder. "You had a fall. Dev's all right," Cord added quickly, knowing that Raine's first concern would be for her horse. "Do you hurt anywhere?"

Raine's head sank back into the loose dirt of the ring as the world whirled around her. When it was still again, she opened her eyes. "I'm fine. Just dizzy. Breath knocked out."

"Tell me if I hurt you," said Cord, running his hands over her body, beginning at her neck and working down, probing for broken bones with surprising skill and gentleness. When he was finished, he looked a silent question at Raine.

"I'm fine," she repeated, her voice stronger.

"You didn't look so fine," said Cord bluntly. "You were face down in the dirt, out cold."

Raine moved her head warily, then winced as she sat up. When Cord put his arm around her, bracing her, she didn't object. "Now that you mention it, I have a bit of a headache. What happened?"

"One of the horses went crazy. Bee sting, probably. He hurtled into another horse, broke through the fence and then slammed into Dev. You were knocked off right into the middle of it. Dev drove away the other horse and then stood over you like a one-ton attack dog."

Raine smiled weakly. "Yeah, he gets a little protective of me when I fall."

Cord's black eyebrows lifted at her understatement.

Suddenly, Raine remembered seeing one of her teammates thrown into the fence. "Jameson," she said, turning suddenly toward the fence, startling Dev. "Is Jameson all right?" called Raine to the people beyond the fence.

Captain Jon was standing next to the American rider. Jameson turned toward the ring. His face was pale and sweaty. Cord didn't need to see the way Jameson held himself to know that the rider's shoulder was either fractured or dislocated, or both.

Captain Jon confirmed Cord's guess with a single, laconic word. "Shoulder."

"What about Show Me?" asked Raine, referring to Jameson's horse.

"Strain, probably. Nothing serious," added Captain Jon. "But Jameson won't be riding for awhile."

Raine exchanged a long look with Captain Jon. The U.S. had to field a minimum number of three contestants in the three-day event. Four was the maximum allowed for a team, and the preferred number, allowing some margin for accident after the beginning of the event. With Jameson out, one of the short-listed riders would move up to take hisplace. There would still be four riders, but not the four that Captain Jon thought had the best chance of winning.

Grimly, Raine started to get to her feet.

"What do you think you're doing?" asked Cord, holding her back.

"I'm getting up," she said, her voice determined. "Either help me or get out of my way."

Cord looked at Raine for a long moment, then pulled her to her feet with startling ease. She hesitated a moment, letting dizziness pass. Then she reached for Dev's reins. Cord didn't release them. She turned on him, angry for no better reason than that a man and a horse had been hurt, undercutting the hopes and dreams and years of hard work by the whole U.S. Equestrian Team.

"Give me the reins," she said curtly.

"I can lead Dev back to the stable," said Cord, his voice reasonable.

"Not yet. First he has to go over the jump."

"What happened wasn't Dev's fault."

"I know. But if he doesn't go over that jump now, there could be hell to pay later."

"She's right, you know," observed Captain Jon, looking shrewdly from Cord to Raine. "It's a matter of the horse's confidence."

"What about the rider's neck," retorted Cord, his voice uninflected, professional, and very cold.

"Event riders rather routinely finish the course with concussions, broken teeth and bashed ribs," said the captain. "Comes with the territory."

Cord hissed a single, explicit word. He bent and turned

suddenly, all but throwing Raine up on Dev. Cord let go of the reins and stepped out of the way. His pale eyes never left Raine's face as she guided Dev back around the ring. He could see her fight dizziness, conquer it, then line up Dev for the jump.

You're Blue's daughter, all right. Stubborn to the bone. Brave, too. But you don't think about that, do you? You just see what has to be done and then you do it. How can anything as sweet and soft as you be so stubborn? But then, I never did like things easy. You've met your match, Baby Blue.

Problem is, so have I.

Cord watched Dev fly over the jumps like the black-maned demon he was. When he landed after the third jump, Raine slumped against his muscular neck. Before she could fall, Cord was there. He lifted her off the blood-bay stallion and into his arms.

"I'm . . . a little . . . dizzy," Raine admitted.

Fortunately, she fainted before she could hear Cord's very blunt reply.

Chapter 7

"AFTERNOON, THORNE. ANYTHING FOR ME?"

"No, suh. Things have been real quiet."

Cord turned to Raine. "Raine, this is Thorne. Thorne, Miss Chandler-Smith."

Raine didn't miss the sudden narrowing of Thorne's eyes, or the instant reassessment of her rumpled, dirty clothes. She smiled wryly, knowing that she looked exactly like what she was—a woman who had just spent several hours in a hospital emergency room being probed, X-rayed and questioned while Cord watched with pale eyes and a mouth that had forgotten how to smile.

"Call me Raine Smith," she said. "Everyone else does."

"Miss Smith," said Thorne, nodding. "Pleased to meet you."

"Raine," she said, stressing her first name.

Cord smiled slightly, knowing that Raine's informality

wouldn't make a dent in Thorne's southern sense of propriety. After three years, Thorne still called Cord "Mister." Cord had given up trying to change Thorne; the man was intelligent, silent, and deadly with any weapon that came to hand. For those qualities, Cord could live with a few social formalities.

"See if you can find a recliner for Raine," said Cord. "You two can sit together under the pepper tree while I bring out her horse. And send someone to check Raine out of her motel."

"What do you think you're doing?" she asked indignantly.

"My job."

Raine opened her mouth, then closed it with a sigh. She'd argue with Cord later, after she had checked Dev. Right now, it was enough just to be standing up. A battle of wits was beyond her.

The feeling of lassitude persisted even after Raine had examined Dev minutely and given Cord careful, unnecessary instructions on how to groom the big stallion. She had held her breath when Cord picked up Dev's steel-shod hoof and cleaned it, but Dev had accepted Cord's attentions without one sign of rebellion.

"It's that damned shaman's voice," Raine said beneath her breath, listening to the mesmerizing music of Cord's words as he worked over the horse. "It's even getting to me."

"Ma'am?" asked Thorne politely.

"Nothing," she sighed.

Raine closed her eyes and settled back into the chaise lounge that Thorne had brought for her. The murmur of Cord's voice mingled with the warm breeze, draining away her tension. Tiredness claimed her, a reaction to the stunning fall earlier combined with all the restless nights since she had shut Cord out of her castle and barred the gates.

"Mr. Elliot," said Thorne quietly.

Cord put down the pick that he had been using on the stallion's hoof and walked quickly to Raine's side. Very gently, Cord's fingertips found her pulse. Slow, steady, deep, like her breathing. Skin neither clammy nor dry, cold nor hot. Cord nodded to Thorne, then returned to Dev's grooming.

The horse stood with his head down, his weight on three legs, his ears utterly relaxed. From time to time he would send his long black tail swishing over his body, brushing away the flies. Sometimes he would snort and rub his head against his foreleg or Cord's chest in order to get rid of the persistent insects.

"Word around the stables is that her horse is a killer," said Thorne after a long time. As he watched Dev with narrow dark eyes, Thorne's hand was never far from the gun he wore at the back of his belt beneath a light cotton jacket.

"He could be," agreed Cord, brushing down Dev's hard-muscled haunch. He used strong, rhythmic strokes, polishing Dev with a soft brush. Dev groaned in a contentment that was almost comical.

"You don't think he's a killer?" asked Thorne softly.

"Never with Raine. Probably not with me, so long as I'm careful. Given enough time," added Cord, smoothing his palm over Dev's satiny coat, "he would come to trust me completely."

Cord stepped back and admired the result of his work. All traces of sweat had been brushed away from Dev's powerful body. Mane and tail shimmered like coarse black silk, emphasizing the blood red of Dev's coat. The unique, pungent scent of horse lingered on Cord's hands, bringing back a rush of memories from his childhood.

"Damn," Cord said softly, "but it's good to work with a horse again. Especially a horse like this one."

Thorne looked from the huge stallion to Cord. "I'm a city boy, myself. I'll take your word for it."

"There's nothing like it," murmured Cord, remembering the long rides, the smell of horses and piñon trees, the feel of the Nevada sun hot on his back and a horse running cleanly between his knees. "Nothing in the world," he added with conviction.

Dev snorted and stamped his front foot, dislodging a fly.

Cord looked over at Thorne, then at Raine sleeping in the lacy shade of the pepper tree. "How long has it been?"

Thorne checked his watch. "Half an hour."

Cord went to the chaise and squatted on his heels beside it like the range rider he once had been. He checked Raine's pulse and breathing. Still deep, even. Slowly he stroked her face, waking her as gently as he could. Before she was fully awake, she turned her lips into his hand, kissing him sleepily. His other hand came up in a slow caress, smoothing her hair away from her face.

"Raine," he whispered. Then, more clearly, "Raine." She stirred again, nuzzling his hand.

"Open your eyes," Cord murmured, wanting to brush his lips over her cheek.

Raine's hand came up in silent protest, discovered Cord's hand on her cheek, and closed around his fingers with a sigh. She shifted again, cradling his hand between her cheek and her palm. Cord bent and put his cheek alongside hers for an instant. He breathed her name too softly for her to hear. Then, reluctantly, he straightened.

"Wake up," Cord whispered. "I have to see the centers

of those beautiful eyes." The caressing pressure of his fingers on her cheek increased. "Wake up, Raine. Look at me."

Long, dark brown lashes stirred, then lifted. Hazel eyes looked out at him, dazed by sleep. Her pupils were dilated, but contracted quickly in the bright light. Quickly and evenly.

"Go back to sleep," Cord said, his voice soothing, velvety, urging Raine back down into the sleep she needed. "Everything is all right. Go to sleep."

"Cord . . . ?" she whispered.

"Go to sleep, little queen. Your soldier is here."

Raine's breath sighed out as she gave herself over to sleep again; but she clung to Cord's hand even then. He waited for several minutes, looking at the silky half circles of her eyelashes, the shimmering wealth of her chestnut hair tumbling over the lounge's pale cushion, the pink curve of her lips and the skin stretched smoothly over her cheekbones. He bent and kissed the hollow of her cheek, then straightened again. Gently, reluctantly, he eased his hand out of hers.

When Cord looked up, Thorne was pointedly looking somewhere else. Always the southern gentleman. Nor did Thorne say any of the sensible things about getting involved with someone whom you were supposed to guard, someone whose father was one of the most powerful men in the government. Thorne kept silent even when Cord carried Raine into the radio room of the motorhome, laid her on his own bed and locked the door. She stirred fitfully, then calmed as soon as Cord bent over and murmured a few words.

Cord went to the swivel chair by the computer, punched in his code and began to update himself on all that had happened in the last half day. Next to him a radio scanner worked ceaselessly, hunting among all local, state and federal law-enforcement frequencies. When the scanner found a channel that was being used, it stopped to listen in on the transmission. Unless Cord intervened, the scanner would monitor the call, then proceed again across the frequencies, picking up disembodied voices.

For the most part, Cord ignored the transmissions, halting the scanner only if he heard certain codes used. Occasionally he would reach for the two-way radio set that was nearby. Like the scanner, the radio was capable of reaching all law-enforcement frequencies. Cord had at his fingertips all of the various police agencies whose responsibility it was to protect Olympic athletes, VIPs and spectators against everything from pickpockets to a full-scale terrorist attack.

Cord worked quietly, sifting through intelligence reports graded according to their reliability and making reports of his own. Every half hour he checked on Raine. Each time he did, she reached for him as she came out of sleep, holding his hand against her and curling around it like a child. Each time, it was harder for Cord to pull away. He wanted to lie down beside Raine, let her burrow against him and sigh with contentment while he held her. He would settle for that. Just holding her. He was lucky to get even that much. She could easily have died in that ring this morning, and she had a dented riding helmet to prove it.

Cord sat next to Raine on his bed, watching her. Her color was normal now, not even a hint of paleness beneath her smooth, translucent skin. Her skin was neither hot nor cold, and still vaguely dusty from her fall in the ring. Her breathing and pulse were normal.

"Raine," he said softly, caressing her cheek with the back of his fingers.

She awakened as before, her hand reaching up to curl

around his. When her lips touched his palm, he felt the heat all the way down his body to his knees.

"Open your eyes," Cord murmured, rubbing his fingers gently through Raine's hair. There were no lumps, no swellings, barely even a tender spot to make her flinch. "That was one hell of a good riding helmet, lady."

Raine's eyes flew open, wide awake and startled. Both pupils were evenly dilated. Both responded with equal quickness to the light level in the room. The tension in Cord eased a few more percentage points.

"Cord?" she asked, her voice husky with sleep. She looked past him, seeing the room for the first time. "Where am I?"

"In the motorhome."

"What time is it?"

"Almost five. Hungry?"

"Starved," said Raine. "Whatever happened to lunch?"

"You turned it down in favor of sleep."

"Do I get a second chance?" she asked. Then she realized she was holding Cord's hand against her cheek. Color spread beneath her skin. She let go of his fingers as though she had been burned. She sat up hurriedly.

"Dizzy?" Cord asked.

"No."

"Headache?"

"A little," she admitted.

"How does your stomach feel now?"

"Predatory."

Cord smiled and stood up. "If you can still tell me that when you're on your feet, I'll fix an omelet for you."

Raine stood up, knowing that Cord's ice-blue eyes noted every hesitation.

"Still not nauseated?" he asked.

"No. Just hungry," she said firmly. "And—does this place come equipped with a bathroom?"

"First door on the left," Cord said, unlocking the door and walking out of the room. Though he seemed not to notice whether Raine followed, he was listening very carefully, ready to turn around and grab her if he heard her stumble. She didn't, though. She was very steady on her feet. Utterly normal.

Raine took one look at herself in the bathroom mirror and shuddered. "Put a hold on that omelet," she called out. "I'm taking a shower right now!"

Cord appeared instantly in the doorway. "Sure you're up to it?"

"Positive."

He hesitated. The shower had a bench and a long-necked movable wand for ease in washing. Still . . . "Don't wash your hair."

"Don't be ridiculous. It will crawl right off my head if I don't."

Cord smiled. "Then I'll wash it." He waited long enough for Raine's expression to get indignant, and then added, "In the sink."

"What?"

"I'll wash your hair in the sink. That way if you get dizzy I'll be right there to catch you."

"That's not necessary. I'm fine. Hardly even a headache."

Cord shrugged. "In the sink or not at all." When she opened her mouth to protest, he added dryly, "I'm bigger than you, if you hadn't noticed."

Muttering beneath her breath, Raine walked two steps to the sink. Cord's razor, toothbrush and aftershave were laid out on the narrow counter. Next to his things, lined up in a neat row, were a squeeze bottle of her shampoo, her toothbrush, toothpaste, hairbrush and comb.

"Cord, what's going on?" asked Raine, keeping her voice level with an effort.

"You refused to stay in the hospital. You need to have someone wake you every hour or so during the night to check that you haven't slipped into a coma. You didn't have a roommate who could do that." Cord shrugged. "So you'll stay here where I can keep an eye on you." He watched with interest as color and anger changed Raine's face. "There's more than one bed in this place," he said calmly. "Just one bathroom, though. Don't worry about it. I may wear a gun, but I'm quite civilized about closed doors." He walked over to the sink. "Do you want your blouse on or off while I wash your hair?"

Raine's eyes widened. Not by any intonation or action did Cord act as though the question were unusual. "On," she said, swallowing quickly.

His hands came up. Before she could protest, he had unbuttoned the first two buttons of her blouse and was folding her collar underneath. She jerked back, entirely too conscious of his fingers brushing over her neck and the hollow of her throat.

"What are you doing!" she demanded.

"Getting your collar out of the way. Or did you want the blouse washed too? If so, it would be easier if you took off the blouse. Not nearly as interesting, though. All in all, I like your idea better. Wash the blouse with you still in it."

Cord's voice was so bland, the implication of his words so outrageous, that he had Raine's head in the sink and was running warm water over her hair before she realized precisely what he had said.

"Cord Elliot," she told the bottom of the sink, "whoever taught you how to talk should have been shot!"

Cord's only answer was a chuckle that could have been the sound of water flowing. Raine muttered a few words she usually reserved for Dev at his worst, then gave in to the luxury of having her hair washed by strong, gentle fingers. The only problem was that water—and soap—kept trying to run into her eyes and nose. The third time she had to come up for air, Cord reached for a towel.

"This isn't going to work," he said, mopping off Raine's face. "Let's try your idea."

"Mffpha?" asked Raine, her face buried in the towel.

"Washing everything at once," explained Cord, smiling wickedly, knowing she couldn't see. He kicked off his shoes and pulled her into the shower. "Sit," he said, pushing her gently down onto the bench and pulling the towel away from her. "Tip your head back so soap won't run in your eyes."

Raine sat, head tilted slightly back, off-balance again. She ruefully admitted to herself that Cord had a definite talent for keeping people off-balance, unsure, a step behind and not very darn likely to catch up. At least, he had that effect on her. The smooth, bland voice coupled with the outrageous words; the gentleness and humor that made her forget the lethal knowledge implicit in the gun he wore; the heat and hunger of his hands opposed to the icy assessment that she had seen in his eyes.

Cord stepped out of the shower, unfastened his holster and beeper with easy motions that spoke of long familiarity, and set them aside. He came back to the shower and stood in front of Raine, legs braced.

Raine watched as he picked up the shower wand, turned on the water, and waited until it was just the right temperature. He had rolled up his sleeves before he tried to wash her hair in the sink; even so, water had splashed over him, turning the shirt's light blue into a rich autumn sky

color that clung to the lines of his chest and arms. Black
hair curled over his tanned skin like a satin shadow. As he
adjusted the faucets, muscles slid and coiled with casual
strength. Raine watched, fascinated by his unself-conscious
grace, remembering the time she had kissed him and her
fingertips had traced the full veins just beneath his skin.

"Close your eyes," said Cord, standing very close to
Raine.

She looked at the lean waist that was only inches from
her, at the shirt that concealed little of Cord's strength, at
the very male lines of his body beneath his close-fitting
jeans. Heat and dizziness swept over her, a reaction that had
nothing to do with her fall. She closed her eyes, but still she
saw him standing only inches away, another memory to
haunt her nights. When his fingers eased into her hair, she
couldn't entirely conceal the shiver of her reaction.

"Cold?" asked Cord, concern clear in his voice.

Numbly, Raine shook her head, not trusting her own
voice. Another picture flashed behind her eyes: a headlong
fall beneath a berserk horse, steel-shod hooves flailing near
her face, just missing her eyes, then the dark dirt of the ring
exploding around her. She had always known that there was
the possibility of serious injury, even death, in the strenu-
ous demands of the three-day event. She thought she had
accepted the danger as simply part of the life she had
chosen.

But now, twice within a few days, her world had been
stood on end and shaken until she fell out, slamming face
first into a new reality. She had learned forcefully that
tomorrow was a matter of faith, not a guaranteed event. The
only guarantee was here and now. That knowledge was
subtly rearranging her thoughts, her expectations, her
self-assurance. Questions she had never asked were turning

in the depths of her mind, demanding answers that were neither easy nor comfortable.

Who was she to smile blithely and talk about forever, to plan for a life-ever-after with some imaginary man she couldn't even see clearly in her dreams? Who was she to play aloof, uncaring queen to the battle-worn soldier at her gate? Who was she to disdain competition madness when it was a fire and an ache in her own body?

Warm water poured through Raine's hair. Cord's strong, lean fingers worked gently over her scalp. Scented liquid soap became mounds of slippery lather. Head tilted back, eyes closed, Raine lived only in the moment, absorbing the sensations of water and warmth, of Cord standing so close that she could feel the occasional brush of his shirt against her face and breathe in his oddly familiar scent. The smell of him haunted her like a half-remembered song.

Then she realized what had happened and began to laugh softly.

"Ticklish?" asked Cord, his voice very deep. He massaged her scalp with slow, powerful strokes while lather slipped and ran through his fingers.

"No." Raine opened her eyes and looked up into his, smiling. "You smell like Dev."

Cord smiled crookedly. "Are you politely suggesting that I need a shower?"

Raine's long eyelashes swept down, concealing the laughter and light of her eyes. "Not at all. On you, essence of Devlin's Waterloo smells . . . sexy."

Cord's hands paused, then resumed their slow massage. Raine made a soft sound of relaxation and pleasure. With another shiver, she turned until she could rest her head against the hard muscles of Cord's stomach.

Cord moved quickly, surely, preventing lather from

sliding into Raine's eyes. He tilted her head back without shifting her away from his body. Warm water poured over her again, removing silver streamers of lather from her hair. Warm water ran over her shoulders, between her breasts, over her stomach and thighs. The sensation of being bathed in warmth while fully clothed was both alien and exquisite.

"Once more," said Cord, his voice deep, almost gritty in its intimacy.

Soap came out of the squeeze bottle in fragrant pulses that sank deeply into Raine's dark hair. Cord's hands moved in slow motion, creating pleasure and iridescent bubbles in equal measure. The changing pressure of his fingers encouraged Raine to put her cheek against his waist. She didn't resist. When she rested against his resilient warmth without hesitation, Cord's fingers shifted and changed subtly, caressing as much as massaging. He stood with eyes closed, rocking her very slowly against his body. For a long time there was no sound but warm water flowing from the wand braced between Cord's knee and the shower bench. Finally, reluctantly, Cord retrieved the wand.

"Not yet," murmured Raine, putting her arms around Cord's hips as unself-consciously as a child. "It's so good just to be held by you."

Cord whispered Raine's name as he cradled her again, gentleness and passion and restraint mingled inextricably in his embrace. She was so vulnerable now. Too vulnerable. He knew enough about the physical and mental aftereffects of trauma to realize that she wasn't wholly responsible for her actions right now. She was off-balance, at the mercy of instincts she didn't understand.

Cord understood them, though. Confronted by death, life reverted to a basic biological strategy: reproduction. He had seen it happen too many times, to too many men and women, choices made in heat and repented in confusion, just another hazard in an already hazardous profession. He would no more take advantage of Raine at this moment than he would deliberately get her drunk and then haul her into his bed and overwhelm whatever reservations alcohol hadn't already drowned.

"You're all wet," Raine said. She pressed her cheek closer to Cord, savoring the warmth radiating through his soaked clothing.

Cord laughed oddly, wondering if Raine had been reading his mind. Without being conscious of it, he let his hands slide down to her neck, her shoulders. The pink of her shirt was dark with water, almost cherry colored. Streamers of lather wound over and between her breasts. Her nipples stood out clearly, defined by water and clinging cloth. He remembered how she had felt in his mouth, hard and soft at once, salt and sweet, utterly feminine, and the soft cries that had come from deep in her throat.

With a soundless curse and a stifled groan, Cord bent and picked up the shower wand. He rinsed Raine's hair careful-ly, trying to ignore the havoc in his nerve endings caused by the careless pressure of her cheek below his waist, the warm water flowing over her, sliding over him, warm water joining them in an intimacy that was fast eroding his control. He turned off the water with quick, hard move-ments. Yet his hands were gentle as he squeezed water out of Raine's hair. And he was very gentle when he loosened her arms from around his hips.

"All done," Cord said, his voice neutral. He turned away quickly, before Raine opened her eyes. He knew that his hunger for her was made very obvious by his clinging wet jeans. "I'll wait out here while you finish your shower. Holler if you need anything."

The shower door closed firmly behind Cord. Raine blinked and rubbed her eyes as though waking from a deep sleep. Confused, she looked at the opaque rectangle of glass and the man silhouetted beyond. She knew Cord had enjoyed touching and holding her as much as she had enjoyed it. Why had he stopped?

"Cord?"

The door opened. Eyes that were oddly smoky, brilliantly blue looked out at her from an expressionless face.

"I feel a little dizzy," Raine said, her voice weak. It wasn't a lie. When Cord looked at her like that, she felt weak and dizzy, hot and cold, hungry to taste and feel the male textures of him.

Cord's expression changed. He moved with startling speed, scooping her off the bench and holding her tightly. "I never should have let you out of bed," he muttered.

Soft, laughing agreement was breathed into Cord's ear as Raine's arms wound around his neck. Cord stood very still for an instant, then set Raine carefully on her feet. He tilted her chin up.

"Nearly being killed is the most potent aphrodisiac known to man," Cord said with a casualness that went no deeper than the expressionless mask of his face. "Don't trust your reactions until tomorrow."

Embarrassment replaced Raine's light laughter. She felt as though she had been dropped into ice water. She turned away from Cord, flushing red and then going very pale.

"Let go of me," she said, her voice as pale as her skin. "I'm fine now. Not the least bit dizzy."

"Raine—"

She refused to look at him. Cord turned her until she had no choice. The sensible words he had been going to say caught in his throat. He hadn't meant to hurt her, hadn't really even believed he could.

"Let go of me, Cord," Raine said quietly, holding

herself together with the same discipline and nerve that had made her a world-class rider. "I've taken enough falls for one day, don't you think?"

"If it were tomorrow," said Cord, holding Raine against the length of his body, no longer caring if she knew how hungry he was for her, "if it were tomorrow, I'd be in that shower with you right now, undressing you and licking water off your skin. Call my name like that tomorrow," he said, his voice husky as he stepped back from her, "and see what happens."

Raine closed her eyes, wondering how she had so badly misread herself, him, everything. Off-balance again. She resented the feeling, and the man who caused it. "Maybe, maybe not," she said, her voice a cool echo of his when he had told her about death and aphrodisiacs. "Competition madness is unpredictable. Besides," she added distinctly, "tomorrow might never come."

"I used to believe that."

"You should. You're the one who taught me."

"I don't believe it anymore. Tomorrow will come for us. When it does, I want it to be right. I want to know that I didn't take you off-balance and more than a little afraid. I'm good at taking people that way. Too good. It's part of my job. But not you," said Cord, his voice deep, a river running through moonlight and darkness down to a warm sea. "I want you in a very special way, Raine. I can wait one more day for that. I've already waited a lifetime."

Raine looked away, unable to meet the hunger and certainty in Cord's eyes. Maybe he was right. Maybe she shouldn't trust her own instincts now. Maybe she shouldn't trust herself at all when she was around him.

"I'll make your omelet while you shower," said Cord, his voice matter-of-fact again as he turned away.

This time Raine didn't call Cord's name when the door shut behind him.

Raine lay on Cord's bed, trying to concentrate on the mystery she had bought at Dulles Airport before she got on the plane to California. So far, the only mysterious thing about the book was why it had been published in the first place. With an unconscious grimace, she started the second chapter for the third time in as many minutes.

Only a few feet away, Cord worked quietly. The computer keyboard made tiny hollow sounds beneath his fingertips. The scanner cast fragments of scratchy dialogue into the room. Sometimes poignant, sometimes urgent, often simply bored, the voices had an eerie unreality that nagged at Raine's attention.

"Delta Blue Light, do you copy?"

Out of the corner of her eye, Raine saw Cord's hand flash out to the scanner and depress the hold button. She realized that each time she had heard those words, Cord had reacted in the same way. Other words, other codes overheard by the scanner seemed to have no interest for him. She tried to make out the meaning of the transmission, but couldn't. The men spoke in a staccato shorthand that might as well have been another language.

Curiosity nibbled at Raine. She hadn't asked any questions after dinner when Cord had brought her back to the radio room and quietly explained to her that she was standing in the midst of a hallucination: the equipment didn't exist; the room didn't exist; and the motorhome itself was only an unfounded rumor. Therefore, the fact that she didn't have the security clearance to be here didn't matter.

Raine had accepted Cord's words without question, concealing her sudden interest. She was, after all, Justin Chandler-Smith's daughter. She was also intelligent. Her

half-formed assumption that Cord was some sort of glori-
fied bodyguard for her father shattered against the high-
tech, high-tension reality of the motorhome. Whatever
Cord did, it was more far-reaching and less obvious than
guarding VIPs.

Doggedly, Raine dragged her thoughts back to the second
chapter for the fourth time, but its clues and red herrings
were less tantalizing than the fragments of conversation
pulled out of the night by the scanner. When the words
"Delta Blue Light" came again, and again Cord stopped
the scanner to listen, Raine put down her book with an
impatient gesture. As soon as the transmission ended, she
looked over at Cord.

"What is Delta Blue Light?"

Cord swiveled his chair to face Raine, but said nothing.

"If the equipment doesn't exist, and the room doesn't
exist," Raine said reasonably, "then *I* don't exist. You
can't break any security rules by telling me about Delta
Blue Light, because I'm not really here at all."

Cord's lips turned up in the shadow of a smile. "You
should have been a lawyer." He hesitated, then shrugged.
"Delta Blue Light is a big secret, badly kept. The newspa-
pers have been hinting about it for eighteen months."

Raine waited, knowing that Cord would tell her what he
thought he should, and no more. She also knew that his
reticence was a way of protecting her, as her father had
protected her mother. Even so, Raine chafed at ignorance in
a way that she never had before. She wanted to know more
about Cord, about what he was, about what he did, about
his thoughts and experiences and dreams. Yet his life was a
closed file kept in a locked cabinet in a guarded room, with
access only on a strict need-to-know basis.

Well, she needed to know. And she would keep asking
until she did know.

"The Pentagon," continued Cord, watching Raine with eyes that were almost colorless, like his voice, "has set aside fifty million dollars for backup in case of another terrorist attack like Munich. Our hole card is Delta Blue Light, a group of hand-picked commandos waiting around outside Las Vegas. If they have to, they'll come down on LA like a hard rain, using all the nasty tricks we've learned from some of the world's nastiest people—terrorists."

Raine was utterly still for a second, caught as much by the violence beneath Cord's words as by the words themselves. Not a bodyguard, not a simple soldier, not like any man she had ever met before, not even like her father.

"Who are you?" she whispered.

Raine saw the subtle, devastating change that swept over Cord at her words. Suddenly he was poised, deadly, waiting for a signal only he would recognize. She held her breath as fear roughened the skin on her arms. Cord was looking at her the way he had the first time, when he hadn't known who she was. He was looking at her as though his pale, uncanny eyes could peel away her soft exterior and see whatever might be hidden beneath. And if he didn't like what he found . . .

His hard smile was no more comforting than his eyes. "I'm Cord Elliot, remember?"

"That's not what I meant," said Raine hurriedly, words tumbling out of her as she tried to explain, to banish the deadly stranger who was looking at her through Cord Elliot's eyes. "Are you local police or federal or military or . . . something else?"

Cord's eyes closed for an instant. When they opened, the stranger was gone. "I'm on your side, Raine. Isn't that enough?"

Cord turned away before Raine could answer. There was a finality to his action that told Raine more clearly than words that the subject of Cord Elliot was closed. With hands that wanted to tremble, Raine picked up her mystery and began the second chapter for the fifth time. This time she was more successful, if success could be measured by the number of pages turning beneath her determined fingers as the darkness outside deepened toward midnight.

The words Raine read were meaningless, the silence and the static cries of the scanner oddly hypnotic. Cord was right. This equipment, this room, she herself didn't exist. Nothing did but darkness and ghostly voices and the man with the pale eyes who sat at the center of everything, listening, waiting.

"—and Ontario. Two-eleven in progress. All cars in vicinity respond code three. Repeat. Two-eleven in progress on corner of—"

Static and silence and the hollow clicking of a computer keyboard. Raine held her breath unconsciously while the scanner searched unknown frequencies.

"—subject turning right on Sunset. Are you on him, Jake? Can you—"

Silence and clicking, scanner searching.

"—and they're at it again. Flip you for it, Martinez. Last time I got between her and her pimp she damn near—"

Silence and static, the faint hiss of voices coming over frequencies layered like cards in a deck, waiting for a dealer to pick them out and give them meaning.

"—repeat. Anyone monitoring this frequency speak Chinese? At least, I think it's Chinese, but I—"

Cord snapped on the hold and waited, listening.

"—can't be sure because I'm no linguist. She looks about six years old, and scared to death in the bargain. This is Kate on Nine. Over."

Cord waited, but no one answered. He picked up the radio, adjusted the frequency, and spoke.

"Kate on Nine," said Cord, omitting his own identification. "Is the girl able to hear me? Over."

"Yes. Over."

Sliding, singsong syllables poured out of Cord. Raine listened in fascination. When he ended with, "Does she understand? Over," the English words were almost jarring.

"Thank God! Yes, she understands you. Over." The woman's relief was evident even through the static.

Cord talked for a while longer, his voice soothing even in the atonal, minor-key phrasing of the language he used. The girl's voice came back to him, high and thin and oddly musical. The exchange continued for a few minutes, then Cord addressed the woman called Kate.

"The girl's name is Mei. She's Vietnamese, ten years old, and has been here only a few weeks. Do you live near Anaheim Stadium? Over."

"A few blocks north. Over."

"Call the stadium security people. She was at an Angel game and she got separated from her parents in the closing crush. Her parents are probably frantic by now, though they won't show it until they have her back. Over."

"What about the police? Shouldn't I call them? Over."

"Only as a last resort. The sight of a uniform might panic her. Where Mei came from, uniforms were worn by enemies. Over."

"Okay. Thanks. What's your name and call number? Over."

"I'll monitor this band for awhile. If you need me, just ask for Mei's friend. Over and out."

Cord set the radio aside, released the scanner and went back to sifting through electronic reports.

Raine picked up her mystery again. For a long time she

lay there, staring at pages she didn't see, wondering about the man called Cord Elliot. A man who could badly frighten her with a single look, and the next instant speak gently to a lost child in her own language, an alien language thousands of miles removed from the reality of the Summer Games. Fear and gentleness flowed from Cord so easily, so naturally. As did hunger and passion and a primal male sensuality that was like nothing Raine had ever known.

After a long time, the mystery novel slipped from Raine's fingers. She drifted in and out of sleep listening to fragments caught by the restless scanner, voices crying in the cosmopolitan wilderness telling of drunk drivers and armed robbers, lost children and freeway accidents, drug deals and domestic disputes, murder and rape, loneliness and violence and a chill seeping into her soul. Woven through it all like a glittering black thread came the clipped, almost brutal humor of the men who spent their lives patrolling civilization's long nights. Men just beyond the castle, walking cold perimeters while fire danced behind the locked gates they guarded, warmth always alluring, always beyond reach.

Half-asleep, half-awake, suspended between dream and reality, Raine turned restlessly, seeking peace. But the voices were still there, scratchy static whispers telling of life beyond the castle walls, life besieged by violence and unhappiness, life that knew the pain of lonely men and of children crying for lost mothers. And one man calling to Raine in a dark shaman's voice, telling her to unlock the gate, to come to him and make a new world where fire would drive away the chill. . . .

Finally, Raine slept, but it was a light sleep, easily disturbed. Cord watched her restless turning, waited until it stilled, then punched a code into his computer.

BLUE MOON CALLING BLUE HERRING.

Within minutes, the special radio phone buzzed. Cord activated it quickly so that it wouldn't wake Raine.

"Blue Moon."

"Blue Herring, buddy. You took your time getting back to me. Heavy date?"

Cord's lips turned in a sardonic curve. "You wouldn't believe me if I told you," he said, thinking of Raine sleeping on his bed only an arm's length away. "What's doing, *compadre?"*

"The usual. Blue is using field boots on everyone in sight. He's worried about Baby."

"Tell Blue that Baby is literally within my reach when her one-ton guard dog isn't on the job."

"Her what?"

Cord laughed softly. "Just tell him. He'll know."

"He's worried about whether she'll cooperate with you. Says she's damn near as stubborn as he is."

"She is," said Cord succinctly. "But she'll cooperate, one way or another."

"Well, at least you won't have to chase Baby through a lot of bedrooms. The book on her is that she likes horses a helluva lot better than men."

"Can't say as I blame her."

"Cynic."

"Realist. Did your worm say anything else about Barracuda and friends?"

"No. He couldn't even positively ID the picture Mitchell managed to take at LAX."

"You don't suppose your worm's turning again?" asked Cord.

"Doubt it. He barely got out alive. His ex-friends don't have any sense of humor. Barracuda personally executed the last three who tried to leave without permission."

"Sometimes they do it just for window dressing," pointed out Cord.

"Yeah, but this time they dressed the wrong window. The worm's girlfriend was five months pregnant when Barracuda scragged her."

Cord heard Raine's gasp. He spun quickly, watching her but saying nothing.

"Believe me, worm can't wriggle enough for us. He wants revenge so bad he sweats thinking about it."

"Anything else?"

"Nothing new, except . . ." Static, soft and scratchy.

"What is it?"

"Bad vibes, buddy. If I were running this show, I'd put a lock on Blue and Baby that an A-bomb couldn't blow. Moving targets are one thing. Sitting ducks are another. Watch your ass, OK? You're the only one I can beat at chess."

"I don't play chess."

"No kidding."

"Neither do you," added Cord, ending the prearranged code that established that each man wasn't acting under coercion of any kind.

"That's a state secret. Hasta la bye-bye, buddy."

"Hasta luego, compadre," said Cord, giving back correct, liquid Spanish for the mangled version of good-bye that Blue Herring had used.

Raine saw Cord replace the special phone. She bit her lip, trying to control the emotions seething inside her. She knew that Blue was her father's code name. Her father had always called her Baby Raine. She loved horses. She had to be the Baby that the scratchy voice had referred to. Had she become a target, too? And who was the poor woman who had been five months pregnant when she was murdered

trying to get away from someone or something called
Barracuda? Who or what was the worm, turning and
twisting under pressures too great for anyone to bear?

And Cord, wearing his gun again . . . Cord in the center
of all that violence, watching it with eyes the color of ice,
colder with every moment, midnight coming down. Even
vicariously, Raine couldn't survive the kind of life Cord
lived. Yet the hunger and need in him called to her in a
language older than castles or civilization. He was a winter
night and she was a fire burning.

Cord stood up slowly, his eyes never leaving Raine. He
unclipped the holster from his belt and tossed the gun into
the empty chair.

Chapter 8

RAINE CLOSED HER EYES, UNABLE TO BEAR THE INTENSITY of Cord's look any longer. Strong, gentle hands closed around her face. Her eyes opened dark and almost wild. Cord was very close, his eyes intent as he tilted her head toward the bedside light.

"What—what are you doing?" asked Raine.

"I'm looking at your eyes," answered Cord matter-of-factly, but his lips curved up in a crooked smile.

"W-why?"

"I'm checking that both your pupils are evenly dilated," explained Cord, his voice patient and very deep.

"Oh. Of course." Raine bit her lip, caught between the aching pleasure of Cord's touch and the knowledge that he was the wrong man for her, he led the wrong life, he would destroy her and never mean to. Yet his hands were very sure, very gentle, and his fingers curved to fit her face perfectly.

"Are they?" Raine asked after a moment.

"Are they what?" said Cord absently as his thumbs traced the sleek brown arch of Raine's eyebrows.

"Evenly dilated."

"Flecks of gold and depths of green, dark amber shadows . . . Do you know what time it is, Raine?"

She could only shake her head mutely, caught between his hands and his tangential question, off-balance again, falling toward him so quickly that she didn't even feel the pressure of her teeth scoring her lower lip.

"It's tomorrow," murmured Cord, bending over Raine until he filled her world.

Cord kissed the corners of Raine's mouth gently, coaxingly. When the tip of his tongue traced the teeth pressed into her lower lip, she couldn't control the tiny shiver that went through her. She was afraid, but not of him. It was his world that frightened her, a world where violence came as surely as midnight. She couldn't be a part of that world.

"Cord," Raine whispered, "it won't work. We're too different."

His tongue slid between her lips, her teeth, a gentle invasion of her mouth that made speech impossible. He savored her slowly, stealing away her unspoken words. The velvet texture of his tongue stroked her, exploring her with a deliberate thoroughness that asked everything of her and concealed nothing of himself. All of his hunger and gentleness and strength were condensed into a single kiss.

"Give it a chance to work," said Cord, his voice as caressing as his tongue. "I need you, Raine. I'm cold without you."

Cord's honesty overwhelmed Raine's few defenses. A wave of longing swept over her, drowning and lifting her up in the same rushing instant. She couldn't live in Cord's world; nor could she deny her world to him any longer. But did it matter? It was only for a few days, a week, until the Summer Games ended and sanity returned. She could live in his world that long, and he in hers. For that long, he would not have to live in cold and darkness.

Raine tried to say Cord's name but the only sound she made came from deep in her throat, a sound of surrender and victory and passionate surprise. Her hands, hungry to feel the rough silk of his hair parting between her wide-spread fingers, came up to his face. She heard her name whispered against her own lips; then her mouth was taken again before she could reply.

The kiss was different this time, a possession that drank her response, filled her, seduced her with slow movements that spoke eloquently of male hunger and the moment when he would hold her body as surely and intimately as he held her mouth. Muscles tightened deep inside Raine as a strange shivering took her. She knew nothing beyond Cord's taste, felt nothing but the heat spreading through her, burning her, burning him.

Cord drank Raine's shivering response as he had her kiss. He felt the fire spreading beneath her skin, fire that he had hungered for since he had first known of its presence. With a single powerful movement he lowered himself onto the bed and lay beside her, pulling her against the ache and hunger of his body. She came to him willingly, fitting herself perfectly to him as though it were the thousandth rather than the first time. He held her, surrounding her, wanting her with a force that shook him. He lifted his mouth from hers, measuring the depth of his need in the strange pain of so simple a thing as ending a kiss.

"Raine, listen to me," said Cord, his voice deep, a shaman casting spells before a shimmering midnight fire. He kissed her between each word, unable to deny himself the taste of her for more than a few seconds at a time. "I can stop if I have to. Now, but not later. Not even a few minutes from now.''

Cord captured Raine's lips again, let his tongue move deeply over hers, felt her liquid movement against his body as she silently answered his unspoken question.

"Tell me in words," said Cord urgently, his hands kneading down Raine's back, pressing her close to the rigid ache and hunger in him. "I have to hear you say that you want me. Do you understand? I don't trust myself to guess, because if I guess wrong I don't know if I can stop."

Before Raine could answer, Cord took her soft mouth again with a controlled passion that made her moan. "I won't hurt you," he promised, velvet voice and tongue touching her. "Don't be afraid of me."

Raine's slender fingers combed through Cord's hair, gently pulling his head back until she could see his eyes. Slivers of blue burning within silver that was smoky, molten. Black, thick eyebrows drawn in waiting; black lashes motionless, waiting. Muscles tight over the male planes of his face, waiting, and his whole powerful body like a coiled spring against her, waiting.

"I'm not afraid," Raine whispered, brushing the back of her fingers over Cord's lips. "Not the way you mean." She hesitated, not wanting to talk about her past but knowing she had to match Cord's honesty. "The one time I was with a man . . . it wasn't very good. My fault. He thought I was experienced. I wasn't. I disappointed both of us." She closed her eyes, unable to look at Cord, not wanting him to see the need in her, and her fear of not being able to please him. "I don't want to disappoint you," she whispered, her voice so soft he could barely hear the words. "I couldn't bear that."

"I had already guessed that you weren't experienced,"

said Cord, smoothing hair away from Raine's face with a gentle hand.

Raine wrenched her head aside as though Cord had struck her. Shame swept through her that her inadequacy as a woman should be so obvious to him after only a few kisses. When Cord's hands tightened, forcing her face back toward his, she struggled against him. It was futile. He was far stronger, far more experienced in using his superior strength.

"Your hesitations told me you weren't experienced," Cord continued, shaman's voice tugging at Raine, unraveling her. "Do you know how sweet it is when you hesitate and then open to me? To feel your surprise when my tongue first moved over yours . . . and then to feel you turn to me, kissing me the way I kissed you, the way I've always wanted to be kissed by a woman."

Raine couldn't conceal the quiver that went through her at Cord's words, at the memories blazing in his eyes and the hunger of his chiseled lips poised so close to hers.

"The kind of 'experience' you're talking about doesn't interest me," he said softly, clearly. "A thousand women could give it to me. I don't want it. I want you. I want your hesitations and surprise and fire. I want to hear the sweet cries you make when I touch you. I want to feel your body change when I make love to you."

Cord shifted with the same smooth power he had used to hold her motionless. Raine felt a premonition of warmth, his breath flowing over her; then his teeth raked lightly over her breast, capturing the nipple, pulling it into the heat of his mouth. Her thin blouse and bra offered no barrier to his caress. She cried out in surprise and passion as her nipple tightened beneath his probing tongue, only to be caught and held with loving finesse between his teeth.

Cord laughed softly and arched like a cat against the unconscious demand of Raine's nails raking down his back, wanting him closer, all of him. "Yes," he whispered, biting her with fierce restraint, "cry for me, want me."

When Raine's nails scored down his spine again, Cord rolled her onto her back swiftly and settled between her legs. His teeth closed again over her breast as his hips moved deliberately, caressingly, letting her know the full measure of his hunger. For an instant Raine hesitated, shocked by the sensations radiating up through her. Then she moaned and moved helplessly, caressing him with her body as he had caressed her.

Cord arched above Raine, inciting her, savoring her soft cries in the instant before he consumed her mouth in a powerful kiss. When he finally tore his mouth away from hers, his breathing was ragged.

"Did you feel like this with him?" Cord asked, biting and licking Raine's lips between each word.

"No," she said, then repeated the word again and again, shivering and burning with each shift of Cord's weight between her legs.

"Do you want me?" Cord asked, moving again over Raine slowly, then lifting himself so that she was free of his weight. He didn't want to release her but knew that if he held her, he would not be able to let go if her answer was no.

Raine made a sound of protest, reaching for Cord even as he freed her. She buried her fingers in his thick hair and tried to pull his lips back to hers.

"Tell me," he whispered. "Don't torture me, Raine."

"Is this torturing you?" she answered, lifting herself until she could move her mouth slowly over his, tracing the line of his lips with the moist tip of her tongue.

"You know damn well it is," he said roughly.

"Now that you've told me, I know." Raine caught Cord's lower lip between her teeth, holding him immobile as he had held her the first time he had kissed her. When she released him, she whispered, "Yes, Cord. Yes and yes and yes."

The shudder that went through Cord surprised Raine, telling her how much he wanted her, and how afraid he had been that she would not want him enough. Cord's hands came up to Raine's face, surrounding her with his strength. Slowly he lowered his head and kissed her with a gentleness that made tears gather behind her eyelashes. As he kissed her, he cradled her against his body carefully, completely, savoring each new point of contact, each new warmth.

Raine put her arms around Cord's waist and smoothed her palms over the long muscles of his back. Cord arched his body into her caress, responding with an honesty that made her breath catch, then come raggedly. She tugged at his shirt, pulling it free of his jeans, and made a throaty sound of pleasure when she felt the sensual heat of his naked skin beneath her fingers.

Cord laughed softly and rubbed against Raine's hands, his muscles twisting and shifting beneath her touch. "Do you like petting me?" he murmured into her ear, his tongue following his words caressingly.

She shivered in response and whispered, "Yes."

Cord laughed again. "Good," he said, his voice husky as he probed her ear with his tongue. "I want you to enjoy me as much as I enjoy you."

Blindly, Raine's hands moved over Cord's back to his waist, then up again, stopping only when she became tangled in the restrictive narrowness of his tailored shirt.

"Unbutton my shirt," said Cord, biting Raine's neck with exquisite restraint, leaving no marks but the spreading flush of passion beneath her skin. "Go on." Then, lifting his head and smiling wickedly down at her, "I promise I'll do the same for you."

Raine hesitated. She had wanted to run her hands over his bare chest since the time her fingertips had slipped between the buttons of his dress shirt in Griffith Park. The silky feel of him had haunted her dreams.

Cord bent swiftly, buried his tongue in Raine's soft mouth, then rolled over onto his back, pulling her with him. "See," he murmured, releasing her, "I'll make it easy for you."

Raine leaned awkwardly across Cord's body as she worked on the first, stubborn button of his shirt.

"Surely an Olympic equestrian can think of a better way to keep her balance," Cord teased, his voice velvet and rough at the same time.

Raine gave him a startled look, then accepted his implicit challenge. With a fluid movement, she settled onto Cord as though he were Dev waiting patiently by the mounting block.

"I do believe," murmured Raine, bending over the buttons again, perfectly balanced, "that I finally have you at my mercy."

"And you like that, don't you?" murmured Cord, his eyes smoky, his pupils very black and wide.

"Considering that I've been off-balance since the first instant I met you, *yes*."

Raine smiled to herself as the buttons on Cord's shirt came undone one by one. As each button opened, she pushed aside the shirt. Eyes nearly closed, lips curved in a sensual smile, she slowly stroked the crisp black hair on his chest with the backs of her fingers. When she brushed over his dark male nipples, she paused, then returned, circling him with sensitive fingertips.

Cord watched Raine's dreamy, absorbed expression with

a concentration as intense as hers. She felt the tightening of his body, heard the breath catch in his chest as her fingertips teased him into hardness. Slowly she bent down, licked each nipple as delicately as a cat, then caught him between her teeth with the tender ferocity he had taught her.

Hunger ripped through Cord, a hot, bittersweet pain raking deep inside him with claws that were neither kind nor wholly cruel. His hands clenched at his sides, because if he had touched Raine in that instant, he would have torn off her clothes and buried himself in her fire. But she was worth every bit of patience he could find, worth every small agony and savage pleasure she innocently gave him while she explored him, becoming as hungry for him as he was for her.

When Raine lifted her head and looked down at Cord, he was smiling. His fingers kneaded through her clean, soft hair as he pulled her mouth down to his for a long kiss. She shivered uncontrollably when his hands cupped her breasts through the thin white shirt she wore. Before the kiss ended, her blouse and bra were open and his hands were caressing her. She tried not to cry out when he gently devoured her, pulling her deeply into his mouth, making fire burst inside her. But in the end she could not help herself, tiny cries pouring out of her with each movement of his tongue over her breast.

The room swung dizzily as Cord shifted without warning, taking Raine down beneath him on the soft bed, his whole body covering her in a single hungry caress. With a hoarse sound, he rolled aside and stood by the bed, looking down at her, seeing the special beauty passion had created. Her eyes were brilliant, her skin flushed, her nipples dark rose, still taut from his hungry mouth.

"I was going to wait," Cord said, his voice husky as he pulled off the rest of his clothes and kicked them aside. His hands moved over Raine's jeans, unsnapping them, sliding them free of her slender legs. "But I have to see you," he said, removing her blouse and bra completely, easing her silky pants down the length of her legs. "I have to touch you."

Raine looked at Cord as he stood beside her, naked as the desire he had for her. Hunger twisted through her, a need to touch him, to have him lie beside her and hold her.

"Cord—"

"Don't be frightened," he murmured, velvet voice and touch soothing Raine. He brought himself back under control with an effort that left him aching. "I won't hurt you."

Raine pulled gently on Cord's hand, urging him back onto the bed. As Cord lay naked beside her, his hand stroked up her body from her ankle to her temple, then back down again. His hand lingered over her breasts, teased the shadowed hollow of her navel, then slid down until his fingers tangled in her dark, springy hair. At the same moment, his mouth caught her breast again, tugging swiftly at its already hard peak.

The twin assaults made Raine shiver and hold Cord's head fiercely against her breast. She felt his fingers ease through her hair to her thighs, then stroke slowly upward. Instinctively she shifted, opening herself to his touch. He whispered her name against her mouth as his fingertips touched the liquid heat of her. Then he groaned and caressed her deeply, only to withdraw with slow pressures that tormented her. He returned again, and then again, exploring her as thoroughly as his tongue explored her mouth.

Raine arched against Cord's deep caress. She had never been touched like that before, never savored and lingered over. She moved languidly, increasing the sensual pressure of Cord's fingers. His voice came to her in shades of darkness, shaman's words of desire murmuring over her, encouraging her. Tiny shudders moved inside Raine, passion gathering with each shared movement, each redoubled caress.

With a low moan, Raine melted in waves of liquid warmth. Surprise froze her. Fragmentary words tumbled from her, confusion and pleasure and apology.

"Shhh," Cord murmured against her lips. "That's what I wanted, Raine." He kissed away her words, stilling her confusion with a caressing tongue. "I came to you for your fire."

Cord moved slowly over her, touching all of her intimately with his hands and mouth until Raine shuddered and clung to him, melting, and he knew her pleasure again. Only then did he take her fully, burying himself in her liquid heat. Her eyes opened in surprise as she felt the extent of his possession. He saw her surprise and smiled down at her, a very male smile through lips drawn back with a need that was too consuming to be called either pain or pleasure. His hips moved and her breath came out in a moan. He moved again, joined with her in an intimacy greater than he had ever known, for her heat was inside him as deeply as he was inside her. He felt her shudder, felt the warmth spreading between their bodies.

"Yes!" said Cord, triumph and passion thickening his voice.

He held back as long as he could, savoring Raine's heat and response. Then he moved slowly within her. Raine felt her body gather itself, tension and heat racing through her, possessing her; and then giving her utterly to Cord. Her cries changed, deepening, urgent, and her nails raked down to his thighs. She clung to him with all her strength, feeling her world shaking apart, shattering into a pleasure so intense she could only surrender to it, to him.

Cord cried out wordlessly, holding Raine hard against his body as he shuddered again and again, giving himself to the heat that he had called from her, letting her fire consume both of them until there was nothing between them but soft sounds of ecstasy; and even he could not say whether the cries came from her or from him.

For a long time after, Cord held Raine, feeling the occasional tremors that swept through her as the world reformed around her, around him. He stroked her hair and kissed her cheek, cradling her as she sighed and nuzzled against him.

"You're . . . beautiful," Raine said, smoothing her cheek against his chest.

He laughed silently. "You have strange ideas of beauty. I'm about as pretty as a rockslide."

"Not pretty," countered Raine, her eyes following her hand down Cord's body. "Beautiful. The way mountains are beautiful. The way Dev is beautiful when he takes an impossible jump—rippling with fierce pleasure and power and purpose."

"Like I said," Cord murmured huskily, "a strange idea of beauty. I have a more conventional idea of beauty. You."

"How did you get this scar?" Raine asked, turning away from Cord's eyes.

"Why do you tighten every time I say you're beautiful?"

"Because I'm not, and I know it."

"Crap."

Raine turned toward Cord, startled by the certainty beneath the lazy sensuality of his voice. "You've never seen my sisters, Cord. They *are* beautiful. Particularly

Alicia. Men quite literally stop and stare when she goes by.''

Cord shrugged, a movement that sent a ripple through his powerful body. "That's one kind of beauty."

"It's the only kind."

"No. It's the least important kind. There's another kind of beauty that only special women have. A fire burning, hot and silky and incredible." Cord's hand came up and turned Raine's face toward him, shaman's voice flowing over her. "It's the kind of beauty that sinks into a man's bones until he can't breathe without remembering how his woman's breath felt on his skin, can't lick his lips without tasting her, can't move without remembering the soft weight of her sliding over him, can't feel anything but her burning around him, can't hear anything but her cries of pleasure. That kind of beauty can make a blind man weep. It's the only kind of beauty that matters, Raine. It's your beauty."

Raine blinked back sudden, unexpected tears. She had known Cord such a short time, yet he had slipped by all of her defenses. He had made her laugh and he had made her cry; he had frightened her and he had protected her; he was dangerous and kind, hard and gentle, aloof and sensual, self-sufficient and hungry for her. Cord was the wrong man for her . . . and he had become as much a part of her as the fire in her that he had found and freed.

"Raine? What's wrong?" Cord asked softly, pushing damp tendrils of hair away from Raine's face.

Raine lowered her eyes. "I thought I knew myself," she whispered.

"Don't you?" asked Cord, shifting until he could see Raine's face.

"Not when you touch me."

"It's the same for me, Raine," murmured Cord. "A new world and a new man experiencing it." Despite Raine's subtle resistance, he pulled her head down until he could brush his lips over hers. "Don't pull back, little rider. Is it so terrible when I make love to you?"

"No . . ." The word came out as a shiver and a sigh.

"Tell me, Raine," Cord murmured, shaman's voice coiling around her like an invisible warm river. "Whatever it is, I'll take care of it. Tell me."

"You're the wrong man," Raine whispered, then could have cried when she saw the change come over Cord, satisfaction and peace turning into tension once again. "No," she said quickly. "That's not true. I'm just the wrong woman."

Cord swore, a single vicious word. Suddenly he rolled over, pinning Raine beneath him. He kissed her harshly, powerfully, expecting her to fight. But she didn't. She put her arms around him and returned the kiss as fiercely as he gave it. His hands clenched in her hair, then gentled even as his mouth softened. The kiss ended very slowly, almost imperceptibly.

Raine held Cord and felt as though she were being torn apart. She could not live in Cord's world. But having met him, having found the other half of herself, she did not know if she could bear to live alone in her world anymore.

And then there were the Summer Games, culmination of a lifetime of dreams and effort. How could she respond to their demands when her world was being shaken apart? Yet she couldn't give less than her best to the Olympics and face herself afterward.

Wrong man. Wrong time. *Wrong.*

And so agonizingly right.

"We have to talk," Cord said quietly, feeling the tension in Raine's body, a tension that had nothing to do with sensual hunger.

"No," said Raine, putting her fingers over Cord's mouth. "I'm not as strong as you," she said simply. "I can't handle everything at once. We'll talk after the Summer Games are over. Until then . . . just be with me when you can, and I'll be with you when I can."

Cord looked at Raine's eyes, hazel and shadows and unexpected brightness of gold. He wanted to argue, to make her accede right now to his claim, to hear her agree once and for all that he had a place by her fire. Yet he sensed her confusion, her fear and her silent, tearing pain. He had deliberately shaken her world to make a place for himself in it, and now she was suffering the aftershocks, unable to realize or admit the extent of the changes he had made.

"Promise you won't run from me," Cord said, his voice deep and gritty with emotion. His hand brushed Raine's cheek with aching tenderness. "I never wanted to frighten you."

Raine closed her eyes against the tears welling, another kind of fire scalding her. She shook her head helplessly, knowing he was the wrong man and she was the wrong woman, and wanting him anyway—wanting him until she was weak with a hunger that only grew deeper with each word, each look, each touch.

"It's all right, Raine," Cord murmured, kissing the tears that gathered and glittered on her lashes. "After the Summer Games you'll see that you don't have to worry about your world or mine. Things will look different then. I promise you."

Raine opened her eyes and saw the certainty in his. She didn't want to question it, to make Cord as unhappy as she was. Better to let go of the cruel future, to live now. Tomorrow was only an expectation, not a guarantee. She had spent her life pursuing tomorrow in one form or another, one world-class competition after another. Tomorrow, beautiful tomorrow. It had always been brighter than today, more vivid and more real, a vision forever dancing just beyond her reach. But it danced no longer, and was dark instead of bright.

With trembling lips, Raine smiled at Cord, hoping for the first time in her life that tomorrow wouldn't come.

Raine and Cord ate breakfast in a companionable silence punctuated by smiles and small moments of touching: his fingertip stroking the back of her hand as she poured coffee, the delicate pressure of her hand on his cheek as she gave him a steaming mug of coffee, the brush of his lips over her palm.

"What's your schedule?" asked Cord softly, reluctant to end the warm silence.

"Dev, Dev and more Dev."

Cord smiled crookedly, not knowing that his smile went into Raine like a knife turning. "Never thought I'd be jealous of a horse."

"Dev doesn't really need that much attention," admitted Raine. "It's more for me than for him."

"What do you mean?"

"Competition madness. Time hanging and clanking around your neck like six iron horseshoes. If you work your horse too much, he'll go stale. If you work yourself too much, you'll lose your edge. So you wait until you're all edges and angles and time moves like it's nailed to the floor." *And a lot of people have affairs while they wait,* Raine added silently. *Like me.*

Yet this didn't feel like an affair to her. It didn't feel like something brief and mildly distracting, a pleasant way to kill time until the main event started. Summer games until

the Games began. Affairs just weren't her style. She almost
wished they were. If only she could learn to give a little and
always hold a lot in reserve, to walk carefully instead of
running headlong through life's obstacle courses. She
should approach life like a dressage rider, always quiet,
always utterly in control. But she never had.

Cord had been right. It was no accident that she had
chosen to buy and tame a half-wild blood-bay stallion called
Devlin's Waterloo. It was no accident that she had found the
risk and adrenaline and challenge of the three-day event to
be irresistible. She gave all to everything she did or she
gave nothing at all. There was no safe, easy, comfortable
in-between for her. She had taken some hard falls in her
life. She would take more. That was the nature of the world
she had chosen. Ride tight or fall hard; victory or defeat; all
or nothing at all.

"I feel like the invisible man," said Cord.

Raine blinked. She had been staring through Cord as she
tried to put the pieces of her world back into place. "Just
planning what to do next," she said.

"And?" he asked, his eyes pale and intent, sensing that
there could be more than one level of meaning to Raine's
words.

"Usually, I'd run a few miles."

"But today isn't usual?" Cord asked softly.

"I'm a bit late," Raine said, looking at her watch. "And
besides, I'm not exactly overflowing with nervous energy at
the moment," she admitted. "I'm feeling lovely and . . .
lazy."

Cord smiled slowly. "I know just what you mean."

Raine gave him a quick look as she realized what she had
said, and remembered the reason for her delicious feeling of
relaxation. She flushed and laughed at the same time.

"Since you aren't going to run, what comes next?" asked Cord, enjoying the color staining Raine's cheeks, remembering a few of the other ways there were to spread heat beneath her smooth skin.

"Clean out Dev's stall. Feed him. Groom him. Walk him a bit. Take him to the ring. Work him. Groom him again. Polish tack. Fret about the endurance course that I can't see for four days. I've a lot of that yet to do—fretting."

Cord frowned. He didn't like thinking about Raine on that course. He had seen the plans, knew the dimensions of each obstacle to the last millimeter. The thought of an exhausted Raine pounding over that course on the back of an equally exhausted stallion made ice condense in Cord's bones.

"The course is worth fretting about," he said quietly, spacing each word for emphasis. "It is one brutal son of a bitch."

Raine looked at Cord's eyes, cold blue and very intent. She knew suddenly that he hated the idea of her riding the endurance course. His reaction startled her; seeing her work through his eyes made it seem somehow more dangerous. She started to explain that it really wasn't that risky, not if she was careful and Dev was healthy, then realized the absurdity of her impulse. There was little she could tell Cord Elliot about danger and safety.

"I'm a good rider," Raine said quietly, "and Dev is one of the ten best event horses in the world."

Cord said nothing, merely lifted Raine's hand to his lips, remembering how Raine had been sprawled unconscious in the dirt while seventeen hands of savage stallion stood over her. "I'm not doubting your skill or Dev's worth," Cord said finally, rubbing his thumb slowly over Raine's palm as he spoke. "There's such a thing as luck, though."

Cord's eyes changed as he remembered the gold coin in

his pocket. Lady Luck. Lady Death. Same coin, different faces . . . and such a terribly thin margin separating them.

"Let's go take care of Dev," said Cord abruptly, pushing back from the table. He swept the dishes into the sink and turned toward Raine, who hadn't gotten up. "Well?"

Raine tilted her head to the side as she studied Cord. "Don't you have to work?"

"I will be working," said Cord.

He turned to pull his denim jacket off a hook. Despite the warmth of the day, he would wear the jacket. He always did, because he always wore a gun. As he turned, Raine caught the blue-steel gleam of the gun holstered in the small of his back. She hadn't noticed the gun, hadn't even seen him put it on. The jacket came down, concealing gun and holster.

"Do you need that just to watch me groom Dev?" asked Raine tightly.

Cord paused before he turned to face Raine. "Anyone who can face that damned endurance course without flinching can face a few other things, too. I was dragged out of my usual work and dumped into the middle of Olympic security for two reasons—to protect your father, and to protect you. You're a tempting target, Raine *Chandler-Smith*. Your father is very powerful. Your mother is the only heir to one of America's great fortunes. You're a favorite news item. Reporters swarm around you because of your family connections and the fact that you're a woman competing in a sport formerly reserved for men only, and military men at that.

"And," continued Cord, his voice as calm and cold as his eyes, "there is the fact that if certain people can't get through me to kill your father, they can always grab you and come in the back door."

Raine listened and felt her world being shaken again. "Is
that what the man on the radio told you?" she asked
angrily, not wanting to believe but knowing Cord wouldn't
lie to her about something like this.

"Which man?"

" 'Hasta la bye-bye,' " quoted Raine sardonically, resenting the unknown man, resenting the other, colder
reality that had been intruding on her world since she was
old enough to recognize and name it.

Cord's smile was brief, very thin. "Good old hasta la
bye-bye," he said, his voice as clipped as hers. "Yes, he
told me. I already knew, though. I just didn't know which
killer was going to be first in line."

Raine rubbed her hands over her arms, suddenly cold.
"You made sure I was cooperative, didn't you?"

"What do you mean?"

"The only bedroom you had to chase me through was
yours," she retorted, remembering the words she had
overheard.

"I caught you, too."

Raine looked away, unable to meet Cord's ice-blue eyes.
"Was that why you installed me in your motorhome? A
simple exercise in tactical economy? Killing two birds with
one bullet as it were."

Strong arms wrapped around Raine, pulling her close to
Cord. "That's not why I made love to you," he said, his
lips against her ear. "Being involved with you makes my
job harder, not easier. When you're out of my sight I worry
about you. And when you're in my sight I want you."

Cord's mouth fastened over Raine's in a kiss that left no
doubts about his hunger. After a moment's hesitation,
Raine put her arms around his waist and kissed him in
return, ignoring the deadly gun her fingers encountered in

the small of his back. It was only for a few days, so few. . . . She could live in his world that long.

"If I don't stop right now," muttered Cord, "the only riding that gets done today will be done right here."

Firmly, Cord put Raine away from him and opened the outside door. Sunlight streamed in, bringing with it the smell of dust and horses, and sprinklers working valiantly against the normal southern California summer drought. Faint voices drifted into the silence, voices too far away to be clearly heard. A car horn honked and somebody shouted a greeting.

Thorne was in his customary spot near the motorhome's side door. With his straw cowboy hat pulled low and his legs stretched out in front of him, crossed at the ankles, he looked as lazy and unalert as a lizard sleeping in the sun. Yet Raine noticed that Thorne's eyes were clear, wide open in the shadow of the hat brim, and he wore a jacket despite the warmth of the sun.

"Morning, Mr. Elliot."

"Morning, Thorne. I'll be with the U.S. Equestrian Team today," said Cord.

"Yes suh." Thorne's eyes switched to Raine. "Good morning, Miss Smith. Captain Jon said to tell you that you're scheduled for an hour later than usual."

"Thank you," said Raine faintly, knowing that she was blushing and helpless to stop it. Women her age spent the night with men all the time and no one blushed over it. But it was new to her, and it showed.

"You going to bring that red devil out here for another combing?" asked Thorne.

"Er, no," Raine said, smiling despite her embarrassment.

"Now that's a shame," drawled Thorne, letting the

languid southern syllables roll off his tongue. "I was looking forward to seeing Mr. Elliot get bit by something meaner than he is."

Raine laughed and shook her head. "He's not that mean."

"Me or Dev?" asked Cord, smiling.

"I'd recommend the Fifth Amendment for that question, Miss Smith," said Thorne smoothly.

"Sold," she said, smiling widely at Thorne, her embarrassment forgotten.

Cord moved to Raine's left side, took her arm and began walking away. After a few steps he dropped behind her, turned and said casually, "Thorne?"

Raine turned around too. She looked at Cord, caught by something hidden just beneath the calm surface of his voice.

"Yes suh?"

Cord's thumb gestured carelessly at the cloudless sky. "Have you noticed? It's a blue day today."

Thorne changed subtly, coming fully alert without shifting his position in the least. "I hear you, suh."

Raine started to ask Cord if he meant Delta Blue, but as she opened her mouth, she saw two people coming out of the shadows between the rows of stalls. From where the people were they could easily have overheard everything that she, Cord and Thorne had said. She waited until the people had passed beyond the range of her voice before she turned back to Cord. He was watching her with narrow, knowing eyes.

"You're Blue's daughter, all right," Cord said approvingly. "Nobody needs to tell you when to talk and when to shut up."

"Would that be Delta Blue you're referring to?" she asked sweetly. "As in the color of the sky today?"

Cord smiled, but it wasn't a comforting gesture. He stepped around Raine, moving once again to her left side. She looked at him curiously, realizing that every time he had walked with her since she had met him in the hills outside Rancho Santa Fe, he had walked at her left side.

"Is there something wrong with my right side?" she asked.

Cord looked blankly at Raine.

"You keep moving to my left side," she pointed out.

He shrugged. "I'm left-handed."

"So?"

"So my holster is slanted for a left-hand draw."

"Oh," said Raine numbly, wishing she hadn't asked. Then, her voice tight, "My God, Cord. How can you stand it?"

"Being left-handed?" he asked coolly, deliberately misunderstanding her question.

"Living like you do. Always having to remember to look around before you say anything, making sure that you can't be overheard. Always having to plan your movements so that your left hand is free to grab the gun you always wear."

"Do you have to remember each one of the hundred little things that help you to keep your seat on Dev?"

"If I did, I'd spend all of my time in the dirt. By now, keeping my seat is a reflex."

"Precisely," said Cord, his voice cool. "Not thought. Reflex."

As they walked toward Dev's stable row, Raine was careful to keep the conversation trivial. She talked about tack and Dev's leg bandages, oat hay versus alfalfa hay; and she watched Cord covertly. His eyes were never still. He was always measuring the people lounging against stable walls or carrying feed up the row, the people who walked horses or groomed them. He looked at roof lines and deep

shadows, knew instantly if someone was coming up behind
him. And he did it all while exchanging greetings with other
people and carrying on a conversation with her. No fuss.
No dramatics. Just years of reflexes honed in the cold world
beyond the castle walls.

A door banged open across the yard, startling Raine.
Before she could do anything more than register the fact of
an unexpected noise, Cord had moved so that he was
between her and the sound. But even as his left hand closed
over the butt of his gun, he recognized that the source of the
sound was harmless, a stall door banging in the wind.
Smoothly, Cord stepped back into place at Raine's side as
though nothing had happened.

And, to him, nothing had.

Raine shivered, feeling the cold of that other world. For a
horrible instant she hadn't known whether the sound was
harmless or deadly, whether to freeze or run, scream or stay
silent. But Cord had known.

Cord's fingers laced between Raine's. "Don't worry,
little rider," he said softly. "I'm as good at my job as you
are at yours."

Raine's fingers tightened in his. She was very glad to
know that Cord was close by. The thought of being a target
had crystallized in her stomach like a lump of ice, chilling
her. She suddenly had a visceral sense of why people built
high castles and higher walls and barred all gates against the
cold darkness beyond. The cold was so great. The fire was
so fragile.

And it was so unfair to ask men to live out there alone
until they froze, never having known warmth.

Chapter 9

THE RADIOPHONE SQUEALED CHILLINGLY, AN ELECTRONIC scream in the deep 3:00 A.M. silence. Even as Raine sat up, heart pounding, Cord was out of bed. In two strides he was at the phone. Soft static and harsh words filled the room:

"Bomb threat at the stables. Smoke spotted. We're moving horses now."

Raine was diving for her clothes before the last word faded into Cord's curse. He turned, reaching for his jeans, and saw her dressing hurriedly.

"Stay here," he snapped. "Thorne will guard you."

Raine ignored Cord. She grabbed for the first shirt she could find. His. She threw it to him and found her own. He grabbed her wrist, ignoring the shirt she had thrown to him.

"You're staying here."

Raine spun to face Cord. "No," she said curtly, buttoning her blouse one-handed. "With all the commotion,

Dev will be an inch away from exploding. If a stranger tries
to lead him out—''

Raine didn't finish. She didn't have to. Cord dropped her
wrist and his objections in the same second. He scooped up
the holster, pulled out the gun, checked its load with a few
practiced motions and secured the gun in the holster. He
clipped it to his belt at the small of his back. The whole
process took no more than five seconds. He was reaching
for his boots in the darkness when a stallion's savage
scream ripped through the night.

"Dev!" cried Raine, leaping for the door.

As fast as Raine moved, Cord was faster. He yanked
open the door and stood to the side, concealed by the
darkness within the trailer. With a single sweeping glance,
he checked the moonlight, shadows and occasional pools of
yellow lamplight for anything unusual. All he saw was
Thorne running toward him. No one else moved or
crouched in ambush. Cord leaped to the ground and landed
running. Raine was a half step behind.

Dev screamed again, shrill and wild, a sound of feral
rage.

Raine ran as she never had before, driven by adrenaline
and fear, bare feet flashing into pale blurs. She knew that
she had to get to Dev before he went crazy with a horse's
instinctive fear of fire. If he couldn't be kept calm, he might
injure himself.

Or kill someone. It was there in his scream, fear and fury
united in a mindless explosion.

She ran, praying silently. She wasn't even aware of Cord
running beside her, his eyes as feral as the stallion's cry.
She ran without feeling the hard ground or the stones that
bruised her feet. She ran without hearing herself call Dev's
name with each breath, a litany of hope and fear. Smoke
curled up on a lazy breeze, darkening pooled lamplight into

Halloween orange. Other horses were neighing now, frightened by smoke, instinctively wanting to flee their oldest enemy—fire.

Raine sprinted heedlessly through the night, dodging the men and horses streaming out of the stable rows. Men swearing and horses shying, their eyes rolling white, sensitive as horses always are to equine and human emotion. Especially fear. Dev's scream was a black wildfire sweeping through the stables, igniting panic despite everyone's efforts to be calm, to move swiftly but without fright, to speak softly to the nervous animals being led out of familiar stalls into the unfamiliar night.

Smoke that was thick and oily billowed darkly toward the moon. Another scream came as Raine and Cord hurtled around the corner leading to Dev's stable row. As one, they saw Captain Jon's slight figure dart through smoke into Dev's stall.

Instants later, Dev reared and plunged wildly, lashing out with deadly front feet. The stallion's mouth was wide open, screaming rage, and his ears lay flat on his skull. Captain Jon held onto the lead rope for one lunge, then the rope whipped through his gloved hands as Dev exploded out of the smoky stall like a devil coming out of hell, running straight for Raine and Cord.

Raine's first thought was to grab a double handful of mane and swing up on Dev's back as he thundered by. But he was already in full stride; he would yank her arms right out of their sockets. Her only hope was the wildly flapping lead rope. If she could grab it and hang on long enough to slow Dev, she could prevent him from injuring himself or someone else in his panicked flight. She turned suddenly, ready to run alongside Dev as she held onto the rope.

Cord saw it all as though in slow motion. Smoke. Captain Jon. Lead rope. Blood-bay stallion rearing. Dev raging free into the night with the white rope whipping alongside, threatening to tangle in the stallion's pounding feet and bring Dev down in a pile of broken legs and agony. Raine at Cord's elbow, reaching out, ready to grab the deadly rope as Dev hurtled by. Thorne running up behind them.

Cord's hands flashed out, snatching Raine away and throwing her into Thorne's arms. "Get her out of here," snarled Cord, never looking away from the stallion hurtling down on him.

Raine fought futilely, a silent clawing fury that Thorne simply, efficiently overwhelmed. And then she watched, utterly still, gripped by a terrible fear as she realized what Cord was going to do—time slowing, crawling, nailed flat to the dusty ground.

Ice-pale eyes measured distance and velocity. Thirty feet. Twenty. Ten. Muscles flexed, body poised—*eight*—arms reaching—*five*—hands tangling—*now*—in Dev's long black mane.

Cord swung up onto the stallion at the same instant that Dev's forward motion wrenched at the hands buried in the flying mane. Cord's powerful legs wrapped around Dev's barrel as he crouched over the stallion's neck, fingers reaching for the flapping lead rope. Dev was in full flight, steel-shod hooves pounding out a drumroll of fear, muscles bunching and sliding, ears flattened. The stallion ran like unleashed hell, too caught up in fear and sudden freedom to register the presence of an unfamiliar weight on his back.

Cord settled deeply into the stallion's stride, letting reflexes ingrained by years on horseback take over. He quickly gathered the flying lead rope, then began pulling back on it with increasing pressure, curbing Dev's freedom as the special halter closed over the horse's flared nostrils. Dev slowed as his breathing was forcibly shortened. His neck bowed rigidly, his hindquarters tightened with resentment, and his gallop became choppy, brutally hard on his rider.

Gradually, Dev calmed enough to realize that it wasn't Raine on his back. The stallion screamed once, raw fear and fury, and then he came apart. His black nose plunged down between his front legs as he bucked and twisted and shuddered, trying with all his huge strength to shake off the hated weight of a man. Cord's legs clamped down like thick steel bands as he simultaneously hauled up on the lead rope, trying to bring up Dev's head so that the stallion couldn't put his full strength into bucking.

Raine and Thorne came running around the stable row and stopped as though they had run into a wall. They stood without moving, barely breathing, riveted by the primitive battle in front of them. Shirtless, barefoot, Cord rode the screaming blood-bay whirlwind. The man's muscles bunched and gleamed in the bright moonlight even as the stallion's did, two powerful, supremely conditioned males fighting for dominance.

Inch by straining inch, Cord brought up Dev's head. His arms knotted with the effort of the fight, but his body remained supple, swaying and meeting each of the stallion's wrenching, twisting bucks with deceptive ease. Inexorably, Dev's head came up until his neck was a tight arch of arrogant rebellion that made each muscle and vein stand out. The stallion lashed out futilely with his heels, shredding shadows and moonlight, screaming in frustration. Elbows tight against his sides, Cord held the lead rope in both hands until Dev's nose was nearly at the man's leg and the stallion turned in tight little circles.

Then Cord began to talk to Dev, shaman's voice filling the darkness, a murmurous warm river of sound curling around the horse, washing away fear. Gradually Dev's circles became fewer, less frantic, his body less bunched with fear, his ears less flat against his skull. The stallion slowed and snorted, his blood-red hide rippling uneasily. He made a final, stiff-legged circle before he paused and sniffed his rider's leg. Dev drank the scent, his nostrils flaring as widely as the special halter allowed.

"That's it, boy," murmured Cord, stroking the stallion's neck with a gentle hand, "go ahead and smell me. You know me, don't you? I've been grooming you for five days, and for five nights your mistress has slept in my arms. I smell like Raine and like me and a little like you after that wild ride you gave me. Here, boy, smell my hand. Take a good, deep drink of me. See? I smell just like the three of us. Nothing to be afraid of, you blood-bay idiot. Just me."

The voice continued, dark velvet reassurance, words and nonsense, praising and petting. Slowly, slowly, Cord eased the pressure on the lead rope, giving Dev back his freedom. The stallion pranced and snorted, his ears swiveling every which way in their own nervous release. Cord's arms gave a few inches, allowing Dev to release the tension of a neck bowed too tightly. The horse stretched gratefully, then a black muzzle came back to tentatively sniff Cord's foot. Nostrils flared widely, fluttered and blew out a warm stream of air, only to flare again, drinking the mixed scent of Cord and Raine and dust from the stable yard.

The shaman's voice continued to cast its spell, winding around Dev like an immaterial net, holding him. The stallion snorted hugely and moved jerkily, uneasy with his strange burden but no longer wild with fear and rage. There was a man on his back, yet there were neither whips nor spurs nor savage bits cutting into him. There was only a hand stroking his neck and a shaman's voice flowing caressingly around him.

When Cord gathered the lead rope and turned Dev toward Raine, the stallion's ears came up. Moving as though walking on eggs, he minced diagonally toward her, dancing through moonlight to the rippling music of a shaman's voice. Raine walked forward a few steps, then stood motionless, entranced by the sight of a shaman riding bareback on a dancing stallion.

A black velvet muzzle moved lightly over Raine's face, drinking her scent. Automatically her hand came up in a familiar caress, rubbing Dev's ears; but her eyes were only for the man on the stallion's back. She touched Cord's leg as though she couldn't believe he was real. Only then did she admit to herself how terrified she had been that Cord would be killed by Dev's rage. With a shuddering sigh she put her cheek against Cord's thigh. Dev lipped at Raine's hair and minced sideways, trying to see her. Cord's hand tightened on the rope, stilling the horse's restive movements.

"Here," said Cord, his voice still low and reassuring. He held out his left hand to Raine and locked his left foot into a rigid platform for Raine to use to mount. "When you're barefoot around this blood-bay lummox, the best place for your toes to be is out of reach."

Raine used Cord's foot like a stirrup as he swung her easily into place behind him. Dev minced a bit at the strange weight, but settled down quickly when he smelled Raine's familiar scent and heard her voice floating down from his back. He snorted, flicked his ears, danced in place and waited for a command from his riders. Raine put her arms around Cord's waist and laid her cheek against his naked back. Even sitting behind him, she couldn't believe that Cord had ridden Dev, was riding him now, and both man and horse were alive, unhurt, radiating the heat of their brief battle into her.

Dev flinched suddenly, startled by the sound of the walkie-talkie that Thorne carried. Raine heard a brief mutter of voices; then Thorne called out to Cord in a calm, low voice.

"It was a smoke bomb. Some bastard's idea of a giggle. He's probably out there somewhere, busting a gut laughing." Thorne's voice left no doubt that he would enjoy getting his hands on the man who had set off the smoke bomb, then called in a bomb threat for good measure.

"We'll keep Dev out here until all the stables are checked and everyone is out of the yard," said Cord.

"Did you see Captain Jon?" asked Raine. "Is he all right?"

"My hands are sore," said Captain Jon, walking up behind Thorne, "but otherwise I'm intact."

"You should have waited for me," Raine said. "Dev nearly killed you."

"I didn't know if Cord would let you come to the stable," said Captain Jon, his voice matter-of-fact. "It would be a fine snare, you running in all worried and all of us running around turning loose horses. And then there was the smoke. I assumed that the fire wasn't far behind. I decided it was better to try to lead Dev out than to leave him in his stall to cook."

Raine said nothing. She was still absorbing the fact that Captain Jon knew that she was a target and Cord was her keeper. She wanted to ask how long the captain had known, but before she could speak, he was talking again, walking toward them slowly.

"Bloody amazing," said Captain Jon, looking at Cord sitting easily on Dev's back. "Bloody, *bloody* amazing."

Dev shied and turned effortlessly, facing the captain.

"I used to ride a lot," Cord offered dryly.

Captain Jon said something beneath his breath. "Bloody rodeo king," was all that Raine caught. She laughed softly, remembering what Cord had told her about his childhood.

"I shipped out before I won the silver buckle for bareback bronc riding," Cord admitted. "The old reflexes are still there, but I'm going to be stiff tomorrow."

Raine stirred, loosening her arms from their tight grip around Cord's waist. "We should walk Dev to make sure *he* doesn't stiffen up," she said quietly. "He has to be supple for the dressage test tomorrow." Her voice dropped as the realization hit her: within six hours, she would be riding in the Olympics. Culmination of a lifetime's effort rushing toward her. Would she be ready? Would she be good enough? Her arms tightened unconsciously around Cord as tension crept over her.

Cord turned toward Thorne, who had stepped back until he was little more than a tall shadow beneath the eaves of a nearby stable. "We're going to walk Dev around the yard," said Cord.

"Yes suh."

That was all either man said, but Raine knew that Thorne would follow them, a shadow watching shadows for movement that shouldn't be there.

"Do you think that the smoke bomb was more than a sick prank?" asked Raine as Cord turned Dev toward a deserted part of the stable yard, avoiding the men and horses who were returning to the area they had so recently abandoned.

"Maybe, but I doubt it. Too dicey with so many people running around. If they just wanted to kill you, the smoke bomb might have worked. But what they really want is to use you to get to your father. For that, you have to be alive."

Raine shivered at Cord's blunt assessment. "What about the rest of my family?"

"They're well guarded against kidnapping," said Cord.

What he didn't say was that there was no foolproof way to guard against assassination. Anybody could be killed, as long as the assassin didn't mind dying too. So far, Barracuda had been more interested in surviving to reap propaganda benefits than in dying a martyr to a blood-drenched cause. But that, too, was going to come to an end. Fishing Barracuda out of troubled international seas would be Cord's parting gift to Justin Chandler-Smith, one of the few men on earth that Cord truly respected. It would also be Cord's gift from the cold violence of the past to a newer, warmer future. Cord did not want to spend the rest of his life looking over his shoulder, watching for a nameless man who was narrow between the eyes.

"Don't worry about your family, Raine," Cord said quietly, bringing her hand up from his waist to his lips. "I'll take care of it."

"How?" she whispered.

Cord didn't answer. Raine didn't ask again.

When Dev was cool, groomed and calm, they left him in the stall and returned to the motorhome. Raine walked quickly, restlessly. She wasn't ready to go back to sleep.

"Worried about Dev?" asked Cord.

"No."

"Competition nerves?" he asked, drawing Raine into the motorhome and locking the door behind.

"Yes," she admitted. "Being awakened like we were didn't help."

"Puts the adrenaline count right over the moon," agreed Cord, stretching again, easing shoulder muscles that wanted to knot and stay knotted.

"I can't groom Dev, which is what I usually do when I get edgy like this. So," Raine concluded brightly, "I'm going to groom you."

Cord's black eyebrows arched in amusement. "I'll bet the brush will tickle like hell," he said, unclipping his holster and putting it aside. "As for the currycomb," he added, slipping out of his jeans and standing naked, hands on hips, "forget it. My hide just isn't that tough."

"Wrong color, too," murmured Raine, looking at the honey-dark skin and shadow patterns of hair gleaming in the subdued light.

"I'm getting a better idea," said Cord, smiling slowly, watching her hazel glance move over his body.

"I can see that," she retorted. "Face down on the bed, Mr. Elliot. It's your turn for a rubdown."

"I wondered why you brought that liniment from the stable," said Cord.

The pungent odor of liniment permeated the room. Oily, sharp, clean, oddly soothing, the smell brought back a rush of memories from Cord's childhood. He lay quietly, remembering horses and men and campfires, the scents and laughter of another world. He asked himself silently why he had ever left that world. There was no answer.

Raine's hands kneaded Cord, loosening tense muscles.

Cord made a long sound of pleasure and relaxed. "I love your hands, little rider," he said very softly. "Strong and . . . womanly."

"Comes of handling my knotheaded stallion," said Raine, leaning into her work, using all of her strength to loosen the long, powerful muscles of Cord's body.

His back moved in silent laughter. "Comes of grooming the red devil, too," he added.

"Wait until you see me work Dev over after the endurance run. I'll spend the night kneading him like a great red-and-black pile of dough."

Cord's only answer was a groan of pure pleasure as liniment and knowing hands made his muscles feel like putty. Raine smiled and leaned harder, probing and kneading until Cord's muscles were supple beneath her hands. Then she slid down and began to work on his legs and hips.

For a long time the only sounds were the slide of her hands over his legs, his occasional groan of contentment, and the erratic mutter of the scanner. The latter sound had become so familiar that Raine didn't even notice it.

At last Raine sighed and sat up, flexing her hands. Cord didn't move. His head was turned away from her and he was breathing evenly, deeply, utterly relaxed and probably asleep. She smiled to herself, stretched, and slid off the bed. She was less on edge than she had been, but still not ready to sleep.

Cord's arm snaked around Raine's leg before she could take a step. "Still restless?" he asked, turning over so that he could see her.

"A little," she admitted.

"What do you do after you've groomed Dev and groomed him again and you're still on edge?" asked Cord.

"I usually get on bareback and take a slow, lazy ride."

Cord smiled as he pulled Raine down, fitting her soft curves over him. "I thought you'd never ask."

Raine awoke to the alarm and the smell of liniment. She rolled over, expecting to find and curl up against Cord's solid presence. He wasn't there. She sat up suddenly, heart pounding.

"Cord?" she called, looking around quickly.

There was no answer.

Vaguely she remembered hearing his beeper go off earlier, remembered him kissing her and saying, "Go back to sleep, little rider." And, amazingly, she had.

Raine dressed and ate without wasting any time. She had only a few hours to polish tack, groom Dev, and groom herself to the elegant standards required by Olympic dressage. Mentally she composed a list of what had to be done before she was ready to ride Dev in front of the three expressionless judges who would decide whether she was a credit or a burden to the U.S. Equestrian Team. She was still juggling chores in her mind when she let herself out of the motorhome. Thorne was in his usual position, a man who apparently had nothing better to do than sit and watch the world go by.

"Morning, Miss Smith."

"Good morning, Thorne," said Raine. "Is Cord around?"

Thorne glanced around. "I don't see him, ma'am."

Raine smiled. It had become a game with her and Thorne. If Cord wasn't around, she would ask about him. Thorne would reply politely and very vaguely, saying nothing at all about the movements of his boss.

"If you see Cord, say hello for me," said Raine.

"I'll do that, ma'am." Thorne smiled. "Count on it."

Ritual completed, Raine started toward the stables. Thorne stood with a lithe speed that belied his outward laziness. He spoke briefly into his walkie-talkie and then caught up with Raine. She looked at Thorne quickly. This wasn't part of their usual morning game.

"Going to watch me comb the red devil?" asked Raine dryly.

"Yes, ma'am, I'm going to do just that."

"I didn't know you liked horses."

"I'm learning," Thorne said in a resigned voice.

Thorne stayed with Raine the rest of the morning. He was never out of sight and rarely out of reach. Unlike Cord, Thorne walked on Raine's right side. He was remarkably discreet, fading into shadows when other members of the equestrian team came to talk to her. If it weren't for the fact that she kept looking up at odd moments, hoping to see Cord, Raine wouldn't have noticed Thorne at all.

At last, Raine admitted that she couldn't put off Dev's

final grooming any longer. Cord had promised to help her, but obviously his electronic leash had led him elsewhere. Not until Raine accepted that Cord wasn't coming did she realize how much she had come to enjoy the long, peaceful hours she and Cord had spent grooming the big stallion or polishing tack until it shone. She had always done everything by herself; Dev simply hadn't tolerated anyone else to the point of relaxing his guard. But the stallion had come to trust Cord.

And she had come to trust Cord too. She really had believed he would be there to help her prepare for her Olympic test. Her disappointment wasn't Cord's fault, though. It was her own.

"Foolish little girl," Raine muttered. "You know better than to trust a man on a leash. He'll do the best he can, but you'll always be second in a two-entry race."

"Ma'am?" asked Thorne, hearing only the sounds, not the meaning.

Raine glanced up, startled. "Er, nothing. I always talk to myself when I work with Dev. It lets him know where I am."

"Wise. That red devil could kick you into next year."

Raine went to the stall door, looked into the yard, and then looked away quickly. Cord would come when and *if* he could. Hanging over the stall door wouldn't bring him to her any faster. Deliberately, she turned her back and began weaving Dev's thick mane into a French braid. When she was finished, there would be nothing but a smooth, textured surface running the length of Dev's neck. There would be neither a wild black fall of mane nor beribboned pigtails to detract from Dev's performance in the Olympic dressage ring. After Raine completed the mane, she brushed Dev's long tail until it was a black waterfall rippling and shimmer-

ing nearly to the floor. She polished each hoof until it was
dark and gleaming.

"Should I send over one of the girls to help you?" asked
Captain Jon as he leaned on the stall door and looked
critically at the stallion.

Raine shook her head. "I've got it under control. How
are we doing in the dressage ring so far?"

"Better than I'd hoped. The Russians are having the
same trouble we are. Their bloody beasts are damned near
jumping out of their skins with health. Their fault scores are
still only fifteen to twenty, though. They take to discipline
better than you Yanks."

Raine smiled at Captain Jon's familiar—and mostly
joking—complaint. Yet the thought of having to hold her
volatile, vibrant stallion to a mere twenty faults was
troubling. Dressage wasn't like jumping, where faults were
quick and obvious. Each dressage exercise could theoreti-
cally be performed to perfection. Perfection, in many ways,
was a matter of opinion. Dev usually got high positive
marks simply because he was beautifully built and had a
commanding presence. He also received relatively high
negative, or fault, marks for obedience. He made up for the
latter on the grueling endurance portion of the three-day
event, however.

Captain Jon cleared his throat uneasily. Then, "Raine?"

She turned to face him, caught by the unusual hesitation
in his voice. "Yes?"

"I could short-list you, if you like. You don't have to go
out there and be a bloody target."

Raine froze. *Short-listed.* Taken off the American Olympic Equestrian Team and replaced by one of the other
American riders who had also trained strenuously for four
years, hoping to make the Olympic cut. Yes, Captain Jon

could short-list her; it was his right. But he had to do it now, before she entered the first competition of the Olympic three-day event. Once she had competed, if she were disqualified for any reason, the Americans would simply have to go on under the handicap of having only three riders on the team rather than four. In a competition that counted the best three out of four team members' scores, having a team member disqualified during the event was a crippling blow.

"Do I have a choice?" asked Raine, her voice careful, colorless.

"Of course."

"I want to compete."

Captain Jon rubbed his cheek thoughtfully. "Even as a target?"

"If you're worried about the team, short-list me. If you're worried about me, don't. I'm a candidate for kidnap, not assassination. Ask Cord."

"I did."

Raine looked up sharply. "And?"

"He said he would feel a lot better if you weren't risking your neck on the endurance run. But he said that was a personal, not a professional, opinion."

Raine closed her eyes, silently thanking Cord. She knew that he was worried about the obstacles on the endurance course. She was very grateful that he hadn't used his professional position to ground her.

"He's an unusual man," added the captain. "Honor isn't just a word to him. And he has a great deal of respect for your skill."

"Yes," said Raine softly, "I know." She looked past the captain automatically, searching for Cord's lithe male figure. He wasn't there, though. Was he going to miss seeing her ride in the dressage competition?

Captain Jon cleared his throat again, accurately guessing where Raine's attention was at the moment. "Go ahead and enjoy Elliot. God knows it's about time you let a man get close to you. But don't let him distract you from your major purpose—the Olympic Games."

Raine flushed. "I won't let the team down, Captain Jon."

He nodded once, abruptly. "If I thought you would, you'd be short-listed right now instead of polishing that bloody great stallion. Give him your best ride, Raine. And don't worry. I don't expect miracles. That horse was born to run, not to make pretty patterns in the sand of a dressage ring."

Raine stepped out of the motorhome and locked the door behind her. She was wearing the formal riding attire of the dressage ring. Black hat and polished English boots, white blouse and carefully tied stock, jodhpurs and a dark, severely tailored riding coat. She carried white gloves in her pocket. They would go on just before she went into the ring. Her hair was twisted up beneath her hat. There would be no flying locks to detract from the calm, measured elegance required by Olympic dressage.

Thorne appeared and walked at Raine's right elbow. She didn't ask him if he had seen Cord. She didn't trust herself to play the small ritual game lightly. It seemed that she had spent a lot of time looking forward to someone coming to see her perform, only to be disappointed at the last minute. She closed her eyes and took a deep breath, putting aside the disappointment as she had learned to in the past. She was about to enter the first event of an Olympic competition. She had worked all her life toward this moment. She would give the games what they demanded and deserved: her best.

When Raine turned the corner at Dev's stable row, she saw her horse bridled and saddled, standing quietly, black muzzle nibbling at Cord's collar. Dev scented her, lifted his head and nickered, tugging at the reins Cord held. Cord turned and held out his hand to Raine. He didn't say where he had been, or why; nor did she ask him. Raine knew that she didn't have the security clearance to know the details of Cord's life.

"You look very cool and elegant," said Cord. His eyes went over Raine's slender figure from her hat to her boots. "Will you be disqualified if I hug you?" he asked in a husky voice.

Raine put her arms around Cord and hugged him. "I'm glad you'll see me ride in the Olympics," she whispered, and felt his arms tighten even more.

Suddenly Raine felt lighter, younger, triumphant, as though she had won the dressage event before she even went into the ring. When Cord lifted her up into the saddle, she smiled down at him and put her hand along his cheek.

"Thank you for saddling Dev."

"For a smile like that, I'd saddle the devil himself," said Cord. He kissed Raine's palm and stepped back.

Cord walked alongside Dev to a practice area where dressage contestants "rode in" their horses, carefully warming up the animals so that their muscles would be supple for the intricate demands of dressage. Cord watched as Raine collected Dev, schooling him, working until the stallion's weight was poised over his hocks and his neck was a smooth, impressive arch balanced lightly against the bit.

When Raine's name was called as the next competitor, she turned Dev and rode him out of the practice area toward the competition ring. Cord watched her go. He could have called out, wishing her luck or some such trivial thing, but he remained silent, understanding that at this instant Raine had to be focused entirely on the Olympic competition.

Raine waited behind the bleachers while the previous rider's scores were flashed on the lighted board. A round of mild applause came, telling her that the French rider had performed adequately but not well. Nervousness turned over coldly in Raine's stomach. She concentrated on the flags of the participating countries flying behind the bleachers, along with the flag bearing the Olympic symbol of five interlocking circles. The bleachers were brimming with an excited, attentive crowd. Three judges sat alone beneath an awning at one end of the freshly raked, sandy rectangle that was the competition ring.

Raine heard her name and country announced over the public address system. At Captain Jon's signal, she took a deep breath, collected Dev, and began the first test of the Olympic three-day event.

With the contest finally begun, Raine's nervousness fell away. She rode Dev into the smooth-surfaced, rectangular performance area, stopped in front of the judges, saluted, turned, and began the preset pattern of dressage exercises which every Olympic competitor had to perform. In the next seven and one-half minutes, the judges would examine horse and rider, looking for a harmony that would be expressed in serene, elegant, yet powerful movements over the freshly raked sand. While Dev changed paces and leads, directions and diagonals, Raine was expected to sit gracefully and not in any way show that she was the one giving the horse its cues.

With horses that were trained and bred only for dressage, there was a docility of body and spirit that greatly aided the rider's appearance of being merely a well-dressed passenger. Event horses, however, were bred and trained for aggressive health and the kind of spirit that wouldn't quit no matter what the obstacle ahead or the exhaustion of the moment.

As a result, Dev didn't want to confine his bursting energies to seven and a half minutes of simple patterns of walk and slow trot, slow canter and fast walk, switch leads and working trot, stand immobile and wait for an invisible signal to move, and so on. The stallion's spirited displeasure showed in his tossing head, his champing at the bit, his constant testing for a weakness in Raine's grip on the reins. For seven and a half minutes, Raine and Devlin's Waterloo fought a sub-rosa battle for control of the bit.

Dev never broke loose or refused a signal; nor did he always show the calm submissiveness that dressage judges favor. At times, Dev required "aids" of a strength that were hardly invisible. On the other hand, the stallion's impressive hindquarters and muscular, arched neck made him appear to be more collected beneath Raine's hands than he often was. There was also the fact that her slender, long-legged grace showed to particular advantage against Dev's huge, coiled body.

With a serene expression and an iron grip on the reins, Raine signaled the last lead change as she turned Dev back toward the judges. She stopped the stallion and held him immobile between the combined pressure of the bit and her knees. Then Raine saluted to the Olympic judges, thus ending the longest seven and a half minutes of her life.

She waited with outward patience until her scores were flashed on the board. She looked only at the faults recorded by each judge: 33; 40; 23.

With no change of expression, Raine turned and rode out of the ring. Considering that the average three-day event horse compiled fifty faults per judge, Dev's and her performance was better than adequate. Considering the

Russian horses so far, though, Dev's and her performance left something to be desired.

Amid loud applause Dev minced out of the ring, pulling eagerly at the bit. He had pleased the audience, if not the judges, and he knew it. Now the stallion wanted nothing more than a good hard run.

"You'll get it, you red devil," muttered Raine, heading Dev toward an open area set aside for exercising horses. "Not as much as you want, though. Just enough to clean out your pipes before we ship you to Rancho Santa Fe for the cross-country. There you'll get all the run you want, and then some."

Shying, prancing, Dev did everything but crawl out of his skin to free himself from the restrictions of the bit and his rider's gentle, implacable hands. Nervous lather was forming on his shoulders and flanks by the time he cakewalked to the area where he would be allowed to run.

Cord was waiting at the gate. He swung it open, allowing the eager stallion inside. "That was a world-class piece of riding," Cord said, admiration clear in his voice. "Dev's a lot of horse to keep the lid on."

"He's going to get his reward now," said Raine rather grimly, settling deeply into the flat saddle as Dev danced sideways. She let out the reins slightly. Dev went from a standing start to a gallop, fighting for control of the bit.

Cord watched, his expression admiring and harsh at the same time. Raine rode with a joy and grace that almost made Cord forget how big Dev was, how fiery and powerful. But Cord never forgot how completely Raine's life depended on the trust between herself and the volatile blood-bay stallion. The upcoming endurance event haunted Cord. In a few hours he would be driving Raine down to Rancho Santa Fe, away from the heat and smog that Prince

Philip had decreed were unsuitable for the cross-country part of the Olympic three-day event . . . Rancho Santa Fe, where an exclusive country club had torn up its golf course and replaced it with obstacles designed to test the courage of horse and rider.

The thought of the cross-country made ice condense in Cord's veins. But there was nothing he could do. Raine had made her choice long ago. He respected that, as he respected her.

Chapter 10

RANCHO SANTA FE'S DRY WINDS COMBED RESTLESSLY through the golden grass and silver-green eucalyptus trees. The sky was blue-white, radiant with heat and sunlight. Yet Raine barely noticed her surroundings as she stood on a hilltop. She was frowning over a steno notebook that contained the condensed wisdom of Captain Jon, herself and her teammates on the subject of the endurance course of the three-day event.

The course was divided into four segments: (A) roads and trails; (B) steeplechase; (C) roads and trails; (D) cross-country. Together, A and C equaled about fifteen miles covered at a canter. Or the rider might choose a combination of walk, canter and gallop that amounted to the average speed of a canter. Pacing was crucial for good performance. There were no points given for going faster than the required times on the roads-and-trails segments; points were deducted for taking too long. A steady canter would be an ideal pace, easy on both horse and rider. The terrain rarely permitted such a pace, though.

It was up to the rider to balance the requirements of the course against the needs of the horse. Too conservative a run would cost time faults. Too fast a run would take too much out of the horse, making the final cross-country segment of the course impossible rather than merely difficult. Any errors at all on roads and trails would erode the team's chance for an Olympic medal. There was simply no excuse for not pacing the horse properly or taking any of the course out of its assigned order.

Raine flipped through her pages of notes, glancing occasionally at the map all contestants had been given when they were officially taken over the course for the first time. Part B, the steeplechase, was about two and a half miles of fast gallop with jumps placed on the average of every thousand feet. These were fixed jumps, not show-ring jumps. If you hit a fence, *you* went down, not the fence. If you went faster than required, you could make up points. If you went too slow, taking twice the required amount of time, you were disqualified. Period. There was no way to spare your horse and still stay in the event. Refusals or falls at the jumps counted heavily against a competitor. Again, in order to have a chance at the gold, horse and rider had to put in a perfect round.

The steeplechase was a test of nerve and speed and judgment. However, it was part D, the cross-country, that was designed to separate the merely fit and skilled horse-and-rider teams from the superbly fit and consummately skilled. A fall within the penalty area around each obstacle cost sixty points. There were many opportunities to fall. The cross-country was five miles of up- and downhill trails over obstacles of the sort that required a horse to trust its rider's judgment. No trust, no jump. The first refusal of an obstacle cost twenty penalty points. The second refusal of the same obstacle cost forty. The third disqualified you. The obstacles averaged one every eight hundred feet. Thirty obstacles. Five miles.

Although none of the obstacles required more than a six-and-a-half-foot drop from the takeoff point, some of the obstacles were diabolically placed in the middle of ponds or just beneath the crest of a hill, on the downside, where the horse must literally jump blind on a signal from its rider. Other obstacles came at the end of a long uphill run, testing the will of the horse to continue. Five miles of scrambling and jumping. And this came on the heels of nearly eighteen miles of hard work for both horse and rider, including the steeplechase. Except for a fifteen-minute break just before the cross-country—when a veterinarian examined the horse to see that it was fit enough to finish the course—horse and rider were tested relentlessly.

As Captain Jon had put it, the endurance event was a "right bastard."

"You aren't supposed to be out here alone," said Cord's voice from behind Raine, startling her.

She looked up from her notes and realized that everyone else had scattered over various parts of the course, measuring yet again what would be required of horse and rider. She looked back at Cord.

"I'm not alone," she said reasonably. "You're here." She smiled and brushed her lips over his. "That didn't take long," she said, looking at her watch. It had been only an hour since the beeper had called him.

Cord's hand slid into Raine's hair. He pulled her close and kissed her hungrily. "Promise you won't go anywhere alone," he said, his voice almost harsh.

Raine looked up at Cord's ice-blue eyes and felt the tension in his shoulders. "What is it?" she whispered.

Cord shook his head and said only, "Promise me."

"I have to walk parts of the course again," said Raine.

"Let's go," Cord said, lacing his right hand through hers.

"Cord—" Raine hesitated, knowing that he wasn't going to like what he heard. "Even if your beeper goes off again and you have to leave, I still have to go over the course. I can't take Dev over obstacles that I haven't had a chance to really study."

Cord's face settled into grim lines. "We'll burn that bridge when we get to it."

Raine wanted to ask what had happened in the last hour to make Cord so wary, so hard, so . . . *angry*. She didn't ask, though. There was no point. He wouldn't tell her any more than he already had: he most definitely did not want her to be alone.

"Where to?" asked Cord.

"Steeplechase. I want to look at the water jump again, as well as the bigger fences."

Cord and Raine walked quickly, saying little as she looked over the steeplechase part of the course. From time to time she made notes. Cord watched silently, measuring the jumps with a shrewd eye. The water jump involved a hefty fence followed by a small, man-made pond. The whole jump was thirteen feet wide. It would take a powerful, well-balanced leap to clear everything. The other obstacles were no easier: mounds of logs nailed together, solid as a house; brush and water jumps. Jumps into shadow and then into sunlight and jump again half-blind. Twist and turn and jump again, two and a half miles at a hard gallop.

Raine stretched fingers cramped from writing, and folded up her notebook. "On to the cross-country."

"All five miles of it?"

"I'll walk fast."

"I'll starve."

Raine reached back and patted her rucksack. "Food."

"Mind if I rummage?" asked Cord.

"Didn't we meet this way, with you so eager to rummage in my rucksack that you knocked me off my feet?"

Cord's lips relaxed into a smile. His thumb moved caressingly over Raine's cheekbone. "If I knew then what I know now, I'd have taken off your clothes and made love to you right there. Maybe I should do that right now, take off your clothes and pull you down into the grass," he said in a gritty voice, "love you until you shiver and burn and cry out my name."

Raine's breath caught at the desire in Cord's eyes. She swayed toward him and he kissed her until she trembled against him. The sound of voices floated up the riverbed. Cord groaned and tore his mouth away from hers.

"Too damn many people," Cord said bitterly.

Raine laughed shakily. "A while ago you were complaining about it being too lonely out here."

"Then I was thinking like a bodyguard. Now"—Cord's eyes looked longingly at Raine's lips, reddened from the force of his kiss—"now I'm thinking like a lover. *I want you.*"

"Don't tempt me," she said huskily. "I happen to know of a perfect little hideaway. It's too heavily wired for my taste, and the background music leaves a lot to be desired, but the locks are the best that money and ingenuity can provide."

"Background music?" asked Cord, smiling crookedly.

"The scanner."

Cord laughed and folded Raine against his body, cradling her, rocking her. "After this morning, I didn't think anything could make me laugh. You're so good for me, little rider," he murmured against Raine's hair. Then he sighed and gently released her. "But I like you in one piece, so let's see the rest of what this 'right bastard course' has in store."

"You've been talking to Captain Jon."

"That's why I came back so soon. I couldn't believe the cross-country segment was as bad as he described it."

The smile faded from Raine's lips. "It's what it's supposed to be—a test."

Cord said nothing, but his mouth was a thin, hard line. He turned her around, unfastened the rucksack and rummaged. After a few moments he asked, "Ham-and-swiss or Italian?"

"Italian," said Raine.

Raine and Cord cut across the course to the last segment, the cross-country. Between bites of Italian sandwich, Raine answered Cord's questions. All of the questions had one thing in common: his blunt concern for her welfare. The more obstacles he viewed, the greater his concern became. Taken by themselves, many of the obstacles were hair-raising, even for a man brought up riding mustangs through broken country. Taken at the end of nearly eighteen miles of exertion, the obstacles were appalling. They were conceived in hell and dedicated to the principle that any horse-and-rider unit could be broken into its component parts. And left that way.

There was one obstacle called the Coffin. It consisted of a sharp downhill approach, a pair of rails built on both sides of an eight-foot-wide stream, and an uphill landing. If horse or rider misjudged at any point, a vicious fall was inevitable. Then there were the steps, a gigantic staircase with each step just wide enough for a horse to land on. There was no space for a stride before the next step loomed ahead. Without perfect timing, willingness and coordination, the horse stood to break a leg and the rider a neck.

The water jumps were no better. Water was soft, yes, but mud made for nasty footing. One of the jumps was styled after the type of obstacle any nineteenth-century military rider might have encountered: a stream sunk between banks that were almost four feet high. The stream was too wide to jump bank to bank, which meant jumping down into water and then back out, jumping blind. There was another obstacle that involved jumping blindly into water. It consisted of a wall of logs that dropped into water on the far side, then two strides in water over the horse's knees and finally a chest-high fence in the middle of the pond. Jumping the fence required a wet, uncertain takeoff and a worse landing.

"What if you fall between obstacles?" asked Cord, looking at a rugged uphill run separating two obstacles. There was a jump at the base of the hill, a jump onto the crest, and another rough jump hidden just below the crest on the far side.

"No penalty points. There are officials at each obstacle to make sure you take it in the right direction and land right side up. If you fall within the penalty area, you loose sixty points."

"Not to mention teeth," muttered Cord, looking at the solid wood rails as thick as his arm.

Raine smiled briefly. "So far, so good. I still have the ones I was born with."

"Broken bones?"

She shrugged. "Sure. It comes with—"

"—the territory," finished Cord, his voice hard.

"Yes," she said evenly. "Like the scar across your left

hip that you won't tell me about. And the other one on your right side. And the third one buried beneath your hair at the back of your head.''

Cord's right hand was clenched in his pocket around the solid-gold coin. He of all people should know just how much abuse the human body could take and still survive. Yet a sense of disaster was riding him, had been riding him since he had talked to Blue Herring that morning. He had felt like this five times before in his life, and three times people had died. Silently Cord cursed the Scots grandmother who had passed on her fey premonitions to him but had not passed on the means to prevent what was sensed through veils of coldness and unease.

Cord would give anything he had or hoped for if Raine wouldn't ride tomorrow.

"Raine, even if it weren't my job, I'd still want to protect you," said Cord quietly. "You're so beautiful, so alive, like a fire burning in a winter world." He was silent for a moment, choosing words carefully for he had never wanted anything quite so much—or been so helpless to attain it. When Cord spoke again, his eyes were focused on his own past. "I know what it is to live out on the edge, to test yourself and find out just what you're made of, to test and test again until you can live freely, sure of your own abilities."

Raine turned and looked at Cord, seeing herself reflected in his eyes, his words.

"But there comes a time," continued Cord, talking slowly, "when the old tests don't teach you anything new. Do you understand what I'm saying?" His eyes changed, focusing on her, silently asking what he would not put into words.

"I have to ride tomorrow," said Raine, touching Cord's cheek, wordlessly asking him to understand. "If it were only me, I might hesitate. For you, Cord. Only for you. But it isn't just you or just me.''

Cord closed his eyes, accepting what he could not change. Very gently he kissed the center of Raine's palm. "I know, little rider. God help me, I know."

And he did, for he was caught in his own responsibilities, a net that was drawing tighter, pulling him away from Raine.

Raine sighed and sat back in her chair. She sipped at the half glass of white Burgundy that was all she had permitted herself. With her fingers, she casually picked a last leaf of lettuce off her salad plate, ate the crunchy green, and neatly licked her fingertips.

"That's the best thing about this restaurant," she said, looking around the motorhome's small dining room. "I can eat with my fingers and no one cares."

Cord smiled and held his hand out to her across the table. "Let me do that."

"Do what?" she asked lazily.

"Lick your fingers."

The fire that was never far beneath Raine's surface when she was with Cord spread through her. "Why do I suddenly feel like dessert?"

"That's funny," said Cord, his voice velvet and dark as his finger traced the line of her neck and throat and breasts, "you don't look like a strawberry waiting to be dipped in chocolate. You're too rich and smooth. More like a life-sized, double-scoop vanilla sundae. Only much better . . . much warmer. I wonder how you'd look with chocolate running all over your creamy skin."

Raine's breath came out in a rush and she felt herself tighten deep inside. Cord saw her nipples harden against the soft navy T-shirt she wore. He wanted to slide out of the chair and kneel in front of her, to undress her and cherish every bit of her sweetness until she melted in his hands, bathing him in her fire.

"We've checked Dev and eaten a meal to warm a nutritionist's heart," said Cord. "Do you have to follow any other rules for the night before the competition, like sleeping alone?"

"No."

"Thank God," said Cord, his voice gritty with restraint. "I don't know if I could keep my hands off you tonight, Raine. Especially knowing that you want me as much as I want you."

He watched her silently, his eyes pale and brooding. The thought of her hurtling over that brutal course tomorrow was riding him mercilessly. A nightmare vision kept recurring: Raine lying crushed at the bottom of a jump that had proved to be one obstacle too many for even Dev's great strength; or an assassin's bullet taking out the secondary target because the primary target was unavailable . . . Raine lying motionless, a casualty in an undeclared war, blood and silence and death.

"I'm not the only nervous one," Raine whispered, seeing the grim play of expressions across Cord's face. "Is it getting very blue outside, Delta Blue?"

Cord's smile was so brief she almost missed it. "Don't worry about it, Raine. You have enough on your mind."

"Why don't I just tell Dad not to come?"

"It's too late. It's been too late since Blue decided he was going to see his Baby Blue ride. Not that I blame him. If you were mine, I'd see you ride tomorrow if I had to take on hell with a garden hose."

Raine whispered Cord's name as her hands came up to frame his hard face. His eyes were like ice, but his mouth was warm and very gentle. She sighed his name again as he reluctantly lifted his lips from hers.

"Shower first," Cord said firmly, picking a piece of straw out of Raine's hair. "I have a call to make."

"You'll pay for that," Raine said in a husky voice.

"What?" he asked innocently.

"Teasing me and then telling me to take a cold shower."

"Try the handle on the left," said Cord. "The one marked *H*."

Raine muttered something succinct and unladylike. She walked toward the shower, shedding clothes with each step. Cord watched until the bare curve of her shoulder emerging from her blouse went into him like a knife, making a floodtide of sweet aching heaviness rise in him. With a curse, he turned away to make his call.

Still muttering, Raine tucked her hair into a green terry-cloth shower turban. She walked into the shower, turned on the water and grabbed the soap. Before she had worked up a decent lather, the shower door opened and Cord stepped in, filling the small enclosure with his male presence.

Raine stood with soap forgotten in one hand, warm water running over her, desire lancing hotly through her. Cord's eyes were silver-blue, smoky, and the tension of passion showed in every line of his hard, naked body.

"What about your call?" asked Raine, her voice throaty, aching with need of him.

"He was out fishing," said Cord, taking the soap from Raine's hand.

Raine smiled as Cord's hands slid slickly over her neck and shoulders, down her back, her hips, her waist, leaving heat and lather in their wake. As his fingers slid up and circled her breasts she groaned softly.

"I've been wanting to do this since I washed your hair," said Cord, his voice husky. He watched Raine change beneath his touch, felt the silky resilience of her breasts and the tempting hardness of her nipples. "Why the hell did I wait so long?"

"I'll play your silly game," Raine murmured, threading her fingers into his hair, feeling the fire inside her in a single rush of liquid heat. "Why did you wait so long?"

"Stupidity," said Cord. He turned Raine toward the pouring water and let the iridescent lather slide down her body. "Sheer, criminal stupidity."

Cord bent and licked the smooth warmth of her neck. Lips and teeth and tongue caressed her, cherishing her as he tried to banish the fey nightmare keening in the back of his mind . . . Raine hurt, dying, and he was too far away to help her. With a groan, Cord spread his hands wide and held her against his hungry body, trying to touch all of her at once, know all of her, hold all of her *now* because tomorrow would come, bringing blood and silence and death.

Cord's mouth moved to her breasts, licking and love-biting, ravishing Raine gently while warm water poured over him, over her, and he slid down until he was kneeling in front of her. His tongue traced her navel while his hands cupped her hips, tilting her toward his caresses. His teeth closed lightly on the curve of her thigh. Her breath came in sharply and she looked down, saw his hair black against the creamy smoothness of her skin, his teeth white and gleaming, the hard tip of his tongue teasing her inner thigh. And then his head turned, seeking her, finding her in a lover's caress that made the breath stop in her throat.

"Cord—" Raine twisted away slightly, surprise and desire shaking her until she could barely stand.

"It's all right, little rider," murmured Cord, smoothing his cheek against her thigh. "Everything is all right."

Cord stood in a single motion. He shut off the water, stepped out and returned in a moment with a soft towel. He rubbed the cloth slowly over Raine's skin, drying her with gentle movements of his hands. When he pulled off her turban, she closed her eyes and leaned against his chest, tangling her fingertips in the black mat of hair that was both coarse and oddly silky to her touch. When she was dry, he carried her to the bed. He set her on the sheet and pushed lightly.

"Roll over," said Cord. "I'll rub the tightness out of your shoulders."

"Cord," said Raine in a soft voice, "I didn't mean . . . you just surprised me."

"I know. I'm sorry."

Water drops gleamed against Cord's skin as he bent over Raine. He hadn't bothered to dry himself, only her. She combed her fingers restlessly through his wet hair, seeking the warmth of his scalp. Gently he disentangled her fingers and rolled her onto her stomach. A clean fragrance filled the air as he poured lotion into his palm. For long, silent minutes, hands that were both gentle and very strong kneaded Raine's back from her waist to her shoulders. When her body was utterly relaxed, Cord's hands changed, caressing where they had been almost impersonal. He spoke softly, his shaman's voice another kind of caress.

"You don't know how beautiful you are to me," Cord murmured, his thumbs smoothing the muscles on either side of Raine's spine. His hands shaped her buttocks, savoring the resilience and warmth of her flesh. With tangible reluctance his fingers moved on, learning each womanly curve of thigh and calf before sliding slowly, inevitably back toward the aching warmth of her.

"Poets always talk about flower petals and cream and peaches," said Cord in his velvet voice. "Nice enough things, I suppose . . . but it makes me wonder if a poet ever touched a woman like you, felt the strength and silk and fire. Soft?" Cord's long fingers traced the shadow cleft of Raine's buttocks until he found the warmth of her. "God, yes, you're soft," he murmured, sliding deeply into her, "but it's a living softness with strength beneath, the strength to hold a man forever."

Raine's breath came out in a ragged sound of desire. She would have turned over, but Cord allowed her to turn only as far as her side. He fitted her back against his chest, her hips against his, his leg between hers, his hand caressing her with slow movements that melted her.

"You're no fragile petal to be bruised at a touch," Cord continued, voice deep, mesmerizing, his breath warm as he lovingly bit Raine's neck, her shoulder, her arm.

Even as Cord's tongue smoothed out the faint marks of his teeth, he felt the fire sweep through her again, felt her body clinging to his touch, wanting him. He moved his hips against her slowly, letting her know his own desire, savoring the heat of her response.

"You're no peach to be picked once, devoured, and thrown away."

As Cord turned Raine over onto her back, he spoke softly, voice and hands and mouth caressing her, drinking her moans and tiny meltings. He found her breasts and ravished them with his mouth until she cried out in passion, knowing nothing but the fire and the man who called it from her.

"You're no bowl of milk, white and bland and still," he said deeply as his tongue found her navel. "You're hot and sweet and seething. I love the taste of you, Raine," he

murmured, his mouth sliding down her body, shaman's
voice enfolding her. "Don't refuse me."

At that moment, Raine could have refused Cord nothing,
least of all herself. When he touched her, her breath came
out in a rush, his name torn out of her by the force of her
response. His answer was a murmur of encouragement,
love words that both soothed and incited her, his hands on
her hips holding her all but immobile as he caressed her.
She twisted slowly against him while heat welled up, a
savage, beautiful fire consuming her even as he did. She
shuddered and arched against him, calling his name again
and again. He answered with a passionate intimacy that
undid her. She gave herself to his lovemaking completely,
accepting everything, holding back nothing of herself.
Waves of ecstasy swept through her, shaking her until she
moaned.

Cord held Raine tightly, savoring every bit of the fire he
had called from her. As the shudders finally, slowly passed,
his hands moved hungrily over her smooth skin. When she
opened her eyes, they were dark and still half-wild. With a
last, loving caress that made her shudder again, Cord slid up
her body and buried the fierce ache of his hunger in her,
needing her as he had never needed anything in his life.

With a sound of pleasure, Raine accepted Cord, holding
him with all her rider's strength. He moved once, slowly,
measuring the depth of his possession and her response.
And then he moved again and again, more quickly each
time until she melted over him, sharing her heat and
ecstasy. He heard her cries as she burned again in his arms,
and he felt fire swelling in him until it burst and he
shuddered with a pleasure so intense that it was almost like
dying, and he could only hold onto her, giving himself to
her.

Raine slowly came back to herself, to the room and the weight of the man lying in her arms. As she smoothed her hands sleepily over Cord's back, an idea condensed out of the silence and intimacy, an idea that had been growing as inevitably in her as love itself. She would make a home for Cord by the fire he had guarded so long and so well. She would give him the very warmth that he had spent a lifetime protecting without ever having for his own.

"Cord . . ."

He rolled onto his side, pulling her with him. "Go to sleep, little rider," he murmured, kissing her slowly, gently. "Tomorrow will be a hard day for you."

Raine curled against Cord, feeling herself falling asleep even as he tucked her head against his shoulder. She started to tell him about his place by her fire, but all that came out of her mouth was a yawn that sounded like his name.

"Tomorrow," Cord said, cradling Raine against his body.

She snuggled into his solid warmth. He was right. She'd tell him tomorrow, after the endurance event was behind her.

Tomorrow.

Cord lay awake, listening to Raine's deep, even breathing. He did not want to sleep, to lose even a moment of time with her. He did not want to close his eyes and see again the nightmare born of his violent past and the unknown future. For a time he wished that Raine had pursued figure skating or target shooting or swimming or pure dressage riding— anything but the dangerous, demanding sport she had chosen. Yet he admired her courage, her skill, her grace and dedication. He wouldn't have changed her if he could. Nor had she asked him to change, though he knew his work lay between them like a winter night, long and black and cold.

There was nothing he could do to change that now, this instant, this night. Her choices were made. So were his.

So Cord did the only thing he could. He held Raine, kissed her very gently, and prayed that once, just this once, tomorrow would never come.

It did, of course. Tomorrow always came.

"You're next," said Captain Jon, his voice clipped.

Raine turned toward Cord, suddenly wanting to feel his arms around her once more. He pulled her close, kissed her with fierce tenderness, and then pressed a gold coin into her hand. She looked at the alien writing and the graceful, equally alien woman on the face of the coin.

"Lady Luck," said Cord, folding Raine's fingers over the gold. "She's brought me out of a few tight places. Let her ride with you."

"Mount up," said Captain Jon.

Raine put the coin deep into her pocket. Cord helped Raine mount Dev and then held the restless stallion. She gathered the reins, checked the watch taped to her wrist outside her riding glove and waited for the official to call her turn, for each rider rode alone, against the clock.

Raine sat, concealing her nervousness behind a quiet facade. She didn't see the crowd seething around the starting point or the masses of people pressed against the ropes along the course. Cord stood very still, looking at Raine as though memorizing her. She turned and looked the same way at him. He touched her hand, then stepped back.

"Gate," said Captain Jon tersely.

Raine went to the starting posts, held the fidgeting stallion, and waited for the endurance event to begin. The instant the Olympic timekeeper signaled her, she punched in her own stopwatch and let Dev out into a canter.

As always, the beginning of the contest ended the nervousness that had claimed her. It didn't calm Dev, however. For the first few miles, the stallion fought against the bit, wanting a faster pace with every hard muscle in his body. Raine held Dev, pacing him through the twists and turns and inviting open spaces of roads and trails, part A.

"Easy, Dev," she murmured, talking to him constantly, checking her watch to see that she was within the time allowed, "you'll wear out both of us before the work really begins."

After the first four miles, Dev accepted the easy cantering pace with more grace. Hill and shadow, twist and turn, dirt road and narrow trail—Dev took all with equal ease despite the weights he carried to bring his load up to the required 165 pounds for tack and rider.

Dev flashed through the timing gate at the end of section A. Thirty seconds under the mark. Score 0, no faults. Raine reset her stopwatch even as she increased Dev's speed. He was warmed up, moving loosely, ready for whatever came next. And what came next was the steeplechase, two and a half miles of gallop and jump, jump and gallop. The crowds would be thick around the jumps, for it was there that the most spectacular action—and accidents—occurred. Solid jumps and solid horses.

Raine checked her watch, loosened the reins slightly, and leaned forward. Dev went from a canter to a gallop in a single stride. His ears came up when he spotted the first jump. Raine felt him tongue the bit, then accede to her control. Ears pricked, hooves digging great clods out of the earth, Dev went over the first fence with a power that brought a low sound of admiration from the crowd.

Raine didn't hear. A tiny corner of her attention noted the presence of Olympic officials and medics off to the side of the jump, but it was only an instant of awareness. She shut

out the crowd, the officials, everything but Dev and the
course. She rode almost without moving, keeping her
weight over Dev's center of gravity, letting him move
freely beneath her, alert for the upcoming jumps.

Captain Jon had warned her about two jumps in particular; despite their innocent appearance, those jumps had
brought down several riders already. One of the trouble-
some jumps was a combination brush-and-water jump. The
horses weren't meant to clear the brush, but rather to jump
through the last few feet of it. If the horses tried to clear
everything, they went too high and too short, landing
awkwardly in the water on the other side. It was a test of the
horse's trust in the rider; jump on the rider's command, for
only the rider knew about the water.

Raine gathered herself as they approached the jump,
sending Dev the multitude of tiny signals that warned she
was in control. "My way, Dev," she muttered, holding the
stallion to a rapid gallop. "Not yet, not yet, not yet—*now!*"

Dev sprang like a great red tiger for the top of the brush,
for he hadn't been permitted to jump as soon as he had
wanted. Tiny branches whipped past his broad chest and
straining muscles. Water rushed below his belly. He landed
cleanly on the far side, well clear of the water, and galloped
off without a break in stride. The crowd cheered wildly.
Raine checked her watch, deaf and blind to all but the
requirements of the course.

"That was a beauty," she murmured, praising Dev. One
ear flicked back to listen to her; the other stayed forward.
He was running easily, breathing deeply, looking for the
next jump. "You were born for this, weren't you?" said
Raine, feeling excitement race through her as Dev cleared
another fence and galloped off after landing easily.

The rest of the jumps flew beneath Dev's black hooves.
When he went through the timing posts at the end of the

steeplechase, sweat had darkened his coat and he was breathing hard. The score flashed out: 0 faults; 20 positive points for coming in under the required time limit.

Raine felt a single thrill of elation, then forced herself to concentrate on sparing Dev through the second round of roads and trails. Despite the demands of the steeplechase, Dev struggled against the reduced pace. Raine didn't give a quarter inch. She intended to take every second of the allotted time for part C.

Dev caught his second wind before two miles were up. He cantered easily, rhythmically, giving the impression that he could do this all day and well into the night. Raine knew that it wasn't true; the course had already demanded a lot of the stallion's strength. She checked her stopwatch regularly, giving Dev every break that the course, careful riding and time allowed.

Even so, when Dev approached the timing posts at the end of part C, he was breathing heavily. Lather gathered whitely down the slope of his shoulders and flanks. His rhythm was still good, though, and his breathing was deep rather than gasping. He was tired, but not exhausted. Not yet. That would come somewhere during the last segment, the cross-country.

Raine dismounted the instant that the timekeeper signaled her arrival at the end of part C. Captain Jon and Cord walked forward quickly. Cord stripped off tack and held Dev while Captain Jon and Raine worked rapidly, washing down the stallion. Normally a stable crew would have worked over Dev while Captain Jon briefed Raine on the state of the course ahead. But with Dev, handling was never normal. So Cord held the restless, adrenaline-loaded stallion while Captain Jon talked and worked and Raine listened and worked.

"Russians have four refusals and a fall so far on the

cross-country," said Jon tersely. "No pattern. One obstacle is just as bloody awful as the next. We have two refusals."

"Dev never refuses," said Raine as she sponged out the stallion's mouth. That was as close to a drink as Dev would get until the endurance event was over and he was cool again.

Captain Jon grunted. "A refusal is cheaper than a fall."

Raine said nothing. She knew better than anyone how hard it was to come out of Dev's more spectacular jumps right side up.

The veterinarian came over, watched Dev move, listened to his breathing, and checked for swelling or injuries to the horse's legs. Cord and Raine held the stallion firmly, her words mingling with the shaman's murmur of Cord's voice. Dev's ears flattened as the vet's hands probed his legs, but Dev tolerated it. Barely.

"Hell of a horse," was the vet's comment as he stepped out of reach. "Steel tendons and a temper to match." He nodded to Raine. "You're in, young lady. Saddle up."

Cord lifted the weight-laden tack to Dev's back and cinched the saddle in place.

"One minute," said the captain, looking at his own watch.

Cord boosted Raine onto the stallion's tall back. Dev was still breathing deeply, but wasn't laboring for air. Not the way he would be in a few miles, as each obstacle demanded more from the stallion's diminishing reserves of stamina and will.

"Jump straight and clean, you tough red bastard," murmured Cord, smoothing Dev's hot neck.

Dev bumped his muzzle against Cord's chest and breathed out twin streams of hot breath. Raine checked her watch, then looked at Cord, wishing there had been time

just to touch him. He looked up at her as though he knew
her thoughts. She saw his lips move as he said three words,
but the meaning was drowned in the roar of the crowd
greeting a new horse and rider.

Three words. Had he said "Good luck, Raine"? Or had
he said "I love you"? She turned to ask, but it was too late.

"To the posts," snapped Captain Jon.

Automatically, Raine obeyed.

As Cord stepped back, his beeper squealed in a series of
coded staccato pulses that made adrenaline pour through
him. *Blue all the way to the moon. Delta Blue.* Quietly,
ruthlessly, Cord pushed his way through the crowd, running toward the helicopter he knew would be waiting for
him.

Raine moved Dev up to the starting posts. As soon as he
stepped between them, the electronic timer would begin
counting off the seconds and minutes that would eventually
add up to part D, the cross-country. Five brutal miles. Just
as she positioned Dev at the posts, she heard the faint,
familiar electronic squeal of Cord's beeper. She wanted to
look over her shoulder but it was too late, her own
electronic leash had shortened. The timer had started, the
course lay before her and she must take Dev over it.

Raine brought Dev out of the posts in a steady canter, a
pace she would try to hold for the next five miles. The
obstacles would make that impossible, of course. That's
what they were designed for—to test horse and rider
relentlessly. Blind jumps to tempt a horse to refuse. Blind
landings to shake a horse's confidence and test the rider's
ability to stay in the saddle. Two falls were permitted,
though heavily penalized. The third fall disqualified horse
and rider.

Raine saw neither the crowds around the obstacles nor the
Olympic officials. She focused only on the harsh require-

ments of the cross-country. The course unrolled in her mind even as it unrolled beneath Dev's feet. Downhill and turn left, jump up onto a bank, two strides, ditch and rail, turn right, long downhill with the Coffin at the bottom—*fly, Dev!*—now uphill uphill uphill and over the top sliding into a blind downhill jump—*easy boy easy No!*—and the terrible shock of a bad landing, Dev nearly pulling her arms off as she fought to keep his head up, keep him on his feet and herself in the saddle.

Raine didn't hear the cries of the crowd as she rode with every bit of her strength and skill, putting Dev right again and herself deep in the saddle, arms and back and legs aching. But that was nothing new, they had been aching since the first miles of the event, time blurring into eternity.

Raine collected Dev and talked to him, praising his courage, letting him feel her confidence despite the bad landing. The stallion's ears came up again. He settled into a rhythmic canter, eager for the next obstacle. Raine checked her watch. Still on schedule; the long-legged stallion's strides ate up distance. She reached up to wipe sweat out of her eyes and saw blood on the riding glove. Somewhere in those wild seconds of nearly falling and then recovering she had cut herself, probably on the buckle at the top of Dev's bridle. If she were lucky, that would be the worst that happened to her today.

Talking to Dev, riding to spare him and not herself, Raine took the stallion over obstacle after obstacle, enduring as he endured, knowing that the landings would be harder each time for each time Dev's strength would be less. The pond was a nightmare, a blind leap into water above Dev's knees, mud sucking at his hooves, Dev sliding, wrenching free, clearing the center jump on sheer guts and determination, landing blind again, cantering out of the pond, spraying sheets of water and mud.

Dev was breathing very hard now, the air groaning in and out of his body, lather running in white streamers down his shoulders and flanks. Yet he cantered with his head up, ears pricked forward, game for whatever lay ahead, a horse in his prime, born for the grueling test. He needed no whip but his own love of extending himself, no goad but his own desire to please the soft-voiced rider on his back.

Raine praised the stallion though her breath was coming as harshly as his and sweat ran from beneath her helmet into her eyes, mingling with blood until she wiped impatiently with her already reddened glove. She saw the next obstacle, chose her approach, and settled in for the last two miles, riding lightly though her muscles ached to sit back and let Dev do the work.

The end of the course came almost as a shock. The last obstacle, the time posts, the cheering crowd. Two scores were posted. The first score was 0, no penalties, a perfect cross-country run. The second score was +20, the total of penalties and plus points for the endurance event. Dev had redeemed his indifferent performance in the dressage event.

Raine pulled Dev down to a walk, praising him lavishly with a voice that had gone hoarse. When the official signaled that she could dismount, Raine slid off Dev and leaned against him for a moment, letting her shaking legs absorb her weight. She undid the cinch and slowly led Dev to the weighing stand. She weighed in, staggering slightly under the weight of lead and leather. The official read the weight aloud and approved it.

The endurance event was over.

As Raine led Dev away, she looked for Cord, wanting nothing more than to feel his arms around her and see the relief in his eyes. Dev had performed brilliantly. She and Dev had finished the brutal course with no more than a cut to show for it. Then Raine remembered hearing Cord's beeper. He probably wouldn't be here. She fought down irrational tears, knowing that they were the aftermath of adrenaline and exhaustion as much as disappointment. She would see Cord later, when he had finished whatever business had called him away. Until then, she had plenty to keep her busy.

"Come on, boy," she said, tugging gently on Dev's reins. "We've got a lot of work to do on you if you're going to be in any shape to jump tomorrow."

Neither Dev nor Raine noticed when people made way for the exhausted stallion and the woman with blood welling down the side of her face. Slowly, very slowly, they walked through the dust and heat back to the stables.

"Have you seen Cord?" asked Raine, unable to keep her voice light.

Thorne shook his head without bothering to look around. He appeared older today, harder, and when he spoke, his voice sounded harsh despite his southern accent. "No, ma'am, I haven't."

Raine climbed down the motorhome's steps without her usual grace. She was stiff from yesterday's trial, but not as stiff as Dev would be. She was also restless and deeply uneasy. She hadn't seen Cord since he had boosted her up onto Dev's back for the last part of the endurance course. It had been Captain Jon, not Cord, who had helped her care for Dev last night. It had been Thorne, not Cord, who had driven the motorhome from Rancho Santa Fe to Santa Anita, where the final part of the Olympic three-day event would be held. It had been Thorne, not Cord, who had discreetly guarded her while she checked on Dev late at night.

And it had been Raine, alone, who had listened to the scanner's erratic mutter and finally fallen into a troubled sleep.

Perhaps Cord had come back while she had showered and dressed. Perhaps Cord was at the stable right now, saddling Dev for stadium jumping, the last competition of the three-day event. The thought that Cord might be waiting for her made Raine turn and run through the lace shadows of pepper trees and down the green rows of stables. Her heart quickened when she saw Dev standing groomed and saddled.

But it was Captain Jon who walked out of the shadows.

"Did you get Dev ready?" she asked.

"Yes. You need your strength for riding. Besides, he was too tired to do more than flatten his ears at me."

Raine schooled her expression as ruthlessly as she would soon be schooling Dev. "Thank you."

"How is your eye?"

She shrugged. "Just a cut."

"Bled like a stuck pig," said Captain Jon bluntly.

Raine shrugged again and fiddled restlessly with the saddle blanket. There were no weights now. They would be added just before Dev went into the ring.

Where was Cord?

"Raine."

She gathered herself and turned toward Captain Jon. "Yes?"

"You didn't let that French rider throw you," said the captain bluntly. "Whether or not Elliot is here, you have an event to ride. You owe it to yourself and your horse. And to us."

Numbly, Raine nodded her head. Then she took a deep breath and let it out slowly. "Don't worry, Captain Jon."

She stepped onto the mounting block, then turned quickly back toward him. "Are we still in the medals?"

He smiled widely. "That's my rider. Yes, we're right up there. The Russians and Brits have knocked down some rails. If your bloody great beast can refrain from knocking down the jumps, you'll have a bloody great medal to show your grandchildren."

Raine managed not to groan as she settled into the saddle. She had only eighty minutes before she was due in the competition ring. She would need every one of them to get Dev loose enough to jump. Once in the practice area, she worked Dev carefully, simple dressage exercises designed to ease the stiffness in his huge body.

By the time Raine's turn came, Dev was willing if not eager to face the jumps. For once, he stood quietly in the opening between the bleachers as Raine waited to be called for her turn in the jump ring. The flags and crowds were as colorful as they had been for the dressage event, but the ring was neither empty nor freshly raked. Instead, the area was filled with brightly painted jumps set in combinations that would force horse and rider to adjust stride and approach for each jump. None of the fences was fixed or high. The horses and riders had already proven themselves yesterday. Today they had only to demonstrate that they were willing and able to take to the field again.

There was a small round of applause for the rider who had preceded Raine. His horse had refused once, costing ten penalty points, knocked down a rail for five points, and gone too slowly. Total, eighteen penalty points. Barely adequate. Zero was the only score worth pursuing. Yet Dev was sluggish beneath Raine, and her own body lacked the strength and flexibility that had helped Dev yesterday.

Raine's name and country were announced. As she

brought Dev into the ring at a slow canter, doubts and nervousness dropped away. The stallion's ears came forward when he spotted all the jumps. His gait was a bit ragged and hard to ride, but otherwise he was willing. She waited for the buzzer that would signal the beginning of the timed event, then turned Dev toward the first jump. He took it easily, not pulling at the bit or fighting for a faster pace, leaving everything to her.

Dev's laissez-faire attitude made the ride much easier on Raine, who was too sore and tired for a tug-of-war with the powerful stallion. Unfortunately, Dev was just a bit too easy going about the jumps. He ticked a bar with his back left hoof. The crowd groaned, but Raine wasn't able to see whether the bar had fallen. She wouldn't know until she saw her score at the end of the event.

A triple jump provided another heart-stopping instant when Dev's hoof clattered against wood and the crowd groaned. Again, Raine couldn't tell whether or not the bar had fallen. She collected Dev and approached the last jumps. He finished with a clean show of agility and strength that brought an approving round of applause. Instantly, Raine turned to look at the scoreboard.

Zero. No penalty points.

Raine smiled triumphantly and threw her arms around Dev's muscular neck.

"Good show!" said Captain Jon as Raine came out of the ring.

Raine sighed and stretched her aching back. "He felt about as lively as a balloon full of water," she said, worried.

The captain smiled and shook his head. "Ease up, Raine. It's over, now. Home free, as you Yanks say."

The words came as a shock.

Over. A lifetime of training, work, hope. Over.

It was an incredible feeling, a volatile combination of triumph and emptiness, and then triumph again, a starburst of realization consuming Raine. She and Dev had completed the most grueling test of horse and rider designed by man; they had ridden to Olympic gold.

Raine looked around slowly, seeing the crowds and the horses and the rippling Olympic flags as though for the first time. Strangers cheering and laughing, applauding Dev's achievement and her own. She smiled and waved, sharing the moment of exhilaration with the crowd. Then Captain Jon led Dev away, leaving the noise and the wild moment of triumph behind.

Yet Raine still looked at each face, searching for . . . something.

Cord. Cord wasn't there.

Dev stumbled tiredly, jarring Raine. The sound of cheering had faded. No one was near except Captain Jon, and soon he would have to return to the ring. Raine was alone.

Over.

Was it all over? All of it? Was that why Cord had left and not come back? Had she used him and he used her to ease the killing pressures of Olympic competition? Had they only played summer games until the Summer Games were over?

"Raine? I say, are you all right?"

Raine pulled the last shreds of her strength together. "I'm fine," she said, her voice flat. "Just tired."

Raine was still tired when she climbed the platform and stood next to her teammates to receive a gold medal. The feeling of exhaustion vanished as she felt, as much as heard, the crowd's accolade, people shouting and cheering until the ground trembled. By the time the National Anthem ended, tears were streaming down Raine's cheeks. She didn't notice. She smiled and waved to the cheering people, transported for the moment by the outpouring of emotion from people she would never know, people who had shared the intense emotions of the American Equestrian Team's ride to gold.

After Raine and her three teammates climbed down, they left the arena and exchanged triumphant hugs all around. They walked away from the cry of thousands upon thousands of well-wishers into noisy, exuberant congratulations of family and friends and reporters. She didn't look around for her own family. She knew without being told that Cord wouldn't allow them in such a public melee. With the ease of long experience, Raine evaded the press. She hugged Captain Jon tightly.

"Thank you, Captain," Raine said, smiling at him. "We never would have gotten past the first obstacle without you."

Captain Jon cleared his throat and returned her hug with a huge smile, his Swiss reserve forgotten for the instant.

Raine released the captain into the bearhugs of her teammates. She stood on tiptoe, searching for a man with black hair and pale eyes, a man who moved like a cat gliding through dusk, silence and strength combined. She saw no one. She eased through the gathering of friends and family, looking for Cord, absently responding to invitations to parties and victory celebrations.

After a few minutes, she was at the edge of the crowd. There was no one standing back in the shadows, waiting for her. She stood absolutely still for an instant, feeling as though she were torn in half. Part of her still thrilled to the triumph of Olympic gold. And part of Raine simply wanted to walk away, to keep walking until there was nothing around her but silence and space. In that moment, she realized that she was tired clear to her soul.

The feeling was not entirely new. It came to Raine after every competition, win or lose. Endings, not beginnings. Yet this time was also different. She had no desire to begin again, for there was nothing *to* begin. The ultimate Game was won, the highest goal achieved.

Olympic gold.

And now it was over. Nothing to fight for, to work for, to train for, to risk for . . . nothing waiting for her. She felt like a balloon released by a careless child, free floating high into the blue, higher and higher until cold shriveled the fragile envelope and it fell back to earth.

Raine walked back to the motorhome, barely feeling the weight of the gold medal around her neck. Thorne was in his usual place, but the motorhome was gone.

"Where's Cord?" asked Raine, her voice trembling despite her attempts to keep it level. She had so hoped that he would be here to see her wearing Olympic gold. She could hardly accept that she was alone, no one to share her triumph with, no one to understand why she suddenly felt empty.

"Ma'am—"

"*Where is Cord?*"

"I'm sorry. I no longer know a man called Cord Elliot."

Chapter 11

RAINE WAITED THREE DAYS BEFORE SHE CALLED HER father. He met her in her motel room, accompanied by two men who moved like Cord, calm and alert and strong.

"Tell them to wait outside," she said tightly.

Justin Chandler-Smith was shorter, thinner and older than the men with him, but a single look was all it took to rout them. They left as quietly as they had come.

Justin walked over and hugged Raine. "They wouldn't let me or any of the family near you during the games. Said it was too great a risk. I didn't mind it for me, but for you—" Justin looked down into his daughter's face, older than it had been when he had watched her through binoculars less than a week ago. "That was a ride and a half, Baby Raine. Scared the hell out of me to watch. I had a good view, too. Whoever scouted the land for me knew what he was doing."

"Cord Elliot," she said curtly.

"What?"

"Cord Elliot scouted the land for you."

"Tell him thanks for me."

"You tell him. I think he's one of yours."

Justin held Raine at arm's length. "What is it, Baby? What's going on?"

"Have I ever asked you for anything, Daddy?" she said, looking at him with hazel eyes that were nearly opaque.

"Not since you were ten and I missed your birthday party," said Justin, his voice sad. "You never asked me for anything after that."

"I'm asking now. Cord Elliot. I want to know where he is. Everyone I ask says, 'Cord who? Never heard of him.'"

Justin looked at Raine shrewdly. "You love him, Baby?"

Raine closed her eyes. She had asked herself that question a hundred times a day. A hundred times a day the answer came back. Yes. Win or lose, *yes*.

And she was a hundred times a fool for loving him. She had wanted to give him a permanent place near her fire, to save him from the freezing cold and night of the other world. But it was a world that he apparently enjoyed more than he enjoyed her. He could have left his work at any time in the past. He hadn't. She had been a fool to misunderstand, to give far more of herself than was called for by their private summer games. But that was the way she was. All or nothing at all.

Raine reached into her pocket and drew out the gold coin Cord had given her. The irony of two gold medals for two different kinds of games made her lips flatten and turn down at the corners. Had Cord meant to be so cold? Or had he simply been trying to tell her that the games, though over, had been world-class?

"Find him," said Raine, looking at her father with eyes as blind as the gold circle gleaming on her outstretched palm. "Give this to him. He needs it more than I do." She turned away. "When you're finished, I'll be here."

Raine waited, hardly noticing the hours heaping silently around her, a day passing, two days. Three. Then the knock on her door, two men searching the room and standing aside until her father entered. A single gesture, and the men withdrew, leaving Raine alone with her father and the dizzying feeling that minutes rather than days had passed.

"Where did you hear the name Cord Elliot?" asked Justin the instant the door closed behind his men.

Raine thought of all the ways to explain—bodyguard and escort, horseman and companion—but there was only one truth that mattered. "He was my lover," she said quietly. "That was the name he gave me."

Justin held out his hand to her. "Baby Raine," he whispered, "when did you grow up on me?"

"Years ago, Daddy. Long years."

"I hope so," he said beneath his breath. "You'll need every bit of it." He sighed. "The man you call Cord Elliot isn't one of mine, though I've worked with him before. He's one of the best, Baby, if that means anything to you. He's an operative with the Defense Intelligence Agency. He's assigned to a part of that agency which has no name, no budget—and no forwarding address."

"You didn't find him?"

"I didn't find a man called Cord Elliot."

Raine noted the evasion and knew that was all she would get from her father. He had broken more rules for her in the last few days than he had in a lifetime. He would break no more. "I understand," she said, her voice so controlled that it sounded like a stranger's. "Thank you." She held out her hand. "I'd like the good-luck piece back."

Justin's eyes narrowed into hazel slits. "I don't have it,

Baby. I gave it to Robert Johnstone. Didn't Cord mention him?''

Raine shook her head numbly. "He was like you, Daddy. No names, no facts, nothing. . . ."

Raine's voice trailed off as the implication sank in: Justin had been in touch with someone who knew not only who Cord was, but where he was. The good-luck piece had been returned to Cord, but there was no message for her. Or maybe there was. Silence is more effective than good-bye, and less awkward.

Had that been the three syllables Cord had said? Not "Good luck, Raine," or "I love you," but *"Good-bye, Raine."* And then had he faded back into the crowd, going on to another job, another challenge, another danger . . . another woman?

"Baby Raine," murmured Justin, holding his daughter, stroking her hair. "Don't look like that. Sometimes things aren't what they seem."

Raine laughed, but there was no humor in the sound. "No, Daddy, things aren't always as bad as they seem. Sometimes they're worse." She stepped out of her father's embrace. "Forgive me. I wasn't thinking very well three days ago. I never should have sent you chasing my former lover through Most Secret files."

Justin started to speak, but years of ingrained silence won out. He watched Raine begin throwing her few things into a suitcase. "Where are you going?"

Raine shrugged. "A vacation. I've earned one."

"But where?"

"I'll think of somewhere," she said indifferently, sweeping up the contents of the bathroom shelf and dumping them into the suitcase.

"Where will you be two weeks from now?" persisted Justin.

"Somewhere."

"How about in three weeks, or four?"

"Somewhere else," said Raine, shutting the suitcase.

"Baby? Why don't you come home?"

"No, Daddy." Her voice was soft, final. "I have a life to make for myself. It's time I grew up and quit playing games."

"What about Dev?"

Raine locked the suitcase with two quick motions. "Captain Jon will make arrangements to have him trailered home."

"Who will take care of Dev if you're not there?"

Raine's hands clenched. She didn't want to go home again. She couldn't. The past would reach up and smother her. "Hire a groom," she said curtly, then realized that with Dev's temperament that would be impossible. *"Damn!"*

"One of the men I know has a ranch in Arizona," said Justin. "He's been overseas so much that he's thinking of selling it. I could arrange for you to trailer Dev there. It's a new place, Raine. All new. Up in the mountains, clean water and grass and pine trees."

Raine blinked back sudden tears. She had never cried when her father had let her down; why did she want to cry simply because he understood her need to put something new between herself and the past?

"Thanks." She hugged her father quickly. "And don't worry. I won't ever ask you to break the rules again."

The air was cool, sweet with the smell of pine and water and grass bending gracefully beneath the wind. Raine stood in the doorway of the guest cabin and watched the granite peaks massed against Arizona's cobalt sky. In the five weeks that she had stayed there, she had felt a sense of homecoming that blended strangely with the desolation of losing a man called Cord Elliot. Each day the loss was new, agonizing, for she woke up with his name on her lips and his dream-presence warm around her. And each day she rose alone to put the past behind her as she stood in the cabin doorway looking out over the huge fenced meadow where Devlin's Waterloo reigned supreme.

Raine walked down the short dusty path to the meadow as she sipped coffee from a thick mug. The cabin had come equipped with all the creature comforts, including a surprisingly modern kitchen and bathroom. It also had the one thing she required: privacy. The main ranch house had the only phone. The house was a half mile away, across the pasture. The retired couple who took care of the ranch in the owner's absence were careful not to interrupt Raine's solitude, though they had made it clear that she was welcome any time she wanted to visit them.

The meadow's split-rail fence was new enough not to have been bleached by summer heat and the brief winter snows that came to the lower mountains. September sunlight had already warmed the wood even though it was only a few hours after dawn. The warmth seeped through the short-sleeved cotton sweater Raine had pulled on. The sweater's deep jade color caught and held sunlight. Her riding pants were the same black as Dev's mane. Her hair fell in soft disarray around her shoulders and tickled her where the pullover's deep V revealed her neck and the gentle swell of her breasts.

Dev's head came up as he scented Raine. He cantered toward the fence, nickering a welcome. She watched as he swept across the pasture, coat gleaming like fire, muscles rippling with strength. He had come back from the three-

day event stronger than ever. She would have to begin
riding him soon, working him. Not for any goal or
competition, but simply because they both enjoyed it.

Like her, Dev had settled into the mountains as though
born there. Getting him to go back to stalls and barns would
be a problem. But there was no rush. Her father had assured
her that the owner was engaged elsewhere. She and Dev
could stay at the ranch as long as they liked. The longer she
stayed, though, the less she wanted to leave.

A velvet muzzle pushed impatiently at Raine's shoulder.

"You're after a carrot, aren't you?" asked Raine, pushing back.

Dev snorted and waited, ears pricked, every inch of him
vibrating with health.

"You win," she sighed, reaching into her back pocket.
"You always do, you red beggar."

While Dev ate the carrot, Raine stroked his neck.

"Would you like to live here, Devlin's Waterloo?" she
murmured. "I've never touched the money G'mom gave
me when I turned twenty-three. I could buy this lovely
green meadow for you, and some lively, leggy mares. I
could spend my life here, raising blood-bay hellions and
training them to fly over fences and streams."

Raine didn't realize she was crying until she felt the tears
sliding down her cheeks. It was Cord who had talked about
putting Dev out to stud and raising red hellions. She had
laughed then, not believing in tomorrow. Tomorrow had
come, though. Just because it had come without Cord was
no reason to abandon all of the dream. She could breed and
train event horses here as well as in Virginia. Better. She
would be more at peace here. With her reputation and Dev's
foals, people would come to the Arizona mountains to look
and to buy.

Maybe Cord would even come some day.

Silently, Raine raged at the thoughts she could not control. Each time she believed that she finally had accepted the fact that she loved a man who did not love her, her mind would turn on her with claws of hope and memory, rending her fragile peace.

Raine heard the helicopter long before she spotted it flying low, sunlight flashing off its white body. No numbers, no name. The kind of helicopter her father always used. With a fury of sound and wind, the machine landed. Raine squinted against the glare of the sun. Though the helicopter was only a few hundred feet away, she couldn't see the passenger through the blinding sun. She slipped between fence rails and ran toward the machine, trying not to think of all the bad news that her father could be bringing with him.

"Dad, what are you—?"

The words died on Raine's lips as she recognized the man silhouetted against the burning sun.

"Cord."

Raine stood, staring, hardly able to believe that what she saw wasn't one more cruel dream from which she would wake, alone. But this couldn't be a dream. Cord was standing not twenty feet away from her, city slacks and no tie, white shirt open at the throat, his slate-gray suitcoat tossed carelessly over his shoulder. He looked thinner, drawn hard and tight, and the sprinkling of silver in his forelock had become a solid slash against his black hair.

The helicopter took off in a whirl of dust and noise. When it was gone, there was only silence and sunlight and Cord standing there, looking at Raine with eyes the color of ice. Then he started walking toward her, and she saw the cane in his right hand.

She ran to him, forgetting her anger and pain and questions, forgetting everything except his presence. She threw her arms around him, unable to say anything more than his name. He held her with a strength that made her ache, his left arm a steel bar across her back, his right arm braced on the cane. Then he kissed her as though she were fire and he were a man chilled all the way to his soul.

Before the kiss ended, Raine knew that it no longer mattered that Cord had hurt her by leaving her without warning. It no longer mattered that he was a man perfectly suited for the dangerous life he had chosen. It no longer mattered that his world could include her for only a few days, a few hours, a single kiss. It no longer mattered that he was the wrong man for her. She loved him. There could be no going back from that simple fact.

"That answers one of my questions," Cord said huskily.

"Which one?" asked Raine as her fingers roved over Cord's face and hair, reassuring herself that he was real.

"If you missed me as much as I missed you."

Raine laughed a little brokenly. Tears blurred her vision. She wiped away the tears impatiently, not wanting to miss a single instant of looking at Cord. "I missed you more."

"That isn't possible."

Raine looked at Cord's ice-blue eyes, saw shadows of longing and pain. "Where were—?" Abruptly she stopped. She didn't have the security clearance to know the details of Cord's life. He was here now. Let yesterday and tomorrow go. She would love him now, while she could.

Raine led Cord toward the cabin, walking slowly because she could see that his leg bothered him. Questions ached in her throat. She ignored them. She opened the door and waited for him to climb the few steps up to the porch. She wanted to help him but knew that he would not want to be helped.

"You look as though you've missed a few meals," Raine said as she watched Cord. She kept her voice light with an effort that made her nails bite into her palms. She shut the door behind him and watched as he crossed the room. He settled on the bed by the fireplace, propping up his leg in obvious relief. Despite his injury, he still radiated the power and grace that had haunted her dreams.

"Are you hungry? Thirsty? Sleepy?" asked Raine, the only questions she would permit herself. "I don't know which time zone you've been in, so I don't know what you need."

"You," said Cord, holding out his hand to her. "I need you."

Raine crossed the room in a few quick strides and lay down beside him. Cord held her gently at first, kissing away the tears that fell no matter how hard she willed them not to. Then his kiss changed, hungry and searching, possessing her with a power that drove every emotion out of her but the yearning for him that had made her nights a torment and her days a nightmare.

"I've dreamed of this for thirty-nine days," said Cord, tasting Raine with tiny bites and licks, his hunger tangible in the hard lines and deep tremors of his body. "Even when they knocked me out, I dreamed of you."

Raine closed her eyes and shivered beneath Cord's sensual assault. She sought the hard male warmth beneath his shirt. When the cloth interfered, she unbuttoned it with almost savage motions, wanting to know the resilience of his flesh. Fingers spread wide, she rubbed her hands slowly across his chest, savoring the man she had never expected to see again outside her dreams.

Cord's pale eyes narrowed with desire as he watched Raine's expression, her face taut yet strangely languid, lips smiling as she lifted her mouth to be kissed. His hands kneaded down her back, drawing her close to the hard ache of his hunger. She fitted herself against him intimately, sending desire ripping through him until he groaned. His hands slid beneath her sweater. He pulled the soft jade knit off her in a single motion. There was nothing underneath it but the smooth, fragrant skin that had haunted him since he had first touched her.

"I've dreamed of this, too," Cord murmured. He kissed her breasts slowly, sipping at their peaks until Raine trembled and cried out softly. "Yes," he said in a gritty voice. "I dreamed that, too. I'd wake up yelling because you were crying for me and then the doctors would knock me out again. But I could still hear you, and it nearly killed me because I couldn't go to you, couldn't do anything but hear you crying."

Raine moaned again, feeling fire leap in her. His arms tightened as he began to roll over onto her. Then he stopped, chained for an instant by the searing pain in his leg.

"Let me," she whispered.

Gently, Raine pushed Cord onto his back. She got off the bed long enough to step out of her own clothes. The hungry, smoky blaze of Cord's eyes as he looked at Raine made her tremble. She knelt on the bed and pulled his shirt free of his body, pausing only long enough to kiss the midnight line of hair that descended to his lean waist. When she turned her back to concentrate on his shoes, his fingertips traced the length of her spine. She pulled off his shoes and dropped them on the floor. His hand slid lower, over her hips, tracing the shadow cleft until he found and touched the hidden fire. Raine's breath came in sharply. Her fingers clenched as desire shook her, making her forget what she had been doing.

Cord made a sound deep in his throat as he felt Raine's heat close around him once again. "I dreamed of this, too. It was cold, everything was cold, winter coming down and fire calling to me but I couldn't move, couldn't even scream. And I wanted to. I wanted to tear down all the castle walls, grind them to dust. But there were straps cinching me to a bed as white and cold as snow, winter freezing me. So I dreamed of you, of fire bathing me.''

Raine shuddered and gave in to the desire coursing through her, liquid heat spreading and swelling until she moaned. Cord's voice caressed her, dark and velvet, asking for her fire, telling her how her tiny meltings pleasured him. She swayed, shaken by passion, and he smiled, watching his dream.

''I'll never get you undressed,'' Raine said, the words as ragged as her breathing. ''I want to see you, to touch you.''

With a reluctance that nearly undid her all over again, Cord released her. Her hands were trembling as they unfastened his slacks. She pushed the cloth down, feeling clumsy next to the masculine power of his legs. Her hand encountered a knot of scar tissue on his thigh. She eased the pants past the recent wound.

''What—?'' she asked, appalled by the raw slash of barely healed flesh.

''Later,'' said Cord, twisting out of his remaining clothes with a speed that mocked even the idea of injury. ''It doesn't hurt nearly as much as wanting you does.'' He rolled toward her, but she saw the instant of hesitation as his wounded leg rebelled.

''Does it bother you when you lie back?'' asked Raine, wanting him, but not at the cost of the pain she had seen on his face for one terrible instant.

Cord smiled crookedly. ''Come to me, little rider.'' But despite the smile, his voice and hands were urgent as he lifted her onto him.

Raine settled over Cord lightly, completely, moving slowly until he groaned. She shuddered deep inside her

body and saw by the narrowing of his eyes that he had felt
it. His smile was utterly male, as was the sudden tightening
of his body as he took complete possession of her fire. She
kissed his lips, his neck, his chest, consuming him with
teeth and tongue as he had once consumed her, spreading
fire wherever she touched him.

Ecstasy swept through her as she caressed him. He
encouraged her with dark words and sensual hands. Her
hips moved slowly, sliding over him until his eyes were
smoky, all but closed, his body tight with anticipation and
need. Small cries escaped her, but she didn't know. She felt
nothing but him as their worlds melted together, flesh on
flesh, tongue on tongue, heat swelling, ecstasy expanding
until it burst over them, consuming and renewing them in
the same endless fire.

It was a long time before Raine stirred and looked at
Cord. He watched her intently, reading her satisfaction in
her languid hazel eyes and flushed cheeks.

"That answers my second question," Cord said quietly.
"It's as good for you as it is for me. Which leaves only one
question: Why didn't you come to me?"

"Come to you? How? Where?"

"In the hospital. The same way the good-luck piece did.
You did send it, didn't you?"

"Yes, but—"

"And you said, 'Give it to him, he needs it more than I
do'?"

"Yes, but—" Raine made a harsh sound. "Cord, I didn't
know where you were!"

"Then how did you know I was dying and needed all the
luck I could get to pull through?"

Raine went pale and swayed as though Cord had struck
her. In that instant all her worst fears congealed, crushing
her, ice and violence and raw scar tissue scored across the

body of the man she loved. She trembled helplessly, realizing how close she had come to losing Cord and never even knowing that he had died. He had called for her, needed her, and she hadn't been there. The thought was agony to her, a pain greater than any she had known before. Lightly, blindly, her fingertips traced his features while tears slid down her cheeks. She tried to tell him how much she loved him but no words could get past the tears filling her throat.

"You didn't know, did you?" whispered Cord, catching Raine's tears with his lips, kissing her again and again.

Numbly, she shook her head.

"Then why did you send back my good-luck piece?" Cord asked coaxingly, kissing her gently, stealing each tear as it fell.

Raine shuddered as the rest of the truth congealed in her; he wasn't hers, not really. He belonged to tomorrow, and sooner or later, tomorrow always came. The reality was like a dry, cold wind, freezing her tears.

"The coin wasn't mine to keep, any more than you were." Her voice was flat, lifeless.

"What are you saying?" asked Cord, his hands suddenly hard around her face. He sensed Raine retreating from him, from any emotion at all, shutting down before his eyes, a castle with all gates closing, all bars being drawn.

"You'll come and go as you always did," said Raine quietly, "no warning, no words, nothing."

"I hadn't planned on getting shot."

Raine flinched. She slid off Cord before he could protest. Very gently, her hand sought the new scar. "A bullet?"

"Yes."

"Will you . . . heal?" she asked, remembering his pain.

Cord stared intently at her. "What did Blue tell you?"

"Nothing."

"What the hell do you mean, *nothing?*" asked Cord savagely.

"Just that," said Raine, her voice as harsh as Cord's. "Nothing. I haven't heard one word about or from you since you disappeared."

Cord closed his eyes for an instant. "Christ . . ." His eyes opened pale blue, very clear, blazing with hidden life. "Yet you ran to me."

"Yes," said Raine, because he waited for her to answer.

"You cried for me."

"Yes," she whispered.

"And you made love with me as though there were no tomorrow."

"There isn't."

Cord's voice was quiet and very sure. "Yes, there is."

"Not for us. For us there's only today, now, this instant. In the next instant you could be gone, or the next."

"No."

Raine turned away, not wanting to fight with Cord, not wanting to face the end of the dream so soon after its beginning. "Have you eaten anything?" she asked, moving to get out of the bed. Cord's hand closed around her arm, chaining her. She turned to him. "Coffee? Black, no sugar, right?"

"Are those the only questions you have for me, Raine?"

"No," she said evenly, "but they are the only ones I'll ask."

"Don't you want to know why I'm here?"

Raine turned her face away, feeling shame crawl redly up her cheeks. "What do they call it?" she said, her voice shaking. "R & R? Yes, that's it. Rest and Recuperation. You know, when the soldiers go to town and pick up whores."

"*Stop it.*"

Raine turned on Cord with more despair than anger. "Don't worry, I can stand the truth. I'm not going to throw you back out into the cold. I'll be here when you get back the next time, and the next, until you find a woman you want more or you're killed or I—" Her voice broke.

"Or what?" Cord demanded savagely. "Until you find a *gentle*man?"

"Until I stop loving you," Raine said, her voice ragged, "whoever you are, whatever your name really is."

Cord's expression changed, gentleness smoothing the harsh edges of his mouth and voice. "My love, my love," he whispered, pulling Raine close again, burying his lips in her hair, drinking her sweetness, "didn't Blue tell you anything at all? I turned in my resignation the day after I made love to you. I knew I had to have you, and I knew that you couldn't live with my work." Cord laughed harshly. "Neither could I. Not any more. One too many battles, one too many wars."

"Why didn't you tell me?" Raine asked, staring at Cord's clear eyes, afraid to believe.

"I couldn't quit instantly. Not until a certain matter had been cleared up. I didn't want that hanging over you—the last battle. You had enough to handle already. And handle it you did," he said admiringly. "I wish I could have seen you. But it went blue all the way to the moon. . . ."

Raine saw the change in Cord, anger and grief and pain. "What is it?" she asked. "What's wrong? Do you have to go back soon? Isn't it finished?"

"It's finished," Cord said tersely. He closed his eyes, remembering the friend who had fought beside him and lost, the man who would never again mangle Spanish phrases and ask after chess games. But Al hadn't died alone. Cord had made sure of that, despite the bright blood pumping out of the wound in his thigh. "Barracuda is dead.

Very dead. Another man died. A good man. The best. So we gave him my identity, and buried him. According to official records, Robert Johnstone and an unnamed passenger died tragically in a light plane crash in the San Gabriel Mountains.''

Raine remembered the name Robert Johnstone and realized that her father had given the good-luck coin directly to Robert Johnstone, alias Cord Elliot. No wonder her father hadn't told her anything; if Cord hadn't mentioned his real name to her, Justin never would.

''Who are you?'' Raine asked, trying to keep her voice calm.

''Cord Elliot,'' he answered quickly, almost fiercely. ''The man who loves you. The man who's going to marry you.''

Raine stared intently at Cord, almost afraid to believe. ''Are you sure?''

He smiled crookedly. ''Yes, I'm sure I love you. Yes, I'm sure I'm going to marry you. And yes, I'm sure my name is Cord Elliot. I have the papers to prove it. Lots and lots of them.''

Raine smiled despite the tears that suddenly appeared on her eyelashes. ''Is the ink dry?''

''Of course,'' Cord said indignantly. ''I worked for the guy who owns the presses.'' His smile faded. ''Will you marry a man with no past, a man whose only marketable skill is a certain knack with knotheaded horses? Not that we'll starve. I haven't had much to spend my money on through the years.''

Raine smiled and kissed Cord slowly. ''I'll marry you on one condition.''

Cord's black eyebrows lifted. ''What's that?''

''That you'll let me buy this ranch for us.''

Cord's expression changed.

"Don't you like it here?" asked Raine quickly. "It's so beautiful. And Dev loves it. We could buy a few mares and train the foals and . . . Cord? What's wrong?"

"Do you really like it here?" he asked.

Raine hesitated, then said honestly, "It was like coming home. If it weren't for the peace these mountains gave me, I would have gone crazy these last weeks. Can you understand that?"

"Oh yes," Cord said softly. "That's why I bought this ranch five years ago. It kept me sane until I could find you. Will you live here with me, raise four- and two-footed hellions with me?"

Raine bent over Cord, letting her kiss be her answer. When she shifted to lie beside him again, she saw the livid scar. She touched his leg very gently. "Will you be able to ride?"

Cord laughed quietly. His hand traced Raine's spine, urging her closer. "In a few months I'll be as good as new. Better." He nuzzled against her neck, tickled her ear with the tip of his tongue.

"We'll spend a lot of time riding together," said Raine, her fingertips tracing the strong muscles of Cord's neck.

"Sometimes," Cord said, smiling crookedly, "we'll even take horses along."

Raine's laugh sounded more like a purr.

Cord's expression changed as he looked at her. "Come to me, little rider. I need that place by your fire."

"It's yours," she whispered, turning toward him. "It always has been. It always will be. All those tomorrows finally belong to us."

Silhouette Classics™

COMING
NEXT MONTH

#19 WIND WHISPERS by Barbara Faith

Joanna Morrow and Carlos Quintana met to work on a mural celebrating an ancient Mexican legend about two tragic lovers. As their own love consumed them, Joanna grew afraid that history would repeat itself, but she was determined to defy fate and find a lasting happiness with the man of her dreams.

#20 TEARS OF YESTERDAY by Mary Lynn Baxter

Paige Morgan had hoped that the love she shared with Lane would endure forever, but the magic—and their marriage—hadn't lasted. Now family troubles had brought them together again, giving them a second chance to find a place where time and sorrow have no meaning, where passion and love are all.

AVAILABLE THIS MONTH:

#17 SUMMER GAMES
Elizabeth Lowell

#18 NEVER GIVE YOUR
HEART
Tracy Sinclair

SET SAIL FOR THE SOUTH SEAS
with
BESTSELLING AUTHOR
EMILIE RICHARDS

Next month Silhouette Intimate Moments begins a very special miniseries by a very special author. *Tales of the Pacific*, by Emilie Richards, will take you to Hawaii, New Zealand and Australia and introduce you to a group of men and women you will never forget.

In Book One, FROM GLOWING EMBERS, share laughter and tears with Julianna Mason and Gray Sheridan as they overcome the pain of the past and rekindle the love that had brought them together in marriage ten years ago and now, amidst the destructive force of a tropical storm, drives them once more into an embrace without end.

FROM GLOWING EMBERS (Intimate Moments #249) will be available next month. And in coming months look for the rest of the series: SMOKESCREEN (November 1988), RAINBOW FIRE (February 1989) and OUT OF THE ASHES (May 1989). They're all coming your way—only in Silhouette Intimate Moments.

IM249

TALES OF THE RISING MOON
A Desire trilogy by Joyce Thies

MOON OF THE RAVEN—June

Conlan Fox was part American Indian and as tough
as the Montana land he rode, but it took fragile yet
strong-willed Kerry Armstrong to make his dreams
come true.

REACH FOR THE MOON—August

It would take a heart of stone for Steven Armstrong
to evict the woman and children living on his land.
But when Steven met Samantha, eviction was the
last thing on his mind!

GYPSY MOON—October

Robert Armstrong met Serena when he returned to
his ancestral estate in Connecticut. Their fiery
temperaments clashed from the start, but despite
himself, Rob was falling under the Gypsy's spell.

Don't miss any of Joyce Thies's enchanting
TALES OF THE RISING MOON,
coming to you from Silhouette Desire.

SD 432

Silhouette Intimate Moments

At Dodd Memorial Hospital, Love is the Best Medicine

When temperatures are rising and pulses are racing, Dodd Memorial Hospital is the place to be. Every doctor, nurse and patient is a heart specialist, and their favorite prescription is a little romance. This month, finish Lucy Hamilton's Dodd Memorial Hospital Trilogy with HEARTBEATS, IM #245.

Nurse Vanessa Rice thought police sergeant Clay Williams was the most annoying man she knew. Then he showed up at Dodd Memorial with a gunshot wound, and the least she could do was be friends with him—if he'd let her. But Clay was interested in something more, and Vanessa didn't want that kind of commitment. She had a career that was important to her, and there was no room in her life for any man. But Clay was determined to show her that they could have a future together—and that there are times when the patient knows best.

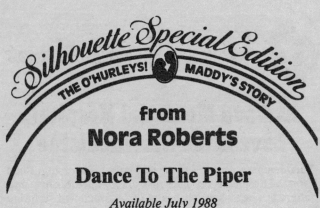

Silhouette Special Edition

THE O'HURLEYS! MADDY'S STORY

from
Nora Roberts

Dance To The Piper

Available July 1988

The second in an exciting new series about the lives and
loves of triplet sisters—

If *The Last Honest Woman* (SE #451) captured your
heart in May, you're sure to want to read about Maddy
and Chantel, Abby's two sisters.

In *Dance to the Piper* (SE #463), it takes some very
fancy footwork to get reserved recording mogul Reed
Valentine dancing to effervescent Maddy's tune....

Then, in *Skin Deep* (SE #475), find out what kind of
heat it takes to melt the glamorous Chantel's icy heart.
Available in September.

THE O'HURLEYS!

**Join the excitement of
Silhouette Special Editions.**

SSE 463-1